BOOKS BY SUZA KATES

The Savannah Coven Series
Whisper of a Witch
Conviction of a Witch
Binding of a Witch
Haunting of a Witch
Possession of a Witch

The She Series
She Who is Hidden

Single Titles
Hallowed Eve
The Penance Stone

THE PENANCE STONE

悔
恨

SUZA KATES

ICASM PRESS
SAVANNAH

Published by Icasm Publishing LLC
5710 Ogechee Rd. Suite 200 #278, Savannah, GA 31405
www.icasmpress.com

Library of Congress Cataloging-in-Publication Data

Kates, Suza
The Penance Stone / Suza Kates
     p. cm.

ISBN-13:978-0-9889809-0-7
ISBN-13:978-0-9889809-1-4 (ebook)
I. Title

Printed and bound in the United States of America

10 9 8 7 6 5 4 3 2 1

To Karen,
for always being strong

ACKNOWLEDGEMENTS

I want to thank the many readers who took a chance on my first book and loved it despite the flaws. As an indie author, I've learned a lot about editing the hard way, and am so grateful for those of you who encouraged me and took the time to contact me with concerns or suggestions. My previous releases are undergoing another edit and will get the proper once-over they should have had before.

This leads into my next round of gratitude! I would like to share my deepest appreciation with Mandi Cranson for bringing her stellar content-editing skills to this project. I am so excited about working with you in the future! I want to thank Donna Wood for proofreading and offering the perspective of a historical romance reader. It's been such fun introducing you to PNR. I also have to say how grateful I am that my husband bumped into Sharyn Cerniglia at last year's RWA convention. While she was unable to work on this project, her expertise as copy editor is much appreciated and will be a great asset to both past and future projects. You are all wonderful, and I am blessed to have you on board!

1

The driver of the taxi smiled over his shoulder from the front, right seat of the British-styled car. He grinned and bobbed his head before facing forward again to jerk the white car back onto the narrow lane. "Chuujitsu," he said, pointing toward the buildings that were coming into view.

Harper nodded to the driver as she met his smiling eyes in the rearview mirror. Then she studied the reflection of her own eyes, the gray deepened by dark circles beneath. Swiping her hair into some semblance of order, she tried to hide the toll of traveling evident in her appearance, and was grateful the long journey was almost over.

The driver was eager to arrive as well, nodding his head as he declared their destination again. "Chuujitsu."

Harper grinned. "Chuujitsu," she repeated. "Hai."

Excitement tingled its way up her arms as she sat up straighter to get a better look. *Chuujitsu*, the name of the village where she would be living for the next six months, and *hai* meaning yes. These two words were the extent of her Japanese vocabulary, but she could hardly wait to get settled into her new home, set up an office space, and dig into her next project.

There would be plenty of time to learn more of the language and the specifics of this rural culture. That's what research was for, and as her editor often accused, the search for new and unusual trivia was Harper's favorite part of the writing process.

The road they'd taken through the narrow pass finally brought them to a valley filled with thick woods. The trees were huge and towering, casting dark shadows to create a primeval forest. Proud evergreens stood straight and tall, yet blended with deciduous trees whose broad leaves and twisted arms declared their strength. Their staying power.

Evergreen samurai against elm wood warriors. She could just imagine how they challenged each other at night, when the people slept and the magic awoke.

Before they drove beneath the trees, Harper studied the rest of the valley. Each side of the open space was barricaded by the towering Chugoku Mountain Range, and judging by the few rooftops she could see, the village was nestled in the middle of it all. Cloistered and protected from the outside world like a hidden heirloom.

Pewter clouds rushed overhead, laying a dark veil over the land, but as Harper took in the high natural borders surrounding the area, she was comforted by the barrier. She could almost breathe in the sense of seclusion. Of isolation. Her favorite state of being.

The road to the village was sheltered by trees, and as the cab drew closer, she saw an imposing manmade structure. Tall, red posts formed an entryway and supported two lateral beams on top. One was straight and square while another above curved its tips toward the sky.

Harper searched her mind for a name and the words snapped into place. A *Shinto* gate. She'd seen pictures on the Internet before leaving the States. The same exotic photos that had inspired a new book idea, and therefore, a new place of residence.

The gate was painted a glossy cherry-red, but the color didn't strike her as bright and happy. Instead, the severe lines of the structure were daunting. Formidable. A happy smile on a threatening mouth.

She chided herself for her overactive imagination and looked away, seeking a prettier picture. Though her sense of the macabre aided her profession, she often had to remind herself to appreciate the less-than-sinister side of life. To remember that most people weren't out to get her. At least, not her specifically.

The taxi rolled through the imposing gate and onto a road that led straight through the heart of the village. The ride was remarkably smooth, since the large gray stones of the street had been beaten into uniformity by both time and usage. Glancing from side to side, Harper noticed the same type of granite had been used for most of the masonry, a resource that ancient villagers had probably dug from surrounding lands.

She couldn't take everything in as the taxi sped down the main street, but she caught glimpses of high stone walls and older architecture off to her left. And were those arched bridges crossing a stream? The road through the mountains had followed a natural waterway, so the same river must divert through the village.

Setting aside her innately reserved and cautious nature, Harper promised herself she'd come to explore the town soon. Maybe take some photos for inspiration.

The taxi driver was on his phone now, speaking quick and sharp Japanese to someone on the other end. He flipped it closed and said, "Hayashi-san come soon." He was referring to the leasing agent, Ms. Hayashi.

"Will she meet us at the house?" Harper asked, leaning against the back side of his seat to gaze out the windshield.

"Hai. Hayashi-san." He gestured to the mountain up ahead where the forest grew thick and dark green. Harper had a hard time envisioning the home that waited for her there, but Ms. Hayashi had promised all of her needs would be met.

The stone road once again gave way to dirt as they traveled through vast fields. A few houses dotted the working farms and while modern in structure, the roofs of the homes were covered with some type of thatch or grass. Spring was upon them, and two men stood on the side of an outlined plot, likely discussing the growing season for rice or potatoes.

The car braked hard, and she had to grab the shoulders of the front seats to keep herself from being thrown forward. The driver muttered under his breath as his city taxi gave right-of-way to a cow crossing the road.

Harper laughed breathlessly as she eased back into her seat. Well, she had requested rural. And that's exactly what she'd gotten.

Patting the Kenneth Cole satchel on the seat beside her, she rubbed the luxurious black and navy leather and told herself she could still shop online. In case of emergency.

Her smile was wry as she mused to herself. What a case study she would make for some young psychologist. The recluse who loved couture. Literally all dressed up with... nope. Too cliché to even complete the thought, and practice made perfect.

Damn. She did it again.

While she wondered how fast Internet access would be out here in the country, the road began to twist and climb into tree-covered foothills. Switchbacks were mild and shallow, long sinuous curves that made ascension more comfortable. While the higher mountains were a darker, bluish-green, the plant life they passed now was warm. Lush.

As they climbed, Harper rested her chin in her hand to look out the side window. There was a gorgeous view of the valley, and from this distance, the farm houses, fields, and village seemed quaint. Not nearly as threatening as the red gate.

Soon the car turned onto a gravel road enshrouded by trees, and at the end of the drive, they found Ms. Hayashi standing outside a tall, stone wall. The leasing agent waved and smiled, tidy and trim in her cream-colored business skirt and jacket.

When the taxi rolled to a stop, Harper reached for the door handle, ready to see what lay beyond the stately enclosure. An elegant wrought iron gate stood open, and she hoped the house was half as nice as the entry implied.

"Ms. Gray," the petite leasing agent said, stepping forward with her arm held out. Her skin was surprisingly warm as the two women shook hands in greeting, and her burgundy manicure was as flawless as her pearl-like complexion. Ms. Hayashi completed her perfect picture with black as midnight hair swept into a smooth chignon. "I hope your trip was comfortable."

Harper nodded slowly. "The flight was long, but the two-hour drive from Oda City gave me a chance to unwind. The countryside is beautiful." She made a small circle and held out her arms to indicate the surrounding forest. "And quiet."

"Just as you requested," Ms. Hayashi said with a serene smile. "Would you like to see the house?"

"I'm dying to," Harper said, cringing inside as she worried the American expression might have come across badly to the woman. Ms. Hayashi seemed unaffected, and given her impeccable English, Harper had a feeling she was fluent enough to grasp the meaning.

"This way," the agent said with an expedient twirl of her short, flair-skirt and a crunch of heels across the gravel. She pushed the black metal gate open to reveal even more greenery.

But at once Harper could see the difference. Here was a true Japanese garden, designed to provide tranquility and help whoever strolled along its paths forget the rest of the world even existed.

The feel was definitely one of simplicity, and every plant or tree had its purpose. How much time had gone into the construction of the unadorned yet well-orchestrated area? The paths alone would have taken hours to put in place, and she recalled something about the curving design. There was a reason for avoiding straight lines, but she couldn't remember it just now.

She sighed as she studied the pond and the flagstone walkway that circled around the water then disappeared behind a wall of bamboo. She would wait and investigate that secret spot later, since Ms. Hayashi was already opening the front door to begin the tour.

"When you described what you wanted, I knew the Saito house would be the right one," the prim agent said as she stepped inside. "The owners are away most of the year and rarely have need or desire to rent. They made an exception for you, since the wife is an avid reader. The husband is from a wealthy Japanese family and built his country palace here for the same reasons you have decided to come." She held the door open for Harper. "Peace and quiet."

"I'm very appreciative," Harper said, slipping off her shoes in imitation of Ms. Hayashi as the agent removed hers. She put them to the side of a square section that was one step below the main floor and covered in dark gray tile.

"This is called the *genkan*," Ms. Hayashi explained. "Outside shoes must be left here, and either socks or slippers are worn in the house. There is no tatami room with reed mats, so you may wear slippers throughout the home."

"All right," Harper said, not understanding the difference between sock and slipper rooms, but grateful she wouldn't have to figure it out. "The floors are gorgeous," she added, noting the wide, shiny slats of dark brown. The hardwood gleamed, and she could tell the home was a mixture of homage to tradition and contemporary comfort.

Ms. Hayashi put on slippers she took from one of several cubby holes next to the front door and walked into the house, motioning for Harper to follow. "The kitchen is quite modern, so you should have no trouble finding your way about. If you do have any trouble, I've put the name and number of your assistant on the counter."

Harper could see the espresso-toned wood and stainless steel from where she stood. The kitchen was in the rear but open to the rest of the house. Ceilings were high and the spacious rooms immaculate. As she walked in, eager to explore, she caught a clean, natural scent, reminiscent of pine trees.

Angling to her right, she found two couches set at an angle from each other, both facing a large square opening in the floor with what looked like a cast iron kettle hanging above. A playful metal fish was on top.

"That's the traditional-style hearth," the agent said with a wave. "The husband insisted." Then she walked toward an open staircase in back. "The upper floor holds a sitting area, master bedroom, and bath. I believe you'll enjoy the balconies, as they flow uninterrupted around the home."

The soft sound of slippers had replaced the agent's clicking heels, but her pace was still as quick and competent. She moved to the left side of the house and another open area with two round chairs and a table.

The chairs faced a wall of Japanese-style screens. "These are shoji," Ms. Hayashi said, pulling apart the ivory screens sectioned into panes by dark wood.

Once the wide panels were moved aside, Harper had a glorious view of the backyard. Another garden was featured, with a view as equally amazing as the one she'd passed through before. She could imagine enjoying her morning coffee right here. The perfect spot.

"You'll have your choice of two rooms for your work space, both on this level. Or you may prefer the sitting area upstairs." Ms. Hayashi was looking at her now.

"I'll figure it out," Harper said, grinning. "I had no idea how big the house would be."

"Is it too much?" the agent asked with a worried frown.

"No, no. I love it." Harper put her satchel down now and whirled. "It's paradise."

"I'm happy you like it." A strange expression flickered in the Japanese woman's eyes, then was gone. She walked to Harper and handed her the keys. "You have my number if you need anything, and I called Mr. Ellis to tell him you had arrived. He should be stopping by within the hour."

Harper stilled. "Mr. Ellis?"

"Yes. He agreed to offer assistance while you are here in Chuujitsu. He is American as well, one of only a few that live here, in fact." The agent tapped a burgundy fingernail to her lips. "What does he do? Ah, yes. He is an archaeologist. No." She put her palms together. "An anthropologist."

Harper's mind buzzed with the unexpected turn of events. She'd anticipated a nice, young girl taking the part-time position. There wasn't much work involved, and the pay was minimal. Why would an academic want to be anyone's assistant?

"Would you like some tea?" Harper asked, hoping to keep Ms. Hayashi around until this Mr. Ellis showed up. She didn't like spending time with people she hadn't met or at least spoken to.

Especially strange men. In her space.

And the house was hers now, reserved and paid in full. She wasn't sure how she felt about having Mr. Ellis running errands for her and coming here when she was alone.

Stop it. She ordered herself to calm her irrational thoughts. The leasing agency set up the arrangement, so the man had to be trustworthy.

"Actually, I have another appointment in the city, and as you know, it is quite a long drive." The agent smiled and lifted her brows as if asking for Harper's approval.

"I understand," Harper said, feeling silly and a bit selfish. "I can't tell you how much I appreciate your finding this place for me. And for coming all the way out here to meet me." She walked with the woman to the front door, to the genkan, and watched as she changed back into her pumps.

Ms. Hayashi pressed her hands together in front of her chest and bowed slightly in standard Japanese fashion. "Please contact me if you need anything."

"Thank you." Wanting to lock the gate behind the woman once she left, Harper slipped into her "outside" shoes and accompanied the agent to her car. She waved goodbye as Ms. Hayashi turned the vehicle around in the gravel and drove off through the woods.

After a moment, Harper realized she could no longer hear the sound of the small car's engine. She stood with her hand on the black iron of the gate and closed her eyes. She took a deep cleansing breath through her nose.

All she could hear was the wind slipping through the trees and a few calling birds.

Ah, yes. She already loved it here.

When she opened her eyes, a slight movement stirred in the bushes. There was a path disappearing downhill into the forest, and she thought she'd seen a darting motion. Like someone ducking quickly out of sight. Someone who didn't want to be seen.

Paranoid, she told herself, clucking her tongue and stepping back inside to close the gate. She was simply jet-lagged and overwhelmed by the many changes that came along with moving to a new place. She had the routine down cold, though. This wasn't her first temporary home, and the private, Japanese manor wouldn't be her last.

She would take a quick tour of the front gardens then find her way around that fancy kitchen. Maybe try her hand at making authentic green tea.

She grimaced. *Then at least I'll have something to offer the strange man when he arrives. Mr. Ellis. Hmph. Sounds pretentious.*

She had a picture in her head of the anthropologist. An older, silver-haired man with a moustache, glasses, and pot-belly. She groaned. Why hadn't she thought to specify a female?

No matter. It was a done deal and he was on his way. She might as well get ready.

Looking through the iron bars one last time, Harper was grateful for the shelter of the trees. The house was beautiful and was exactly what she needed. Mr. Ellis would do fine, too. Probably just a friendly guy who missed being around another English speaker. No worries.

Everything would be okay.

Glancing again to the path in the woods where she thought she'd seen movement, Harper fought indecision. Then, even though she knew Mr. Ellis would be arriving soon, she opted for safety. As always.

And locked the gate behind her.

2

Harper was frowning at the royal blue tea kettle when she heard a knock on the front door. She set the pot aside and moved toward the front of the house, a chill rolling down her spine as she slowed to peer through the glass squares on each side of the entryway.

She'd locked the gate, hadn't she? How had this man, who she presumed was Mr. Ellis, gotten inside the yard? All she could see was the bend of one elbow, encased in a long, navy-colored sleeve, and she didn't want to appear foolish by sticking her face up to the windows to get a better look.

Steeling herself, she heaved a reluctant sigh. She would make polite chit-chat briefly then offer the excuse of being travel-weary to send him on his way. Harper opened the door. The man smiling at her from the other side wasn't nearly as old as she'd expected. And there was definitely no pot-belly beneath his shirt.

"Ms. Gray," he said in greeting. "I'm Reid Ellis." He stuck out his hand, so Harper had no choice but to grasp his long, sturdy fingers with her own and shake.

She was still staring at him, wondering how she might describe the color of his dark green eyes, when he held up a set of keys and said, "I let myself in the gate." He angled around her, since she was blocking the doorway, and started unlacing his hiking boots.

Stepping out of them, he grabbed a man-sized pair of inside shoes. He appeared to have practiced the routine before and knew exactly which cubby held shoes in his size.

A gnawing suspicion started in Harper's gut, and she didn't like the feel of it. "You have a set of keys to the gate?"

He flashed her an even smile that made those forest-green eyes curve at the edges. "And to the house. I was the one who stocked you up on necessities and basic food items."

He finally noticed her dismay and turned his head slightly to one side with eyes narrowed quizzically. "Ms. Hayashi did tell you I'd be stopping by, didn't she?"

"Yes. Yes, she did, but she failed to mention you would have a set of keys to the house. It makes sense that you would have needed access to the house before I arrived, but now that I'm here…" She didn't finish the sentence but held out her open palm.

When he only stared at her, she looked pointedly at the keys he still held and lifted her brows to drive home the expectation.

Slowly, as if he were trying to grasp her reasoning, Reid handed her the clinking set of keys and nodded. "I understand. Strange man. Strange environment." His previous affability had apparently frozen up, and now he didn't seem to know what to do.

And it's no wonder. This is the person hired to help me get around, the man who is familiar with the village and the language, and I've practically accused him of breaking and entering. Harper sighed and let her shoulders relax. "I apologize." She worked up a light smile. "I'm not used to other people having access to my home. I didn't mean to be rude."

Reid lifted one side of his mouth and nodded. "But you're still keeping those keys."

She gave the keychain a short toss in the air. "I am." Remembering the tea she'd been preparing, she decided to start over, to salvage what she could of one of the few relationships she would have for the next six months. "I was making some tea but got tripped up by the mechanics. Would you like some?"

"Sure. There's still a bite in the air, and I walked up from my place." He followed her to the kitchen and stood nearby as she picked up the kettle again. She had yet to learn her way around the streamlined room with its mixture of gleaming wood and stainless steel and was unsettled by the fact that someone else was more familiar with her private space than she was.

Harper focused on the lovely tea pot again and tried to keep her gaze off of her guest. Reid Ellis wasn't exactly hard to look at and had a certain outdoorsman quality. His tawny hair was straight and clean cut, and his eyes were the purest green she'd ever seen.

He wore jeans with the navy shirt he filled out so well, and Harper's previous image of an anthropologist exploded into a million pieces to be swiftly replaced by the sexier version of academia standing right beside her.

"What part were you having trouble with?" he asked over her shoulder. Harper jumped to hear the deep timbre so near her ear.

"I... um... wasn't sure where to put the tea leaves. Do I just dump them in when the water boils?" She felt like a complete idiot instead of someone who wrote novels for a living. Foiled by the oh-so-complicated tea kettle. "Won't the leaves pour into the cup?"

"You're missing the infuser," he said, taking the pot from her hands and turning on the faucet. "Why don't you take a seat? I'll give you a tutorial." He gave her that smile again, and Harper suspected she was being teased.

"Well, now that there's an infuser, it all makes perfect sense." Meeting his humor with some of her own, she walked around the counter to pull out one of the wooden stools. The wood was stained dark brown with seats that curved up slightly on both ends.

The design of the stools echoed the *Shinto* gate she'd passed through before, and a sudden chill had her rubbing her arms. Why had that gate bothered her so much? They were everywhere in Japan.

Perhaps it had been the towering, red structure's very clear message. *Beyond this portal is our village. Our rules.*

"Straight green tea?" Reid held up the box to confirm Harper's pick. "No fruity additives to ease you into the flavor? No sweeteners?"

Harper lifted her shoulders. "I'm fearless that way." Inside she called herself a liar, but he didn't have to know that. As soon as he was gone, she would lock the doors again and take a nice hot bath in her brand new sanctuary.

"How much caffeine is in this tea?" she asked, reaching for the box. She'd left her satchel on the counter earlier, and now she rooted inside for the case that held her eyeglasses. She slipped them on and read the back of the box. "It's in Japanese."

Reid grinned. "Green tea doesn't have as much caffeine as coffee or even black tea, but I won't let it steep too long. I'll make it a light brew."

Chagrined by her own ignorance, Harper left her glasses in place, a small shield and only in the psychological sense. "Tell me, Mr. Ellis, what does your work here entail?" Her voice sounded so stiff, so formal. All the better to keep an appropriate distance between them.

"My dissertation deals with the changing demographics of the rural Japanese village and their loss of younger generations. More and more of the children are growing up and moving to cities. I've spent some time in other places, but the final part of my research will focus on Chuujitsu."

He leaned back against the counter casually, as if he and Harper had been friends for years. "This place is different, and I'm trying to identify the reason."

"How is the village different?"

"Very few of their young people leave for good. Some may branch out to get an education, but most return, either to take up the family farm or business." He reached for the kettle when it started to steam, setting it aside and glancing at the clock to time the brew. "I don't have my Ph.D. yet, but I'm almost there."

Harper pondered the strange workings of the universe that had brought her to this moment. He was the oddest assistant she could have imagined. He would help do her grocery shopping, and was now making her tea in a pretty little pot, yet he was still one of the most virile men she'd ever met.

His physique told her he was no stranger to heavy lifting, and with broad shoulders and height of at least six feet, Reid almost-doctor Ellis seemed to overwhelm the refined kitchen.

She watched his strong hands move with efficiency as he poured the pale tea into two matching blue cups. He offered her one with steam curling its way into the air, and she could smell the grassy scent.

Allowing a small smile, Harper cautiously sipped the hot tea and rolled it over her tongue to appreciate the full effect.

Reid watched quietly as Harper experienced the beverage. And experience was the right word, because she didn't just take a taste and declare it "interesting" or "nice." Instead, she immersed herself in the drink, closing her eyes to ensure she didn't miss any nuance of aroma or flavor.

He waited patiently for those gray eyes to open again, and yeah, he'd noticed the unique color right away, stone gray with flecks of blue. She'd been staring into the light when she'd opened the door to meet him with the vigilant stance of a sentry on guard duty. Other than her eyes, the brown hair falling to her shoulders had been the only soft element about her.

She'd come across as cautious, almost hostile, but as soon as she'd asked for his set of keys, he realized there was a bit of anxiety operating there as well. Even after he'd given her back the keys to her castle, she'd remained aloof. Prickly.

He lifted his chin in question when she finally looked at him again. "What do you think?"

"It's good," she admitted, sounding surprised.

"You'll like it more each time," he told her. *And maybe you'll start getting used to me, too.*

After a moment of companionable silence and tea drinking, Reid said, "The rest of your belongings should arrive tomorrow or the day after. I'll keep checking and bring them up as soon as they reach the EMS office in town."

He lifted his cup. "I'll be your go-to guy."

She nudged her glasses into place and said, "Actually, you'll be more like a come-to guy. I don't leave the house much, which is part of why I needed help." She flicked her eyes up and down to take him in before saying, "You aren't exactly what I had in mind, and frankly, you seem an odd choice for anyone's assistant."

Reid wanted to reach out and straighten the glasses for her, rectangle frames of tortoiseshell with jade green on the inside. They looked expensive, just like the rest of her attire, a white shirt with a neckline that went straight across from shoulder to shoulder and dark pink pants that only reached to mid-calf.

"I've never been an assistant before, and to be honest, you didn't have much of a choice." He went to the sink to wash out his cup and set it upside down on the wood rack to dry.

Harper waited quietly as if expecting him to elaborate. So he did. "I didn't take this job for the money, and, no offense, but I'm not exactly a fan, either. I don't read love stories. Give me a good adventure book or a political thriller any day."

"We all have our preferences," she said, clearly unperturbed by his dismissal of her work. "Was no one else interested in the position?"

"No. The villagers keep to themselves." He reached for her empty cup intending to wash it, too, but she held onto it and shook her head. "Don't get me wrong," he continued. "You won't have any trouble with the people here, but they don't go out of their way to welcome strangers."

"Ms. Hayashi was very friendly."

"That's her job, and I'm sure she was thrilled to rent this place for a while. Not everyone can afford the Saito house, especially for such a long time."

Harper bristled at the implication and narrowed her eyes at him. "I'm not on vacation, Mr. Ellis. This is my home now."

"Call me Reid," he said, dodging the mild rebuke and returning to a friendlier tone. "You don't have a house or apartment somewhere else?"

She shrugged and eased off the stool to go to the sink and clean her own cup. "I don't do permanent."

"Fair enough." He could feel the tension radiating from her and knew the time had come for him to make an exit.

He'd been telling the truth when he said he didn't need this job, but now that he'd met the mysterious lady writer, he was more intrigued than before. He wanted to keep the position. To learn more about the woman with the thorny exterior and guarded, gray eyes.

"My number is on the counter there." Reid gestured to the piece of paper. "After you've gotten comfortable, you can let me know if you need anything else. We might not be able to get your usual food items locally, but I have to make occasional trips to the city."

Bobbing her head, she said primly, "I appreciate everything you've done, and I'll try not to pull you away from your work too often."

"I'm sure we'll work out a routine."

"Yes." She walked him to the door and stood back as he changed into his boots again. "You live within walking distance?" she asked, and she didn't look pleased that he might be close by.

"A long walk, so don't worry. I won't be dropping by unexpectedly." He smiled when her mouth puckered, and her eyes grew concerned. "You need your privacy," he said. "I get it, and I'm not offended."

He opened the door to an evening that had grown considerably colder. Spring had just come to the mountain village so chilly nights held on stubbornly. "But, Harper," he said, using her name as a final attempt to build a small, if unstable, bridge between them. "Promise you'll call and won't try to do everything yourself. I'm here to make the transition easier."

"All right," she conceded as he stepped outside. "I will."

As he crossed through the garden and out of the tall gate, Reid considered the woman and her ways. He was a sociable person himself, and had never shied away from new people or new experiences. Life was to be lived, and for him, it was also to be studied. Picked apart until he understood why others did what they did and the impact their choices had on their society.

Or their families. But that was a different story. His own, and one he rarely revisited.

Turning to get a look at the Japanese manor tucked away in the woods, he saw Harper lock the gate behind him and return to the house. A moment later, a light came on upstairs, and he wondered what she was doing.

And why anyone would want to spend all their time alone.

3

Harper stretched and rolled over to snuggle back into the soft, white pillow. Her eyes cracked open to examine the Egyptian cotton, and then swept the rest of the bedroom. She sat up, trying to clear her head and remember where she was.

A glance to her left granted her a view of trees through room-length windows. Young leaves covered the branches, unfurling like millions of tiny, green flags. Now she recognized the view. The Saito house in all its luxury.

Not a bad place to wake up.

Harper brushed a long tendril of bark brown hair from her face and smiled. Now that she was rested, she could explore the house and grounds at her leisure. The night before had quickly turned to an exhausted blur, and she barely remembered taking a quick shower before crawling into the soothing, clean sheets.

Wearing satin pajamas of midnight blue, she rolled from the bed and went straight for the sliding glass doors that led to her bedroom's balcony. The back walls of the upper level were almost all glass, as well as the side of the house that opened to the wraparound terrace.

The temperature outside was warmer than she'd anticipated, and the level of light told her she'd slept late. No matter, she consoled herself. *I have a few days before the countdown truly begins.*

She'd learned the hard way that procrastination was a writer's worst enemy, and the word *deadline* at the start of a project was like a distant, dreamy figure in the clouds. After she'd pissed away two months doing any and everything but writing, however, *deadline* transformed into a tall cement wall that came closer and closer each day until its shadow overwhelmed every aspect of normal life.

And Harper had never performed well under pressure. Just ask anyone who'd read her third release.

Walking at a snail's pace, she took a stroll around the top floor, amazed by how truly secluded the house was. From the front, she could make out the curve of the river and a few of the farms on the north side of the valley, but the village was hidden from view by treetops.

Birds twittering in Japanese woods sounded just like those in any other place, but still she allowed a few minutes to lean against the railing and enjoy the quiet that surrounded her. Branches swayed and bounced in the mountainside breeze. Sun warmed the wood beneath her feet.

And her hungry stomach rumbled.

Intent on solving the problem, she made her way back to the bedroom, stepping over the reed mats near the doors. An overhang created an outside room and the ideal spot for meditation, especially on a rainy day.

Moving through the bedroom with its wide bed and contemporary wood art on the wall, she made a left into the bathroom to find the bathtub in silhouette against another picture window. She promptly decided to end this day with a long, hot soak.

The tub was a massive, white rectangle inset into a raised platform. The floor surrounding the tub was golden wood, as were the two steps she would have to climb to step down into the basin. Dark stones surrounded the tub and had been polished to smooth, round forms by either nature or man. A lone orchid of pale purple grew from one side of the rocks, and Harper counted herself lucky to have arrived while it was blooming.

Happy to linger, she took her time washing her face and brushing her hair. In this room, she could better appreciate the Japanese culture and their desire to allow nature into every room. Never had her morning toilette been so pleasant or calming.

Grabbing her phone from the side table where she'd left it the night before, Harper breezed through the sitting room and down the open staircase, then on to the kitchen to hunt up breakfast. It was already one in the afternoon, but she felt no guilt. Her internal clock would line up with the one on the wall soon enough.

Her first line of business was to fire up the coffee-maker and say a quick word of thanks that there was one. Green tea would be fine for an afternoon break, but her body needed hot, black adrenaline when she woke.

She'd brought her favorite mug with her, but now she was considering using one of the dainty, hand-painted cups she spied in the cabinets. The tall, slim cup with pink cherry blossoms was in theme, both with the house and the plans for her book. She might be more inspired by the Japanese design, so her sturdy black mug was temporarily relieved of duty.

As she listened to the hiss-drip combo of her favorite drug being brewed, she pulled two pieces of bread from a bag. Pleased to find the toaster operated just like the American-made versions, she set out butter and a jar of what she assumed was jelly, if the label's smiling strawberry was any indication.

By the time the coffee was ready, Harper had just finished preparing her toast, so she loaded it all on a tray and carried her breakfast to the area with the two round chairs and table.

Since there was no other furniture in the vicinity, she surmised the setup was for reflection and enjoying the back garden. She slid the two tatami screens aside, and was thrilled to see the garden was even more beautiful than she'd recalled.

A wooden walkway wound around the lower level of the house and could be accessed from every room. A pond stretched from in front of the open doors and to her right where the kitchen would be. She would have to remember to open the shutters on the windows so she could see the pond and garden when she made meals.

A hollow sounding *plunk* drew her eye to a water feature of two thick bamboo canes. One had a stream of water running into the open end of the other. When the second piece became full enough, the cane tipped over to spill its bounty before popping back up to its original position.

Harper sat and took a good-sized slug of her coffee and would swear she felt an immediate jolt. She whiled away the next thirty minutes, sitting and absorbing the absolute serenity before the caffeine from her second cup hit and she was ready to get moving.

Now that she had daylight and her eyes weren't blurry from lack of sleep, she'd indulge herself with a tour of the house. She loved getting to know a new space, learning its secret nooks and hidden crannies.

The house was utopia, not only because of the surrounding gardens, but amenities that made the country hideaway as convenient and comfortable as a penthouse in the city.

The main part of the house was already familiar to her, so she went to inspect the two sections that jutted off each end. Taking the outside walkway, she made her way around to the end of the house to get a good look at the Zen garden waiting there. Pebbles covered the ground instead of grass with a few sparsely planted ferns.

The simplicity here was apparent, no distractions or colorful flowers, just a lone Japanese lantern of granite and a large, triangular rock with symbols etched into its side. She had no idea what the writing said. In fact, she thought, tucking her hair behind one ear, she didn't even know what the writing style was called.

She promised herself she'd look it up as soon as she had her workspace laid out. Continuing her exploration, she followed the curving flagstone path to one of the rooms off the corner of the main building.

The outside door was still locked when she tried to open it, so she ended up going back around to the sliding screens she'd left open. Cutting across that end of the house and through an inner hallway, she made her way to the room. She stepped inside and surveyed the area, taking note of its office-potential.

The first thing she realized was how dark the space was. The only windows here were thin rectangles high on one wall of the room. When she faced the shelving unit to her right, though, she understood the need for shadow. Among the decorations, books, and picture frames, sat a large television, and a well-lit room would cast too much glare.

Given the curving sectional with reclining seats, she checked this room off of her list right away. A desk wouldn't fit in here, and the mood wasn't right. Way too dark. But, she told herself with a smile, at least she had a theater for when she needed to escape from work for a while.

Having learned from her first mistake, Harper cut a straight line through the inside of the house to the room that was on the opposite corner and at the other end, near the kitchen. She followed a similar hallway to the room and knew as soon as she opened the door that she'd found her spot.

A large desk already sat on the far wall and to her right were more tatami screens. By now she understood the architecture and had a good idea what lay on the other side. She slid one screen open slightly and was elated to find a courtyard.

Judging by the position, she knew the front room with the traditional hearth opened up here as well. Several ornamental trees gave the area a botanical quality, and they were interspersed with more of the large, craggy rocks. A flagstone path would take visitors on a winding tour, in and out of the evergreens, and around the lone maple boasting new leaves of vibrant purple.

Another lantern, taller than the last, stood in one corner, and a candle inside told her the stone statue was also functional. She imagined the flickering flame might be mysterious in a nighttime garden. The final detail that confirmed her decision.

She'd found her office.

Now to the arrangement. The desk would have to change positions, since she wanted her back to the courtyard and her computer against a plain wall. Excited about personalizing the space, she hunted up some linens and removed four washcloths to place under the legs of the desk. She couldn't risk scratching the glossy, dark floors.

Still in her pajamas, she positioned the cloths and muscled the heavy desk to the wall she'd chosen. The small table and chair that had been there would go to the now-empty space where the desk had been. A sitting area to enjoy the view.

Now all she had to do was organize her things on top of the wide piece of wood she suspected was teak. The desk was substantial in size yet plain in design, but she would soon personalize it with her own items.

Laptop, legal pads, pens, and highlighters of every available color. These were just a few of her essentials, and she was happy to find storage space in the drawer spanning the front of what was now her writing table. She couldn't abide clutter.

And after her printer and other things arrived, she would set up another table in the corner. She'd seen a sideboard in one of the front rooms that would do, but she could worry about that later. Now she went back inside the main area to dig through the luggage she'd left sitting in the *genkan*.

She opened the smaller bag to pull out the things she'd need to work, all packaged into tight little bundles, except of course, for the laptop. That was in her satchel, too fragile to be tossed underneath an airplane and crushed by heavier suitcases.

The leather bag was atop one of the stools at the kitchen island, and she opened the specially-padded side made for a computer. She set the laptop on the counter for the time being, and opened a pocket inside the satchel that was zipped closed.

As she'd told herself before, the most fragile, most important items were kept at her side when she traveled. Things she couldn't afford to lose. Like the picture frame she now held in her hand.

The silvered frame wasn't terribly expensive, but the picture inside was one of her most cherished possessions. Of course, she'd already made a copy and stored it in a safe place, but the original was still special to her. It had been a gift.

Running the pad of her finger over the glass, Harper felt a familiar clutch just beneath her heart. The same small tug of sorrow she always had in response to seeing the two smiling faces in the photo. She and her sister, arms wrapped around each other's waists with watch-out-world gleams in their eyes. So young. So hopeful.

And so brave.

Drawing a breath that caught on the lump in her throat, Harper stood with the frame in her hand and looked around. Before she would be able to concentrate on setting up the office, she needed to find the right place for the picture.

She didn't consider the kitchen, and the hearth room was too empty. Too austere. The shelves set into the walls were nice, but they were too... cold. She turned and eased her way back up the stairs, stopping in the sitting room on the second level.

Here was a cozy place that was multi-functional with its comfortable sofa and coffee table. And it was just outside her bedroom, so she would pass through every day.

One wall held shelves, so she removed a doll in a silk dress and set it on the other side. Then she placed the picture frame in the vacant spot. A beam of sunlight fell across the glass and highlighted a smudge left by her finger, so she wiped it off with the tail of her pajama shirt and put the picture back. In the sunbeam.

With the pang of loss receding, Harper moved to look outside. The sitting room also had a spread of windows, and the view of the gardens and forest beyond was spectacular.

A quick jerk of movement drew her attention to the base of a tall tree. She was sure she'd seen something. Just like yesterday. Only this time, she couldn't chalk it up to paranoia or imagination. As she stared at the tree and underbrush surrounding it, a person with black hair crept from behind the trunk.

Her skin rippled with unease, and like a doe caught in headlights, she watched the person move with intentional stealth. Sneaking around, hoping they wouldn't be seen.

Only dumb luck had brought Harper upstairs to the ideal vantage point. She could just as easily have remained downstairs, in the office or kitchen, surrounded by the tall stone wall that surrounded the manor. Where she would have never seen the intruder.

Suddenly, the person turned their face up to the trees, and Harper was both shocked and relieved to see that the prowler was a young girl. Relief warred with annoyance. She was glad to realize the person out there posed no threat, but still irritated by the idea of having her privacy violated.

Don't be such a grouch. She imagined an older, gray-haired version of herself raising a fist in the air and yelling, "Damn pesky kids!" It was bad enough she had become a semi-recluse. She didn't have to be a shrew on top of it.

Besides, the girl probably didn't know anyone was living in the house now. The place had been empty for months, and the kid was likely just taking a walk in the woods.

Although… she seemed to be creeping around with a purpose.

Deciding to let her know she'd been busted, Harper knocked on the window and almost laughed to see the girl's head whip toward the house, then up higher until her eyes locked with Harper's.

She immediately felt remorseful. The girl's dark eyes widened with fear and her mouth fell open as she stood frozen in place.

Feeling guilty that she'd scared the girl, Harper smiled and waved. Instead of relaxing, the girl started shaking her head, taking small uneven steps backward. Then she turned and bolted into the thick forest.

Well. Harper crossed her arms and continued to gaze into the green. *I guess she won't be coming back.*

4

Reid pushed the bicycle the last few feet and leaned it against the high stone wall. Then, like a good assistant, he went to the gate and pressed the button that would ring a bell inside the house. He tested the gate, just in case he was wrong, but as he'd suspected, Harper had it locked up tight.

His cell phone buzzed in his pocket, so he pulled it out while he waited. When he glanced down, his morning cheer dissipated like droplets on a hot stove. His mother's number was on the screen.

Very few things could eradicate Reid's usual composure. Most things just weren't that bad, and if they were, he did his best to dodge the drama and move on. Parents, however—he heaved a breath—were a constant.

He wasn't in the right frame of mind or the right place to talk with his mother just now, so he thumbed the ignore button and shoved the phone back in his pants. Harper would be out in a minute, and he didn't want to greet her with a snarl in his voice.

The writer with her own bite, as he thought of her, wasn't a trusting soul, and he wondered again why she viewed the world as one big collection of possible enemies. That was his take, anyway, given her insistence on barring him and everyone else from her refuge.

Maybe she just spent so much time inside her own head

that other voices were an interruption. Reid had known people like that, especially scientific types who focused solely on their experiments and analyses. Workaholics who were ambitious and single-minded, to the exclusion of any social life, romance, and sometimes, unfortunately, even basic hygiene.

Harper didn't have that problem, he recalled with a smile. A pleasing scent had floated around her that first day, noticeable but not overwhelming. Just a bit spicy with floral undertones he couldn't place.

Maybe he should ask her what she wore. He'd enjoy seeing her response.

Then Harper stepped out the front door with a humorless expression and strode toward the gate. *Not today.* Reid noticed her measured stride. *I'll ask her some other time.* If he irritated her too much too soon, she might fire him. Then he wouldn't have an excuse to see her.

And he liked seeing her. Which was surprising, because she wasn't the type he usually went for. Typically Reid dated fun girls, outgoing and ready for any adventure or debauchery, depending on where the day or night took them.

Looks weren't important—okay, they were somewhat important—but what mattered most was their willingness to go and do. Their drive to experience and revel in the wonders of the world.

Harper Gray didn't come across that way at all. She was locked up as tight as the iron gate he stood before. Still, Reid couldn't get her out of his head.

Her early morning call for transportation to the village had been unexpected, but gave him an opportunity to stop by. He hoped to prove he was dependable and that his presence shouldn't be perceived as a threat.

She was looking at him like she might an unwanted snag in the fancy blue shirt she wore. And all he'd done was show up.

"Good morning," he said, as she opened the gate. "So you've

decided to get out and see the local life." He hoped the smile he gave her was friendly and not as carnal as he felt, now that he was seeing her up close and personal again.

"Yes," was all she said, apparently in no mood to expound on her plans for the day. She wasn't classically pretty but had a face that leaned toward interesting. Features layered with character.

Reid imagined she, like most women, would hate being described that way, but in her case it was true. Straight eyebrows could have been harsh but were delicate enough to provide the perfect frame for her eyes, that intense gray flecked with blue. So unique they were worthy of a second glance. Just like her.

Her upper lip was a bit too large, but he found the top-heavy look seductive. And with her warm brown hair pulled back in some strange twist, she definitely gave off the sexy librarian vibe. Too bad she wasn't wearing her glasses.

Her straight nose turned up a bit at the tip and helped balance the strong angle of her jaw. The one that was currently clamped tight with impatience as she stared at him expectantly.

"Where's the car?" she asked, leaning around him to search the area.

"Car?" He grinned. "No. I brought you a bike."

Such horror crossed her face that Reid almost laughed. Instead, he swallowed it and cleared his throat to cover the sound. "I need my car today, but I promise you'll be better off with the bicycle. And the fresh air will do you good."

"I'll judge what's good for me."

The arms crossed over her chest served as a makeshift shield, so Reid told himself to tread lightly. To sound reasonable. "If I drop you off in the village, there will be too much ground to cover on foot, and I won't be available to pick you up until later this afternoon. What if you want to come home before then?"

Her lips pressed together as she considered her change in

situation, giving Reid a chance to study her more closely. She wore a silver necklace with two Celtic knots on a single chain. Now that he noticed the jewelry, he recalled her having it on the last time he'd seen her. A favorite piece?

His eyes continued down her body and landed on the black skirt that fell to mid-thigh then the strappy shoes showcasing delicate ankles. The heels were low, but not low enough for bike-riding.

Tearing his eyes away from her lean legs, he pointed out the obvious. "You should change clothes."

"I'm aware. Thank you," she said coolly, before an exasperated breath rushed from her pink lips.

Then she shrugged and surprised him by saying, "Well, maybe you're right." She looked up at the sky. "It is a nice day."

Before he could respond, concern marred her brow. "But if I need you, will I be able to reach you by phone?"

"Of course." He wasn't sure what had inspired the flash of fear in her eyes, but he had to remind himself that she was new here, to the village as well as its inhabitants. The villagers had their own unique way of living *and* interacting. Especially with strangers.

"You'll be fine," he encouraged her. "The locals aren't very sociable with outsiders, but they won't hurt you. The worst thing that might happen is you get snubbed or ignored, but not by any of the merchants. Believe me. Once they see your American face, they'll be more than happy to sell to you."

She rolled her shoulders and said, "Okay. I'll be fine." Walking over to the white bike, she patted its seat. "Do you need this back soon?"

"No. It's yours for the duration." Reid was glad to see he hadn't ruined her day after all, and he thought he saw a small smile tugging at her lips when she tested the silver bell on the handlebars.

"I haven't ridden a bike in years. Not since I was a kid." She flicked her eyes up to him. "I should thank you for bringing it by."

"And now you have." Reid let the moment of silence hang between them. He wished he could spend more time talking to her, but he had an interview setup that he couldn't miss. The village historian had finally agreed to meet with him, and there was no way he was going to blow it.

Even for a pair of pretty gray eyes.

He would have to count today's brief interlude as a victory. "You know how to reach me," he said, heading for the trail that would lead down the mountain and through the woods to his cabin.

As if they'd said everything they needed to, Harper lifted her hand in both thanks and farewell. Efficient and without a waste of words. Just what he'd expect from her.

Reid turned back to the path and strolled away with a grin.

Harper's eyes followed Reid's long strides as he walked off into the forest, not quite sure what to make of her outside-the-box assistant. The title hardly seemed appropriate anymore since during their discussion, she'd felt like *he* was the one giving orders. Yet he'd done it in such an expert and caring fashion that Harper had barely noticed.

No matter. She wasn't one to quibble over circumstances that couldn't be changed, and she would be wise to remember what he'd told her. Why he'd decided to work with her.

Because no one else would.

She was beginning to appreciate his easy manner. Even though she'd taken his key to her house and made her distrust abundantly clear, Reid Ellis still chose to work for her. Rather, he was working *with* her.

The distinction didn't bother Harper. Instead, she was grateful for his kindness. If she had to tackle all of this alone— a new place, different customs, a foreign language—then she would spend all her time struggling to make any headway. And she would likely starve.

Admiring his lanky yet muscular build as he was swallowed by the mountain greenery, Harper thought she wouldn't mind using him as a model for her hero. She could let his blonde hair and fallen-angel good looks light a fire in her belly.

But only creatively speaking, and only to fuel her imagination. She would never let real life get tangled up in fantasy. No matter how many smoldering looks he sent her with those pure green eyes. *No, Mr. Ellis. I didn't miss those signals.*

A quiet tremble ran through her as she remembered how his eyes had skimmed over her before coming to rest on her face. The smile he'd given her had been slow and warm, as if he already knew every one of her dark secrets. And approved.

He'd been so nonchalant and patient. As if he recognized her type and planned to wait her out.

Poor guy, Harper thought as she sighed. He didn't know a bulwark when he saw one.

Fifteen minutes later, she was appropriately attired in black capris and a black, boat-neck shirt. She did her best to channel Audrey Hepburn but could only aspire to that legend's sleek, chic style.

Far too often, Harper found herself running frustrated fingers through her hair or tying it up in a quick, messy tail. Now even her French-twist from earlier was falling apart as she breezed down the curvy, mountain road.

At the bottom of the hill, she rolled onto flatter roads, mostly dirt, but mixed with enough gravel to keep the dust in check. Soon the trees gave way to farming fields, and the same two men were laying out long rows of what looked like string or twine. One of the men lifted his head, so Harper smiled and waved. He didn't wave back.

Reid had warned her she might not be welcomed by all. Besides, the farmers were busy ensuring their livelihood, the protection of their families, so she didn't mind the rebuff.

And the day was absolutely glorious, sunny with a fair temperature. She had to give Reid credit for suggesting the bicycle. The fresh air was doing her good.

The road led her through the fields and back into the thick forest. The tall trees filled most of the valley and cocooned the village. Pedaling up a slight incline, Harper stood to put her legs into it and was rewarded when she crested the rise.

The streets were neat and tidy, gray stones clean of all debris. Most of the buildings were built on the edge of the road and covered in dark brown wood, clapboard-style. Stonework similar to that found in the streets could be seen in foundations and dividing walls.

The mix of materials added a sense of continuity and belonging, and lent the village a certain charm. Like something out of a fairy tale. A Japanese fairy tale.

Harper had no clear plan or places she needed to go. She had wanted a day out of the house, to get a feel for life in the village and maybe take a few pictures to help her describe the setting.

Rolling the bike along the narrow street, she noticed an area with several other bicycles parked in a row. She couldn't picture more than one car fitting on the main road at the same time, so the two-wheeled transports made sense.

When she drew closer and kicked out the stand, she realized none of the other bicycles were locked down. "This can't be right," she murmured, glancing around as if the answer would pop out any moment. No one had guarded against theft. The bicycles could be taken by anyone who wandered by.

"You can leave it there. Nobody will bother it."

Harper stopped staring at the front wheel and looked up to find a Japanese woman looking at her with her head tilted and a bemused smile on her glossy lips. "There's no crime in Chuujitsu," the woman added, shaking her head as if to emphasize the point. "No one is going to trade their hand for someone else's bike."

Harper felt the blood rush from her face to congeal in her heart. "You can't be serious."

The woman shrugged. "That's the story, anyway." Her deep, brown eyes lit with mischief. "And who's going to break a law to find out if the rumors are true or not?"

She stepped forward just as Harper did, and they both laughed as their feet bumped. "Now I'm terrified to go shopping," Harper said. She scrutinized the woman's clothing and surmised she wasn't from around here.

She wore a nice white shirt with a shock of red lace peeking out where the top buttons lay open. Trim, beige pants completed the outfit. "I'm Saya," she said, "and I'm going to guess that you are Harper Gray."

"Is it that obvious?"

"Mm-hm. Not only are you one of three Americans in the whole village, I also heard about your arrival." Saya put one hand on her hip. "And I'll admit, after I heard you were coming, I went online and found your website."

"I see." The idea of being recognized in a place so far off the map would normally have bothered Harper, but something about Saya's candor and straightforwardness put her at ease. Plus, she sparkled in that special way some people have, as if she embraced each day and was simply happy to be alive.

Together they walked down the street. Harper didn't really know where she was going but was fairly certain she wouldn't get lost. If she did, all she would have to do is look for the foothill where she lived and head toward that end of town.

"I've met Reid," Harper said, "so if I'm the second American, who's the third?"

Saya held out her arms. "You're looking at her."

"But you're... sorry. I didn't mean..."

Saya waved her apology away. "I'm Japanese, through and through, but I was born and raised in Ohio. My parents own a company and have moved back to the motherland to open a new office."

She ran her fingers through her hair, and Harper took note of the well-cut layers of black silk that just brushed the top of her shoulders. Saya was a city girl. "What are you doing in Chuujitsu?"

"I wanted to see more of the land," Saya explained, "so I moved here to teach ESL at the local school. English as a second language. I have a small apartment over a shop on the other side of the village. Near the school. I was over this way to pick up some throw pillows I've had my eye on."

Harper grinned as she listened to the talkative woman and found herself walking in the same direction. Metal lanterns hung near the doors, and residences were interspersed with businesses. Food items and clothing were on display, and several of the stores had colorful strips of fabric hanging outside to be teased and tossed by the wind.

"We're in the main shopping area, but the specialty store I need is one street over." Saya paused and asked, "Would you like to come? I can give you the layout of the village." Her smile was as wicked as the still-present shine in her eyes. "I wanted to take the job as your assistant, but my schedule wouldn't permit. At least this way I can show Reid up a little bit. Beat him to his duties."

Harper found herself laughing. This woman was anything but shy, and her exuberance was infectious. "You and he don't get along?"

"What? No, no. I adore Reid. He and I are the two founding members of the interloper club." Saya nodded at an older woman who passed by and frowned at her and Harper. "And you, dear Ms. Gray, are now our newest member."

"Lovely," Harper said. First Reid had warned her about strangers being unwelcome in the village, and now Saya said the same. But the two of them seemed to be living here happily enough.

And they both still had their hands.

The two women took a right turn between buildings and came out on a boulevard that overlooked the river. Harper had gotten a glimpse of the arched bridges on her first day, but now she saw they were part of an older, and apparently more elite, section of the village.

On the other side of the bridges were large houses, mostly constructed of the same gray stones found in the streets. Behind the first row of homes rose a taller building with several stories and the unique curved architecture that declared its Japanese design.

"What's that?" Harper asked, stopping in the lane so that Saya halted as well. "The building that rises above all the others."

Saya looked and said, "That's the *Shinto* temple. I don't know what their particular version of the religion is, and that's the way they like it here."

"What do you mean?"

"I mean if you really want to be on the receiving end of village hospitality, try getting inside that place. We can go across the bridges and see the houses, but only villagers may enter the temple. Like I said," Saya added, "they have their own practices and beliefs."

Now Harper was intrigued, and the secrecy of an ancient religion had her imagination working double-time.

Saya turned to the store windows behind them. "Those are my pillows," she said, indicating a set of white and black throw pillows with flowers embroidered in lilac.

"I'll tell you what." Saya spoke to Harper as she moved toward the door of the shop. "After this, I'll give you a full tour, and then we can pick up some groceries. I'll cook you a welcome-to-the-neighborhood dinner."

"Oh, well..."

"As long as it's at your place," Saya said, as if Harper were trying to persuade her and not the other way around. "I've always wanted to get a look inside the Saito house." She angled her head to the side and gave Harper a winning smile. "What do you say?"

Unable to summon a single viable argument, Harper lifted her hands. "I say sure."

Saya did a tiny dance of joy before floating inside the store and leaving Harper alone to look around. Her attention returned to the amazing structures across the waterway. The masonry had to be centuries-old, in both the huge homes and the bridges.

She looked down at the cobbles beneath her feet. They were probably just as ancient, and the idea of standing exactly where a real samurai might have stood sent a ripple through her veins. Had servants once washed *kimonos* in the same flowing river? Had *geishas* lived in one of the smaller buildings in this part of town, or had they been elevated to the more opulent life on the other side?

The tops of trees poked their heads above the elegant roofs, surrounding the temple and expensive homes just as they did the rest of the village. Harper took a deep breath and smelled meat cooking with a tantalizing hint of herbs.

She reveled in the adventure of where she was and, surprisingly, found herself looking forward to a meal with Saya. She couldn't remember the last time she'd invited a virtual stranger to her home, and there was a certain irony that she was now doing so in a strange country. And on pure impulse.

Harper was rarely impulsive.

A few streets down, she saw a procession coming from the opposite side of the river. Several men in brown robes were walking in pairs. She suspected they'd come from the temple, given their solemn faces and measured steps. They reminded her of monks.

She wanted to whip out her camera and take a picture, but something about the stillness of the gathered villagers made her pause. As the men passed by, people halted whatever they were doing, dropped their hands to their sides, and stopped talking. They didn't lower their heads in any sort of reverence, but they diverted their eyes from the robed men.

The actions were not overt, but a hush seemed to follow in the wake of the procession. Harper was about to follow suit, because she didn't want to offend them, but a glimpse of white amidst the brown robes made her take another furtive look.

Her gaze fixed on the figure in the middle of the men. A young girl walked among them, protected on all sides as if she were royalty. Guarded from the average commoner on the street.

Then Harper got a clear look at the girl's face and recognized the same scared teenager who'd been sneaking around her house. The one who'd run away when Harper spotted her.

The men were almost upon Harper now, their metronome footsteps pounding as firmly as her heart. In one swift motion, she whirled around to face the river. To stare at the rushing water and lock her gaze on the rolling waves.

For reasons she couldn't name and intuition she didn't understand, Harper's skin prickled with unease. And she wouldn't dare look back.

5

Harper's cheeks were wind-chapped pink by the time she and Saya finished combing the streets of Chuujitsu. Not every corner of the small village was as modern as the decorating store Saya had visited, but what the place lacked in convenience, it more than made up for with mystique and old-world allure.

After pulling up to the Saito house, Harper took her bicycle from the rack on Saya's car. She parked the bike, then helped her new acquaintance carry in the shopping bags.

Harper spared a glance for the woman and re-evaluated. Saya Oshiro was more than just an acquaintance now. The spunky woman was impossible not to like, and had already declared them good friends.

Oddly enough, Harper was still managing to keep pace with Saya's indomitable stride. She never knew what the outspoken woman might say next, but enjoyed the anticipation. The Japanese woman's unique blend of humor and impudence kept the conversation interesting.

She'd even convinced Harper to buy hair sticks, insisting she should be somewhat in character herself if she was going to write a book with a Japanese setting. So when Harper spotted the lacquered drinking glasses of sapphire blue, she had to have those as well. For inspiration, of course.

Harper had absolutely no clue what to do with the groceries they carried, but Saya had promised a feast fit for an empress.

Now Harper found herself looking forward to a real meal, especially since she'd been nuking her way through the past two days.

After making their way inside and taking off their shoes, both women opted for bare feet instead of slippers. "If your feet get too cold on these floors I can get you some socks," Harper offered.

"Nah. I'm good," Saya said, positioning herself in the middle of the main floor and taking a slow turn with her arms out wide. "This place is huge. I'm so jealous."

It was on the tip of Harper's tongue to tell her she could visit again or even stay the night, but the sudden compulsion startled her into silence. Caution choked the offer before it could slip past her throat.

Saya seemed nice enough, but Harper didn't really know her.

Probably wiser to stay reserved. That was how she usually avoided forming attachments, because even friendships could get messy. Any relationship could result in loss or hurt feelings, and it was Harper's habit never to set down permanent roots anywhere. Even the flesh and blood kind.

Still, she watched with an amused expression as Saya rambled from room to room, stopping to slide a screen back and admire the courtyard before hurrying to the other end of the house to disappear down the hall.

When Saya came back, she looked dazed. "My entire apartment would fit into the TV room." Then her quirky grin flared to life. "But I like things cozy." She pointed to the stairs. "Do you mind?"

"No," Harper said on a laugh. "I don't think I left it too messy up there." She followed Saya upstairs and into the sitting room. Like a bloodhound who'd found its mark, Saya zeroed in on the photo of Harper and her sister.

Harper braced for the questions she knew would come next.

"Nice picture," Saya said, casting a small smile over her shoulder as she replaced the frame. "Are you two as close as people say twins are, or is it total sibling rivalry?"

Harper saw Haley's face in her mind. The gentle patience and constant optimism. No, she and her sister were far too different to have ever been rivals. Haley had always been the good sister. The sunshine to Harper's moon.

"Close," was all Harper said. "Wait until you see the bathtub," she added to get Saya moving. To get her off the topic of her sister. Her twin. Who she never discussed.

"Oh!" Saya exclaimed, standing inside the doorway and admiring the bathroom and its luxurious tub. Then she held up a hand in a silencing motion. "Your toilet is inside the bathroom. That's not normally done here." Then she shrugged. "The owner's wife is British, so she must have won that argument."

She backed out and veered into the bedroom, then Harper heard the sound of the glass door sliding open. Followed by a distant squeal. Saya had found the view.

She waited while her guest took a walk around the terrace then Saya walked back inside and said, "This place is amazing. Thank you for letting me be nosy."

"My pleasure. In fact, I think your reactions were payment enough for the grand tour."

Saya nodded. "Good. And I'm still adding food to the bargain."

When they went back downstairs, Harper asked one of the many questions that had been circling in her mind since she'd seen the temple in town. "Saya, you said the villagers have their own type of *Shinto*. Tell me more about that."

Saya opened a bag on the kitchen island and started pulling out the items she'd purchased. "Let me get the meal started first. I talk better when I cook."

Better? Harper thought with a smile. She climbed onto a stool to watch as Saya washed a head of cabbage and sliced it up before setting the pieces aside to dry. Next she removed the pork she'd been so choosy about at the butcher's and cut it into strips. They were to have steamed cabbage and pork, along with some sort of rice bowls and leafy green plants with a name Harper couldn't pronounce.

"Now," Saya said, searching the shelves until she found the pantry and chose a bottle of oil from the two that sat side by side. "You want to know about *Shinto*." Her brown eyes were so dark they seemed like pools of liquid when they fastened on Harper. "Is this for your book?"

Maybe, Harper thought, but "Yes," is what she said. She added nothing else, only waited, using an interviewer's most reliable tool. Silence.

"All right." Saya put a large pot of water on to boil then started adding ingredients to a frying pan. Soy sauce, sugar, and *mirin*. *Mirin* was a rice wine similar to *sake*. Just one of the many things Harper had learned today.

"*Shinto*," Saya said, "is the most prevalent religious tradition in Japan. The word comes from two others that mean 'the way of the divine being.' The origins go back further than the earliest history of Japan, so no one really knows who founded the practice."

"You said the village has its own version," Harper interjected. "Isn't *Shinto* one religion?"

"No." Saya opened two cabinets before she found the wine glasses. She opened the bottle of Cabernet she'd retrieved from her apartment, their last stop before returning to Harper's place. The wine was from Saya's "private stash," as she'd called it. "There are basic fundamentals of *Shinto*, like dances, shrines, rituals, but they can be tailored to fit whatever *kami* is worshipped."

Saya held up a finger, poured them two glasses of deep red indulgence, and finally said, "You're about to ask me what *kami* means."

Harper nodded, sipped her wine, and smiled over the rim. "This is my kind of history lesson."

"We're here to please." Saya winked. "*Kami* may refer to a singular spirit, god, or angel, depending again on the specific religion, or it may mean several different divinities. The *kami* might be a natural phenomenon like thunder, or a physical thing like the sun, a stream, or a tree. Even animals."

"So the *kami* could be any central object of worship?" Harper twirled the stem of her glass between her fingers. "Sounds ambiguous."

"Customized to the needs of the followers. For example, if you're a fisherman, you might show devotion to the sea in return for blessings. A good catch that will feed your family." Saya stirred the contents of the pan as it heated up beside another. Saya coated the second pan with oil, then laid out pieces of cabbage before placing a strip of pork on each.

"And you have no idea what Chuujitsu worships? Harper asked. "They have a pretty big temple, and the building looked old. So did the other homes on the far side of the river."

"Like I said, the villagers are very secretive, but that may be part of their purity practices. Keeping it in the family, so to speak. The oldest families in the village live on the eastern side. Ancient lineages in ancient homes. But the temple was only built about five hundred years ago."

"Only?" Harper squeaked.

"Uh-huh." One side of Saya's mouth lifted. "I know. We forget how young America is. But you can tell the temple was built no earlier than the *Sengoku* period, because the *tenshu* wasn't around until then."

Harper choked on her wine and put her hand to her lips to wipe any that might have spewed. "I'm going to require another level of translation for that."

Now Saya laughed out loud. "Sorry. The *tenshu* is a central tower. They were built in castles and were a sign of prosperity.

You know, my *tenshu* is bigger than yours." Saya gave her an all-female grin.

"Fascinating," Harper whispered, staring at the reflective surface of her ruby-colored drink. Then she looked up to ask Saya, "Do you practice any type of *Shinto*?" She wondered if the question was too personal, but her new acquaintance remained unfazed.

"I'm not particularly religious. What I mean is, I have my beliefs, but I'm not much of a joiner. I tend to keep things private, if you know what I mean."

Harper nodded.

"But I guess everyone has their own way of finding hope, or peace. We all need something to help fight off the fears of the world." Saya tilted her head. "You know, someone or something to keep us going. Help us escape."

"My writing helps me escape." Harper felt her cheeks warm as soon as the words left her mouth. That was a personal admission for her, and she was surprised she'd let it flow right out without pause or stutter. Maybe it was the wine.

Or the open-minded woman she was growing much too fond of. Saya's personality was like a beautiful painting, upbeat music, and a bar of chocolate all rolled into one. She put Harper at ease, and after only a few short hours.

Then her ever-present worry rushed back in and turned the wine's aftertaste from sweet to sour. Harper reassured herself that indulging in one night of fellowship wasn't an abandonment of her normally rigid code of conduct. It was only one night.

Whenever she traveled, she met people, colorful characters who were memorable and exciting. They always ended up a picture in her computerized scrapbook. Fond memories, but distant, two-dimensional ones.

Saya would be relegated to smiling pixels one day, but for tonight, Harper was enjoying the company. She wasn't antisocial. She just liked her alone time. In fact, she craved it.

She was simply introspective. Perfectly normal.

And just because her track record revealed an absence of any long-term relationships, it had nothing to do with how dangerous and unpredictable life could be. Absolutely nothing.

"How does writing help you escape?" Saya asked, jarring Harper from her musings and back to their conversation. She was spooning the food onto square, onyx plates that shone under the lights. Saya's creation smelled delicious.

Harper debated for only a second before deciding to be honest. "I can control what happens." She shrugged. "If I want to spend time in a beautiful house, I write one. If I want to go to the beach, I envision the rolling whitecaps and rippling lines in the sand."

"And if you want a hot guy...," Saya said with a brow wiggle.

"That doesn't work quite the same way." Laughter bubbled from Harper's chest. "Those men are strictly for the heroines. I'm just the voyeur."

"I'll drink to that."

Harper shook her head but lifted her glass to clink with the other woman's. "That's part of why I love it so much," she said, as Saya slid a plate in front of her and topped off her wine.

When her eyes began to sting and the kitchen went hazy at the edges, Harper blinked quickly and coughed. She was letting herself get too emotional.

"Finish what you were saying," Saya urged. Her gaze was soft and accepting. "What is it you love?"

Sighing and staring back at the brazen woman who'd somehow wrangled herself an invitation into her home, kitchen, and now her most secret thoughts, Harper smiled. "The happy endings. That's why I write romance."

"That's why I read them." Saya suddenly looked dreamy-eyed, too. And a little bit guilty. "Okay. I have a confession. I never read your books before I found out you were coming to the village, but I ordered your first one last week."

"Ouch." Harper grimaced. "Be gentle with me, and remember it was my first."

"I will." Saya laughed and took a bite of her rice. After chewing for a moment, she said, "I also wanted to tell you that I know you like your privacy, so you don't have to worry about me dropping in unexpectedly."

Harper formulated her words carefully. "I might like to get together again sometime." She left it at that. No specifics. No promises.

"I'd love that." Saya lifted one side of her mouth again in a half-smile. "Sure. I like to socialize, but I can also just be by myself, no problem. Reid, on the other hand...," she said, catching Harper off-guard with the sudden departure of topic.

"Reid?"

"Yeah. He's the ultimate people person. That's why he does so well in his field. He gets people to open up. Share their lives, their history, their stories."

Harper tasted some rice and pictured how the tall, blonde man had looked this morning. She had to admit, he made a handsome picture, all rugged but scholarly at the same time. "The gift of getting people to talk is probably handy for an anthropologist. Always studying new places. New cultures."

Saya bobbed her head slowly. "Everyone opens up to Reid."

Not me. Harper wondered where the defensiveness in her inner voice had come from. So far, Reid was respecting her wish for solitude. He hadn't bothered her or even called. So why was her back up like a nervous cat?

"Yeah, even some of the hard cases who won't even speak to me will tell him their whole life story," Saya said. "But not about the *Shinto*. Even Reid can't get that out of them. Luckily, he's just studying the number of young people in the village. Or something like that."

Saya waved her hand in the air. "People can be strange.

That's why I like children better. Always have. They're so honest and... unguarded."

The mention of young people reminded Harper of the parade of holy men she'd witnessed in the village. And the girl she'd seen both today in town and in the woods outside her house her first morning here. "When you were in that store, four men in brown robes went by."

"Priests," Saya confirmed.

"There was a young girl with them. She was right in the middle and kept her head down. What is that about?"

"I don't know any details, since it's part of their religion. Why do you ask?" Saya sipped her wine and met Harper's stare.

"I just wondered who she was." Harper stirred the green leaves on her plate. The ones she couldn't pronounce. "Have you ever seen her?"

"Maybe." Saya pursed her lips together while looking up and to the side. She was thinking. "There is this one girl. I think she's the only one I've ever seen in that parade, but I've seen her other places as well. She moves around like anyone would."

I've seen her other places, too. Harper smiled. "The villagers reacted oddly when she and the priests passed by. That's all. Probably just another custom."

"Mm-hm." Saya swallowed a bite of cabbage and said. "Now that you mention it, I think they've been gearing up for something. It is spring. Time to start praying for a good harvest. The girl might be a shrine maiden."

She snapped her fingers then and made Harper jerk upright. "Emi. That's her name. I heard someone call out to her one day. Yes, I remember now. Emi. How could I forget?"

"Why?" Harper leaned forward on the counter and realized Saya had been standing for the entire meal. "Did something happen?"

"No. Not really. It's just that once you meet Emi or spend any time around her, she's sort of hard to forget."

"In what way?" Harper wasn't sure why she wanted to know more about this Emi. The sweet-faced girl she'd startled so badly. The one who'd been draped in white, walking with her head bowed to everyone else.

"They say Emi is special. I'm not exactly sure why, but I got the impression she was... mentally challenged. Maybe autistic." Sadness or pity flashed across Saya's countenance as she spoke. "She seemed sweet, but it was hard to tell."

"Why was that?"

Saya met Harper's eyes. "Because she doesn't talk."

6

Reid's notes were a scattered mess, and that's exactly how he liked them. While most of his house was clean, organized, and traveling-man sparse, his desk looked like a sticky-note monster had vomited all over the top of it.

Some were crumpled, others stuck to each other because the ideas scribbled across them were related, and still a few of the yellow squares were stuck to pages of his dissertation. He would add information or make corrections when he revised the paper.

Assuming he ever finished in the first place.

Sucking down his second cup of black coffee, he waited for energy and clarity to arrive. This was his least favorite part of becoming a Ph.D. Writing papers. And mornings were the only time he seemed to be able to get any typing done.

Oh, he had plenty of drive as the day wore on, but by then, he preferred to be out of the house, visiting people and places, and gathering information. Then he'd come back to his cabin in the woods and try to make sense of the notes he'd made that day. If he didn't get them somewhat organized before the next morning rolled around, he would have an even harder time putting words onto paper.

Still waiting for the caffeine to transform him into a genius, Reid let his gaze travel out the window in front of his desk. He stared at the tall cypress trees and wondered what Harper's routine was like.

He didn't consider himself a writer—not at all—because the truth was he hated it. But he enjoyed envisioning the fussy romance author and speculating how she might spend her hours alone all day. He wondered if she wore the chic, sexy clothes while she sat around working.

Then he switched gears and pictured those glasses of hers. He'd love to slip them off and unbind her hair. To see if he could leave her speechless. Somehow, he doubted that.

Lost in his semi-dirty daydream, he lifted his coffee to take a drink, but found his mug empty. He'd been so absorbed in his fantasy, he hadn't realized he'd finished it off. With a frown, he got up to pour another cup from the Japanese version of Mr. Coffee.

As he trudged over, he scolded himself for thinking of Harper the way he had been. Technically, he worked for her, even if he was only doing so out of a mixture of curiosity and expat loyalty.

He certainly didn't need the money and couldn't really spare the time, but the idea of letting a woman come to Chuujitsu to flounder all by herself had guilt-punched him in the gut. He didn't want her to feel like an outcast, like there was no one she could turn to.

That's the only reason he'd sent her a present this morning. Just a small gift, really, with local flair and hopefully, special meaning for the recipient. It did him no good to second-guess the act or his motives. She might see it as a friendly gesture. Or as flirtation.

He could honestly say he'd intended a little of both. Why should that bother him? He was a man, and she was a woman. They were both single and, as he'd discovered via an Internet search, she was only a year younger.

Even if she acted like she was at least a decade older.

Just as he returned to his chair to write about yesterday's

long-awaited interview, his cell phone started vibrating on his desk. He had to push back a few piles of haphazard papers but finally found it at the bottom, buzzing and hopping against the old, scarred wood.

He bit back a curse when he saw his mother was calling. This was her second attempt to reach him in as many days. He might as well answer.

"Hello, Mother," he said, shoving as much cheer into his voice as he could manage. And it was all he had time to say before she began.

"Reid. I need you to do something for me." Her tone was tense. Angry. She didn't ask how her only son was doing in a foreign country. Had anything amazing happened to him lately? Anything tragic? No, his mother didn't ask. She never did.

Without allowing him to answer, she launched into what she wanted—no, what she *expected* Reid to do. "You have got to speak with your father for me." There was a pause. "Do you know where he is?"

Reid sighed and set his cup down before he broke the handle by clenching it too hard. "No. I don't know where he is." He hated to ask. Knew he would regret it. But he did anyway. "Are you and Father fighting again?"

"Why do you say *again*? I don't appreciate the implication. I really don't."

You mean you don't appreciate the honesty, Mother. He didn't say the words out loud, because he had done so before to both of his parents. Many times. His attempts to point out how destructive their relationship was had fallen on deaf ears.

Not only did his parents constantly hurt each other over trivial matters, but they had done the same to him. The appearance of a perfect family had always taken precedence over the actuality of one.

Unconditional love wasn't a concept his parents embraced,

so he'd railed, he'd pleaded, and as a final, desperate attempt to save himself, he'd blocked them out completely.

Not that either of them had noticed.

"Are you in Boston?" he asked, trying to make sense of what was happening, though it was merely a different version of the same story. The one that had been repeating itself his entire life.

Both of his parents had come from old money, and plenty of it. Their answer to any problem was to go on a trip or buy something expensive. Never to address the issue head-on.

Reid had often felt like an interesting piece they'd picked up on vacation. An *objet d'art* left over from that place called Parenthood. He'd been a prized trophy to be shown off to their friends, a burden relegated to boarding school, or a pawn in his parents' never-ending battle for the upper hand.

But never the simplest of roles and the one he wanted most. Never a beloved child.

"I am *not* in Boston," his mother finally spit out. She didn't volunteer her location.

"If Father isn't answering his phone, then I don't know what you think I can do. The last I heard, you were both going to spend the summer in Antwerp." Reid glanced up and saw a note he'd written about familial traditions and shared values. His chest tightened as his mother droned on.

One day he would make his own traditions. He'd build his own family. And he sure as hell wouldn't have the same set of values as the two callous people he'd been born to.

The resentment he harbored might seem harsh to some, but then, they hadn't been *monetarily supported* by Elizabeth and Daniel Ellis. To say they'd raised him was an insult to good parents everywhere.

He was grateful for the funds that gave him the freedom to pursue his career, but he'd long passed the point of dependency. One of his mother's favorite threats was disinheritance. Reid no longer cared. In fact, he often considered giving all the money to a couple of good causes if his parents ever did bequeath their fortune to him.

Charity was still charity, wasn't it? Even if performed out of spite.

"I know you're protecting him!" she suddenly wailed, just as Reid detected the familiar sound of ice clinking in a tumbler. He could almost smell the gin and French perfume. His mother's signature scent.

He grew nauseated and lifted the coffee to take a deep sniff, driving away the olfactory recall. "I'm not protecting him. I don't know where he is, and I refuse to be dragged into another battle between the two of you."

Reid drew a quick breath and continued before she could argue or cajole. "If I hear from him, I'll let you know. Good-bye, Mother." He hung up on the sound of her gasp and didn't feel a shred of guilt.

That, too, was a thing of the past.

Shuffling through a stack of papers, he pretended to read what was in front of him, but anger was still clutching his throat and hazing his mind. He wouldn't be able to concentrate until the let the steam seep out.

Reid was not a temperamental man and was difficult to rile. He avoided confrontation and drama whenever possible. His parents, however, always seemed to ratchet his blood pressure up with a single word.

He could live his life just fine without them, and he preferred not to be reminded of their selfishness. Their complete indifference when it came to him. Their son.

Forget about her. About them. You've done it a hundred times before. The coffee was still hot and the morning still glorious, so Reid sat back in his chair and focused on the deep green needles of the cypress outside his cabin.

He could force his parents from his thoughts and get through the day. Depend totally upon himself for any need—emotional, physical, or financial—that the elder Ellises either couldn't, or wouldn't, provide.

Yes, he was capable of that. Because he'd done it so many times before.

悔
恨

"I need a break," Harper said to herself, pushing aside the poster board where she'd outlined a potential plot. The first attempt was always messy, and she liked using the large poster for visualization. She could glance between plot points and scenes without flipping pages.

She'd tried the software programs designed for this very purpose, but the click of a button just didn't connect her to the project the way holding notes and pictures in her own hands did. She was old-school that way.

Rubbing her lower back—achy from sitting at the kitchen island to work—she went to her office with the intention of searching the Internet for a while. But as soon as she spied the moonlight falling on the courtyard, the glowing white pebbles, and tranquil setting, she opted for a walk outside.

She slid the glass doors open, since the paper screens had already been moved aside. She appreciated the fact the owners had made two layers, one of glass to keep out the cold, yet still allowing a view of the garden.

The quiet spring air, the ornamental cedar trees, and sweeping paths were soothing. The Japanese garden was meant to be uncluttered, to allow meditation, and the plants and huge rocks used as décor were always in threes or fives. Never even numbers, because symmetry wasn't found in the natural world.

Structured yet fluid, the courtyard was stunning beneath

the starry sky. And Harper couldn't refuse.

The path led her between the end of the house and the high stone wall that enclosed the property. She moved toward the back until she came to the edge of the small pond. The kitchen light was still on, and she could see the silk screen that hung on one wall, depicting a gnarled, old tree covered with birds.

Pivoting, she let her eyes wander to the wall, about forty feet from the back of the house. She thought of the woods, and the girl she'd seen there. Emi. Now that she knew her name, Harper was even more puzzled about why the girl had been here, especially when she'd been surrounded by such stern priests that day in the village.

She'd essentially been shielded from exposure to other people, and all the villagers had lowered their gazes in deference.

Harper stopped in her stroll through the back garden. Was that why the girl had been so horrified when Harper saw her? That a stranger had not only stared straight at her, but smiled and waved?

The girl had probably expected to be safe from prying eyes out here on the mountain, in the solitude of the woods. She might not have known the Saito house was currently occupied.

Harper was having a hard time getting started on the book, especially when it came to thinking of characters. Every time she thought of the village or its people, her mind automatically drifted back to Emi and those priests. She tried to imagine what could be so special about their religion that it had to be kept such a secret.

She had no idea what rule she'd broken by looking directly at Emi, but she hoped it was nothing too serious. Rubbing her arms against the chill that was setting in, she decided to go back inside where it was warm.

When she got back to the courtyard, she stepped up on the wooden walkway and took her shoes off at the door. Wearing only socks, she padded through her office and back to the kitchen.

An idea had come to her while she'd been perusing the gardens, and she wanted to write it down before she forgot. When she entered the main section of the house, her senses went on high alert. Something was different.

Her breath grew heavy in her lungs as she stopped and stared. She could feel a change in the environment, but couldn't pinpoint what it was. After standing still and concentrating hard for any sound or sign of what was bothering her, Harper finally sighed to release the terrible anxiety.

Then she glanced around the open floor plan again, sure that something was off. Feeling braver, she moved past the kitchen and looked toward the other side of the house. That's when she saw it.

The lower level could be sectioned off at any time by pulling *shoji* screens from the walls. They were nestled inside the walls, but could be pulled out to meet each other in the middle, essentially creating a partition.

One of those screens had been pulled halfway out, and Harper hugged herself as she walked closer. She tested the makeshift door, nudging the screen as it glided smoothly back into the wall. The *shoji* panel slid easily into place and stayed there.

Harper stomped her foot, wondering if the mild vibration would be enough to jar the screen and cause it to ease back out. When the screen remained immobile, she pounded the wall for the same reason. The *shoji* didn't move.

"There must have been a draft when I opened the outside doors in my office," she said, well aware she was trying to convince herself. Experiencing a cold tingle on her nape, she turned in place and scrutinized every corner.

Then, sucking in a breath for courage, she hurried to the television room and flipped on a wall light. Nothing there but the couch, shelves, and huge flat-screen TV. She checked the doors that opened to the outside, but they were locked.

The laugh that came from her was light and shaky. "I'm being neurotic. That's all." She shook her head and turned out the light. She'd make a late night snack then get back to work. There was nothing like a good scare to get the adrenaline flowing, so she might as well put the burst of energy to good use.

She longed for a mozzarella cheese stick, but they were hard to come by. She'd had the forethought to ship herself some things from the States before her trip, so at least she had her favorite crackers, enough to last a few months. If she was frugal.

As the herb-flavored triangles tumbled into a bowl, Harper wondered about the screen and why it had moved. She felt the stab of anxiety again but quickly convinced herself she was just over analyzing. Being too cautious.

Why would someone sneak into her house and move a screen? The notion seemed ridiculous, but Harper also knew that a fine line separated needless worry and dangerous ignorance.

Unfortunately, a person only realized they'd been ignorant afterwards. When they were already in trouble.

Okay, get out of your head and back to reality. This is the here and now, and you're all alone. No one sneaked inside to... to what? The screen wasn't even pulled all the way out. She picked up the bowl and said, "Par-a-noid," before popping a cracker into her mouth.

Maybe if she'd been cautious when it really mattered, she wouldn't be like this now. If she'd only known to be worried. If she'd called one minute earlier... *Don't. Don't go there.*

Slamming the bowl back down, Harper told herself that playing the *What if?* game was a one-way ticket to insanity. And she wasn't the sort of person who would talk to a shrink. She'd never had therapy, despite the encouragement of family and friends.

Instead, she'd begun writing. Immersing herself in make-believe characters and all of their stories created the perfect diversion. Heroic saviors and witty heroines helped her forget her own life. Her own tragic tale.

Because she hated tragedies.

Harper still blamed herself and probably always would, but she'd learned to put away the remorse and self-accusations. To take them out at a time of her choosing, when she'd wallow in the pain and anger, letting the emotions wash through her until she cried out every spare tear her body could produce.

Then she would start again. She would put the memories back in their cubicle.

Sometimes there was no stopping the memories, and that horrible night would suddenly rush back. If she passed a particular type of man on the street, or heard a story about a college campus, or saw a girl with brown hair in a French braid.

These were only a few of the things that could force Harper to remember. The world was not a safe place, and the more removed she was from those unpredictable hazards, the better.

Instead of returning to her work, she let her mind go blank. She leaned against the counter and finished off the crackers, angry at herself for getting so worked up over the screen. Her miniature meltdown had been completely uncalled for.

She moved to the sink and turned the water on hot, letting it heat up as she stared out back. How quickly the serenity from her walk had been crushed. Her mood was so foul now, that she might as well go to bed. She wouldn't get any more work done tonight.

As steam lifted from the faucet, the bottom of the window clouded over, drawing Harper's attention to the glass. She noticed a streak forming in the condensation, a place where the steam refused to adhere.

She swung the arm of the faucet around, so the water ran

against the back of the sink. The steam rose quickly to the window, revealing more of the image. Strange lines had been marked on the glass.

Not just lines, but a symbol.

Puzzling over the presence of writing on the window, Harper reached without thinking and ran her finger across the writing. She erased the center.

Because it had been drawn on the inside.

Stumbling back from the sink, she could almost hear puzzle pieces clicking together in her brain. The screen. The symbol. Both things had happened inside the house. Was there a connection? When had the symbol been written?

Struggling for calm, Harper reached across the sink to shut off the water. She opened a drawer and grabbed a large knife from inside.

Here was where that fine line got blurry. Was she overreacting? Or would chalking things up to coincidence only leave her vulnerable?

She'd rather be foolish than end up dead. Or worse.

With the knife clutched tightly in her hand, she went back to her office to make sure the door was locked. She would search room by room, inside closets and bathrooms, until she was certain her home was secure.

As soon as she got to the sliding glass door, she threw the lock and glanced around the courtyard. Not long ago, she'd enjoyed the mystery of the shadows. Now they looked ominous, every dark place a spot for someone to hide. To wait.

Remembering the outside light, she flipped the switch and cast golden light over everything. No attackers hiding in the courtyard. The blush of embarrassment made Harper's neck warm. *So what if I'm acting crazy? No one's around to see.*

Just as she declared this end of the house safe, she noticed light condensation on the outside of the door. A typical phenomenon when a cool night followed a warm day. Still, it made her think of the kitchen window, so she bent closer and opened her mouth to huff hot air onto the glass.

Nothing appeared. Smiling now, and calling herself ten kinds of ridiculous, she blew closer to the center, and was relieved when nothing showed up. She laughed as her muscles relaxed and tension fled. She couldn't believe how good it felt to be wrong.

Then, just to be thorough, she exhaled on the glass in the exact middle, where the two doors came together. A symbol emerged when her hot breath met the cool glass. The same drawing she'd seen in the kitchen.

With renewed urgency, Harper searched the rest of the house. She performed the exact same routine, flipping on the lights and checking every place a person might have room to hide. But now she'd added one more step to the process, checking the windows or doors for the symbol

By the time she'd inspected the entire lower level, she was caught somewhere between rationalization and mindless terror. Her good sense told her there was nothing to be afraid of, while her innate sense of self-preservation made hairs stand up on her arms.

Leaving every single light burning, she ran up the stairs and performed the same test in the sitting room. Then the picture windows in the bath. Finally, she made sure her balcony doors were locked tight before climbing in bed with her knife.

The bedroom was the only place she turned off the light. The yellow glow seeping in from the hallway bathed her room in just enough light, while still leaving her in the shadows. So she could see if anyone was coming.

With her mind racing for any reasonable explanation, Harper huddled under the covers with her back propped up on pillows against the wall. She sat upright, since she doubted she would sleep.

There was no way for her to tell how long the symbols had

been in her house, and for all she knew, they could be some sort of protection, blessing, or wish for good luck. But with the chill in the air and darkness over the mountainside, she was having a hard time seeing anything positive in the strange markings.

Whether they had been put there recently or two months ago. Whether they were a happy charm or an awful curse. Harper didn't know.

All she knew was that every window or glass door in the house had been marked. Whatever the meaning of the mysterious symbols, they were everywhere. On each level and in every room.

She was surrounded.

7

Harper slept fitfully throughout the night, occasionally dozing off, only to bolt upright every time she heard the faintest sound. Eventually, a rainstorm swept across the mountains and valley of Chuujitsu, and the steady roar of pummeling rain finally lulled her to sleep.

She woke now to the last plaintive drops of the dying storm, and to the weak, pale light slipping through the lingering cloud cover. The day outside looked and felt gray. Moody, like a grieving woman who couldn't let go of a dark past.

Since no one had entered her bedroom to strangle or stab her in the night, Harper felt comfortable stumbling from bed and performing her morning bathroom routine. Luckily, she'd already been wearing her pajamas when she'd spooked herself into hiding in bed.

After she'd washed her face and brushed her teeth, she took cautious steps downstairs and stopped at the bottom to look around.

Everything was as it should be. And the *shoji* screen was still in its proper place.

She decided to skip breakfast this morning but did stop in the kitchen long enough to start a pot of coffee. While it brewed, she went to her office and jiggled the mouse to wake up the laptop on her desk.

The screens in her office were also as she'd left them—open, so she could see outside. Wisps of fog floated in the courtyard and around the stone lantern, like ghostly fingers searching for warmth.

Ignoring the eerie scene in the garden, she sat down to her computer and opened a browser online. She'd planned to research Japanese writing anyway, the styles, history, and any interesting details she might come cross.

After last night, this task had become her top priority. She would find the symbol that had been written all over her house, and once she understood its meaning, she could decide her next move.

After fifteen minutes of various word searches, Harper had learned very little. The characters drawn on her windows were called *kanji* and were one of three forms of Japanese writing. The symbols were called ideograms, meaning a simple picture that represented an object, a thing, or a quality.

She'd also learned that the symbol for fire looked a lot like Gumby, but after that, it was all pretty confusing.

She'd tried typing in various versions of the words "*kanji*" combined with "blessing," "curse," and even "drawn on windows." So far, she had yet to see anything resembling the symbols she'd discovered.

Her first instinct was to clean every glass surface in the house. Now that irritation had surfaced, she felt the need to reclaim her territory. Harper sighed and closed the web browser. She couldn't remove the writing yet. Not if she wanted someone else to look at them and tell her what they meant.

There were different styles of *kanji* writing, but none of the ones she'd found online were quite the same as the ones on her windows and doors. The styles used here had been more elegant, almost fluid. And she knew when to admit she was way out of her wheelhouse.

Internet research on the Japanese way of life did not make her fluent in their millennia-old style of writing.

As she swiveled in her chair, slowly back and forth, she rubbed her chin and considered her options. Then she let her gaze fall to the scroll Reid had sent her as a house-warming gift. The one she'd immediately added to her desk necessities. In a prominent position.

The scroll was approximately five-by-five inches square, and had been singed at the edges for an aged effect. The symbol on the paper— she now could identify as *kanji*— had been done with a type of calligraphy and most likely by a local artist. The style of painting took great practice, she knew, and was undeniably considered an art form.

Below the symbol was its meaning written in English. *Perseverance.*

She didn't know what had prompted Reid to send her the small but thoughtful present, yet he'd chosen an eerily appropriate word. Harper was the master of pushing herself through the dark times. Day by day.

By day.

Deciding the mysterious and unexpected Reid Ellis was far more observant than she'd initially given him credit for, Harper decided to put him to the test. He apparently knew more about the symbols than she did, and he had, after all, been hired to help her navigate the village and Japanese customs.

She might as well ask him if he recognized the symbol. The worst thing he could do is say he didn't.

Using a computer program that allowed her to paint electronically, Harper did her best to draw an image of the symbol before saving it to her documents. She would email the drawing to Reid and get his opinion.

Why hadn't she thought of this earlier? Harper happily hit the Enter button and smiled at the laptop. This way, she wouldn't even have to leave the house.

She opened her email and stopped with her hands poised in the air over her keyboard. She didn't have his email address.

She'd have to call him.

Whirling in the chair, she let out a groan and sprung to her feet. The coffee would be ready by now, so she'd pour a cup and make the call.

Why was she trying so hard to avoid any and all contact with the man? That's all he was. Just a man. And the more she got to know him, the more he seemed to be a considerate and attentive person.

He certainly wasn't a threat. So why did the thought of him make her blush? Was it because there was so much more to him than what met the eye?

She shook her head and filled her mug. What met her eye wasn't bad, either. Not. At. All. And that was also part of the problem.

Ignoring the nervous twist in her small intestine, Harper picked up her cell and dialed. Deep breath in. Deep breath out. She listened to the rings like a teenager calling her high school crush.

And when his deep, velvety voice said, "Hello," what little bravado she had popped and flew away, like a balloon that had sprung a leak.

"Reid," she said quickly. "It's Harper Gray. I'm sorry to bother you, but I need you to look at something."

She would swear his voice sounded like he was smiling when he said, "I'll be right over." Then he hung up.

"No, wait." Harper spoke into the phone, but no one was on the other end. She bit her bottom lip and jiggled her right leg. Should she call him back and tell him she just needed his email address? Maybe she should just text him.

"Oh, get over it already," she chastised herself. "This isn't a date."

Then, remembering she was still wearing pajamas, she raced upstairs to get cleaned up. Whether Reid was a hot date or simply her male assistant, there was no way she was meeting him in a state of undress.

As it turned out, she needn't have hurried. A full twenty minutes passed before she heard the gate bell ring. She'd already unlocked it for his arrival and swung out the front door to wave him in. The fog had dissipated slightly, but a thin mist still clung to the air, touching her face with its cool, wet kiss.

"I didn't mean for you to come all this way," she called as he approached. Then he was in the *genkan*, so she stepped back to give him some space.

"I was in the mood for a walk anyway," he said, trading out his shoes as she'd seen him do before.

"In this weather?"

Reid gave her a look. "What's wrong with it?"

"Nothing. Never mind." The flash of leaf-green eyes and Reid's accompanying smile had forced all rational arguments from her head. So, she led him inside and got straight to the point. "I was going to email you a picture, but since you're here, I'll just pull it up on the computer."

She talked over her shoulder as Reid followed her to her office. "I'm hoping you can tell me what this *kanji* means."

"Look who's picking up the language," he said, and again, Harper was struck by how rich his voice was. She could almost feel it stroking her skin. And the dampness of the day seemed to make his scent more pronounced. Definitely male, and the only other word that came to mind was *alpine*.

She was sure he'd love that description.

"Here it is," she said, turning her mind from his easygoing smile and back to the symbol that had terrorized her the previous night. Would she be as frightened when the sun set this evening? She hoped not. This was supposed to be her paradise. Her sanctuary.

So getting an answer to the tortuous riddle was imperative.

Reid leaned down to study the character she'd duplicated on her laptop.

"And here's what I drew by hand. I wouldn't get a passing grade for penmanship, but I think I have the basic shapes right." She watched as he shook his head.

"I speak Japanese moderately well, but I'm still a rookie when it comes to their writing. I don't recognize this symbol." His eyes flicked to hers. "And the style is different from most."

"Most?" Harper prompted.

"I think I've seen similar *kanji* in the village, but I can't say where. I just remember seeing this odd curl here." He pointed to the bottom of the character. "As far as I know, this form of writing is unique to Chuujitsu. I've never seen it anywhere else."

"Someone should know what it means, though." Harper picked up the drawing. "Maybe Saya can translate this for me, but thanks for trying. Oh," she said suddenly. "I also wanted to thank you for the scroll."

She looked at Reid's gift sitting on her desk, so he did the same. Then he smiled and her chest started to feel funny. Too tight. Too breathless.

"I'm glad you like it," he said, scrutinizing her rigid posture before crossing his arms and giving her an appraising look. "And I'm glad you met Saya. You two are a good fit."

Recalling the confident and colorful Japanese woman, Harper laughed. "Hardly. Why would you say that?"

"Because you're polar opposites." He looked down to her bare feet then dragged his slow, heated perusal back up, taking in her pin-striped skinny jeans and white shirt. "Except for your love of fashion."

"I'm sure you think it's odd that I dress up just to stay home all day, but sometimes I need to feel like I'm going to work." Harper put her hands against her thighs, unsure why she was explaining herself.

"I get that," he told her without a hint of mockery. "But if you're not doing anything now, why don't you join me on that walk? Get to know the area better. There's a lot more to Chuujitsu than what you saw in town." Reid stepped closer to her. "Just promise you'll wear your glasses."

"My..." Harper stuttered, caught off guard. "My what?"

"You know, smart looking little rectangles, brown and green." His smile turned sinful. "You look good in them."

Her mouth dropped open. "Are you flirting with me?"

"Do you want me to be flirting with you?"

Shaking her head, Harper said, "That just isn't a good idea."

"And that is not an answer." Reid had edged closer without her realizing it. "I can quit working for you if it will make you feel better."

"What? No. That's not fair." Harper crossed her arms. "You know I need you." She moved past him and headed toward the front of the house, calling out as she went. "This is like sexual harassment in reverse."

"Where are you going?" he asked, trailing her as she moved through the rooms and to the stairs.

"To get my tennis shoes." She didn't look back, because she knew he'd be wearing a look of smug victory. That, and she didn't want him to see her face and the different emotions flashing there.

She wasn't really upset and was sure he could tell. Still, she shouldn't encourage him or send him the wrong signals. They were going to be working together, even if only sporadically, for the next six months. Harper tried not to get too deeply involved with anyone, but especially men.

Especially a man who was supposed to be her assistant. Not that Reid Ellis was even behaving like one. The man didn't have a subservient bone in his body. He was so self-assured, smiling every time she frowned and just expecting her to come around to his frame of mind.

Harper sighed as she retrieved her shoes from the closet then got a pair of socks from a drawer. Apparently, she was going hiking, so she also changed into a more comfortable pair of brown pants.

She went to the bathroom to put her hair up in a clip, and smudged a dot of gloss on her lips. Rubbing them together, she grabbed the edge of the counter and stared hard at her reflection.

"Keep calm and take a walk." She tugged on her shirt to straighten it and remonstrated herself one more time. "This is *still* not a date."

8

"Where did you find that symbol?" Reid asked when he and Harper stopped to look out over the valley. There was a break in the trees, so they took advantage of the open expanse to take in the layout from farming plots, river bend, and on to the village.

He noticed Harper bite her bottom lip before she turned to him with a response. "I was wondering if it might be some sort of blessing."

She had evaded his question, and that, added to her uneasy behavior, told him there was more to her interest in the *kanji* character than simple curiosity or even research for her book. "Where did you see it?" he asked again.

Harper might be a wordsmith, but he interviewed people on a regular basis, most of whom didn't want to tell him anything in the first place. By the time the interview concluded, they usually ended up thanking him for the conversation.

Many didn't realize how badly they needed to share their stories, troubles, or sometimes, even their shame.

He didn't expect great revelations from Harper, but he wanted to know why she lived in seclusion. Compared to the locals he'd encountered in the village, he assumed her armor would be thin. And since she preferred to isolate herself, she probably wasn't used to fending off questions.

The look she turned on him then was surprising, as if she

knew his game and didn't appreciate him playing it with her. "Do you think hammering me with the same question is going to make me get all fluttery and nervous? That enough persistence could ever make me tell you something I have chosen not to?"

Well, color Reid surprised. Perhaps her greatest defense was illusion, because not only was her armor thick, it had just sprung barbs.

"Yes," he admitted. "That's precisely what I thought."

She huffed and stared out at the landscape dotted with farmhouses. "At least you're honest."

"That," he said, "and I can't help you if I don't know what you're really after."

Reid wondered again why he found her so attractive. Her features were such a collage, delicate nose, chiseled jaw and cheeks, and the most amazing eyes he'd ever seen. He still didn't find her beautiful, and pretty was too soft a word for Harper Gray.

Yet she was intriguing, and the more he looked, the more her warm brown hair and serious gray eyes captivated him.

And damn, that top-heavy mouth was her kill shot.

"Someone marked every window and glass door in the Saito house with that symbol."

Reid snapped his wandering gaze back to her. Now she had his attention. "What do you mean? When?"

She shrugged. "That's the question. Maybe the owners did it before they left, but I never noticed them until last night. The condensation on the glass made them more visible."

Reid heard her nonchalant tone, but what he saw when she swallowed was anxiety. "I'm sure it's nothing to worry about, and like you said, the Saito family probably did it before they left. Or they might have hired a superstitious housekeeper from the village. *Kanji* are used all over the place."

When she faced him now, he saw a mix of relief and gratitude. "You're right. I just spooked myself last night. You know, all alone in the woods with strange markings literally all around me." She shivered. "I felt like a marked man."

"Or protected," he suggested.

Her lips spread into a smile, and Reid's hand itched to reach out and feel the hair that lay over the front of one shoulder. To see if it was as silky as its shine suggested. "There's a path we can take through the forest that will come out overlooking the other end of the village." He paused, waiting for her to agree. He'd demanded enough for one day.

"I can do that. Now that we're out," she lifted the camera that hung from her neck, "I might as well get some good shots." She pointed the camera back to the valley and adjusted her lens before snapping the shutter several times.

With a nod from her to indicate she was finished, Reid headed back into the woods with Harper at his side. "You'll be more at ease if you know your surroundings," he said. "Nothing is as scary once you see it in the light."

Harper didn't say anything in response, because she didn't agree with him. She'd seen bad things during the day, and the sun shining down on horror didn't make things better. Just macabre in a different way.

But she wouldn't tell Reid how wrong he was. It would only prompt him to ask more questions, and she sensed the determination in him to seek out every answer. Whether it applied to his research or not.

There wasn't much light in the forest to speak of, since the sky was overcast and trees absorbed what was left of the falling beams. Still, there was peace in the quiet woods, as if even the birds had decided to take a lazy day.

Harper enjoyed the hush. She let it surround her, with only the soft thud of their footsteps on the dirt trail. Soon they started up a mild incline and came upon a divergence in the path. A tall, thin stone sat at the corner, like a street sign from three hundred years ago.

The marker had obviously been hewn by hand, carved into the unnatural shape. More *kanji* were etched into the front, and Harper knew the long line would be read from the top of the stone to the bottom.

"I can't tell you exactly what this says," Reid gestured to the stone, "but at the end of this footpath is an old mine entrance. The village used to dig for silver, but the mine has been shut down for a long time."

"Why?" Harper asked, running her hand over the ancient marker and marveling over the smooth surface.

"I'm not sure. Maybe the silver ran out. The locals don't think much of this place anymore, so they don't talk about it."

"Can we go in?"

He shook his head. "It's boarded up for safety."

Light scuffs against the ground told them someone else was approaching, and a man appeared shortly after. He was wearing a different version of the robes Harper had seen on the priests in town. The top was sleeveless, and the bottom part of the robe opened to reveal pants beneath, but the color and material seemed identical.

She sensed Reid's movement, but the shift in his position was barely noticeable. He'd angled himself in front of her as the priest advanced, then bowed his head before facing Harper.

When she would have spoken, Reid gently touched her arm. The gesture and the set of his mouth told her to wait and stay silent. She gave the barest of nods to let him know she understood, but she couldn't stop herself from tracking the man as he passed.

The neckline of his robe hung loosely, similar to a cowl, and Harper saw the edge of an intricate design on his skin. From the curve, she guessed the tattoo circled from his chest around to his back.

Deferring to Reid, the specialist when it came to local etiquette, Harper looked back at him and met his steady gaze.

She might have been safer watching the priest. The green of Reid's eyes smoldered as he stared at her, and there was nothing cautious or restrained about it.

He was clearly interested in being a lot more than her assistant, and the raw sensuality he emanated made her chest squeeze in on itself. When she was able to find her breath again, Harper realized his hand was still on her arm, but the light hold on her shirt was gone. Now he held her wrist.

His grip was loose but provocative, and the bracelet of his fingers scorched the sensitive skin on the underside of her arm. His thumb rested on her pulse point, and the small connection was suddenly too intimate.

"Why did you turn away?" she asked, steering the topic to a more benign subject. Even a creepy, village priest seemed less dangerous to her than the heat rolling off of Reid. "You had already looked at him."

A disgruntled wrinkle formed on his forehead before he relaxed and let her go. "Looking at them isn't forbidden, but they don't want any type of interaction between themselves and those who don't directly serve the temple. Especially with—"

"Outsiders," Harper finished for him. "I think I'm getting the picture. So looking at him for a long time would have been considered too much contact." She tilted her head. "And rude, since you couldn't speak to him, either."

She chanced a look at him again and thankfully found only his usual carefree smile. "I try not to be rude if I can help it."

Harper's expression said she wasn't sure she believed him. "I don't suppose you've ever seen their tattoos? Do you know what they are?"

"Ancient temple secret," he said, taking a few backward steps up the trail. "Come on, you still haven't seen the best view."

Harper was happy to continue on. His promise of a panoramic vista was enticing, and she felt refreshed by the crisp, moist air.

The forest colors ranged from dark, glossy ferns with emerald fronds, to the tall cedars with their needles of dark blue-green. In contrast, the bark of the towering trees was red, and Harper imagined herself exploring enchanted woods.

"Where'd you get your name?" Reid asked, stopping several yards ahead so she could catch up. "Harper. Family name?"

At last, a question she didn't mind answering. Every time she told the story, she thought of her father. Tall and lanky, medium-brown hair, and reading glasses like her, but his were simple wire-rims. He was a true bibliophile, a lover of books—again, like his eldest daughter.

"Not a family name," she said, smiling softly as she watched her steps on the rocky ground. "At least, not in the way you mean. My father had the honor of naming me, and he's a literature professor at UNC."

"I see where this is going," Reid told her. "Let me think. I'm guessing your dad likes the classics, right?"

She nodded.

"I tend to stick to adventure books myself, especially if there's a submarine involved." He stopped and lifted his head as if looking at the sky. "An author named Harper." He frowned and shook his head. "Doesn't help me all that much."

She surprised herself by laughing. "My full name is Harper Lee Gray. You could say my dad had high aspirations for me, and I'm just lucky I wasn't named Boo or Scout."

"He must have had some foresight, since you became a writer." Reid's smile was genuine when he said, "He must be proud."

"He is, though he occasionally reminds me that bursting corsets do not an American classic make."

"But you're happy, right?"

The moment of levity fell flat as Harper took his question to heart. Of course, she was pleased with her success and glad she could finally support herself doing what she loved, but happy wasn't the right word for what she was.

Content. Secure. Comfortable. Those descriptions might apply.

But no. Harper couldn't claim to be happy and probably never would. Some people weren't dealt a full hand in life, so instead, she would make do with the cards she'd been given. Or at least, the ones she still held onto.

She hiked her brows and squeezed out a smile for Reid, but she saw the way his expression changed. Luckily, the ridge he'd mentioned came into view, so she hurried toward the break in the trees.

When she stopped on the rocky outcropping, a mere two feet from the edge and a long drop below, Harper was able to shake off the gloom she'd felt before.

A few, strong sunbeams had broken through the clouds, and they slanted their glorious light across the valley. From where she and Reid stood, the village looked like a painting. Antiquated buildings and stone streets were gilded by the glow.

Harper took several pictures, and neither she nor Reid spoke for a while. Eventually, she dropped the camera against her chest and studied the rest of the village. "What is that group of buildings on the east end?" The structures had broken windows and were overgrown with vegetation.

"That's where they processed the silver. They're not used anymore, either."

"Seems like a waste." Harper looked back toward the village. More modern buildings were on the east side, farthest from the older and more expensive area on the west end. Where the temple and large, stone homes sat.

From here, the delineation between those who controlled the village and those who simply existed was apparent. The magnificent stone buildings whispered of a tumultuous history and the strength that had sustained them. Those who'd lived in the grand structures had likely wielded power for centuries.

Harper wondered if they still did, or if they'd simply been blessed with the inheritance of great estates.

When lightning slashed abruptly from the darkening clouds, she flinched, then wished she'd had the camera poised. The whip of electricity had been a brilliant white and would have made a magnificent picture as it struck somewhere in the dense forest below.

"That's our cue to go," Reid said. "The sky's been threatening us all day, and I guess she's finally delivering."

Thunder rolled after them as they made their way back into the cover of trees. So far, the rain was holding back, but the impending storm continued to clap and rumble with authority. They picked up their pace as if they were being pursued.

"I can handle a little rain," Harper told him. "We don't have to rush."

Reid slowed and let her move up beside him, so he could see her face. "If the bottom falls out too soon, are you going to let me stay with you until it passes?"

"I'm not heartless," she said on a huff, but she couldn't hold his gaze.

Reid had managed to make her nervous, so with or without pelting rain, he knew he'd be returning to his own home. He wouldn't invade her personal space again today. Not in her home, anyway.

To save time, they didn't speak for the rest of the way, both hurrying down the path toward her house. There were many routes one could take on this mountain, with trails splitting off to the right and left, but Reid knew his way and led her quickly back to shelter.

When they came out of the woods and onto the drive leading to her house, Harper said, "That was fast."

"The return trip always is." He took long strides, eating up the ground to the iron gate. He waited while she opened the lock.

Hesitating, she perused the dark skies. She took a breath and clapped turbulent gray eyes on his. "Do you want to stay?"

"I'm pretty sure I'll beat the storm. But if I don't," he grinned at her, "I can handle a little rain."

Hearing her words tossed back at her, Harper smiled, too.

"But to answer your question," Reid angled his body closer to hers, not touching, not threatening, but just so he could speak in a low voice, "I do want to stay."

Her bottom lip fell slightly open as if she were at a loss for words. Guess he could make her speechless after all.

"But I won't," he added quickly, a quiet thrill running through him at how easily he could throw her off her stride. "I just wanted to make sure you understood." *That I want to kiss you. But I won't do that, either. Not today.*

Her eyes grew as dark as the angry clouds above, and he could see her mind churning just as quickly. She understood, all right, and if he were any judge of people, Reid would bet she wasn't sure how she felt about his intentions.

"I'd better run," he said, backing away from her as thunder boomed from the valley behind him. But this time, he noticed, Harper didn't flinch. This time, she held her ground.

9

Harper made herself some green tea and went to watch the rain fall on the back garden. She slid the glass doors open so she could appreciate the patter of drops on leaves and the languid rhythm of the bamboo water feature. Without fail, the hollow cane filled and emptied, the predictable *plunk* soothing her mind.

And a troubled mind it was, thanks to Reid's unapologetic declaration that he was interested in her romantically. Okay, so he hadn't said it in so many words, but he'd hinted and emoted so much she'd have to be blind or willfully oblivious not to catch on.

She sipped the hot tea, appreciating the vegetal taste on her tongue, another thing she'd give him credit for. He'd told her she would get used to the drink without artificial additives and come to enjoy the natural sweetness. And indeed she had.

Here she was with her legs crossed lotus style, in a round, low-to-the-floor chair, watching her Zen garden get doused by rain while she drank green tea. She felt like she'd truly adopted a new lifestyle and had to admit serenity was easily found here.

The Japanese countryside had made its way to the top of her list of places to escape. Though next time, she might avoid villages with strange religions that didn't welcome visitors.

After almost an hour, the storm began to let up, but she wasn't ready to do anything terribly productive. A hot bath sounded like a good idea, followed by lunch afterwards.

She was in no mood to tackle work just yet, but she often found her second burst of energy in the afternoon anyway. The day wasn't completely wasted. Not yet.

She went upstairs, passing through the sitting room on the way to draw her bath, when she happened to glance casually out the back windows. And froze. She couldn't believe what she saw.

The girl was back again.

With furtive movements, Harper ducked lower and watched from where she stood. She hunched over like a poorly-trained spy.

The uninvited visitor was wandering through the trees as if she had nothing on her mind but a tour of the grounds. Her face was blank—not happy or sad—simply expressionless. Harper knew from previous research into mental illness that Emi would be described as having a "flat affect."

Then she remembered what Saya had told her. That Emi didn't speak.

Well, she didn't want to harm the girl, or even scare her, but she had to be told she couldn't come to the house and slip around the yard whenever she wanted. Or come inside and make symbols on the windows.

No, Harper decided, there's no way this girl did anything like that. She looked too innocent. Sweet, even.

Regardless, Harper didn't like the idea of her lurking outside all the time. Who knew how often she was creeping around the house? Harper might not even realize she was there, because the upper floor had the only vantage point that would allow her to see over the back wall.

Harper made her decision. She'd go downstairs, quietly, and meet the girl in the yard. She would be kind and gentle, and maybe she could communicate with the girl. Find out what she wanted. There were several village families who spoke English, so it was possible Emi came from one.

Would the girl listen to her? More importantly, should Harper even attempt to draw Emi into conversation? If looking at Emi broke some sort of temple rule, then engaging her in conversation was surely an unforgivable sin.

Harper stood ramrod stiff and edged her way to the stairs, back against the wall where she was positive the shadows would cover her. This was her home, and she wouldn't hide inside unless that was her choice.

Now that she'd made up her mind, urgency rode her back as she hurried down the stairs. She didn't want anyone outside when she didn't know about it, and she wanted a chance to speak to the girl. Emi had been at the center of almost every strange occurrence that had happened to Harper since her arrival.

She wanted to put the Emi mystery to bed so she could move on and stop worrying. She might even get an explanation for those symbols.

She hurried across the glossy wood floor in her slippers and cursed softly when she had to stop for the inside-shoes-outside-shoes swap. Then she put her sneakers on and was out the door.

Realizing the last dregs of falling rain would cover any noise she made, Harper experienced a moment of guilt for the subterfuge. Then she reminded herself she was technically in her own yard. She wasn't the trespasser.

Emi might not mean any harm, but if she was so afraid of being seen by Harper, why did she keep coming back?

The gate made a soft creak when it swung open, and Harper stiffened. Was the noise due to the wet weather, or had she just never noticed it before? Well, if she'd given herself away, she might as well skirt the corner of the wall and see if she could spot the girl from here.

She peered around the stone wall but couldn't see anything.

Emi had been farther back, so Harper had no choice but to slip along the wall until she cleared the side and could get a better view. She tried to be quiet, but between rocks and forest debris, every step made a light crunching sound.

When she rounded the back corner, she came face to face with the girl. Like the time before, Emi's eyes went wide and she shook her head frantically. Last time Harper had assumed the action was reflexive.

Now she believed Emi was trying to tell Harper not to look at her.

Instinctively, Harper turned her head and shielded her eyes. "I'm sorry," she said, still unsure if Emi would understand English. She didn't hear anything, no movement or the pounding of fleeing footsteps. No words. In any language.

She waited a few more seconds, but she didn't want to stare at the ground all day.

"I want to know why you're coming here," Harper said gently, waiting for an answer or gesture. For something. Anything. Receiving no indication she'd been understood or if she'd even been heard, she slowly started to turn her head toward the girl. Giving her plenty of warning, and time to hide her face.

Two wide, nervous eyes were staring at Harper when she finally looked up. Emi's eyes were light brown with black brows in a sweeping arch. Her face was pale and her lips were pursed in a tight bow from either fear or indecision.

Her midnight hair was pulled back in a ponytail with one long strand free to hang down the left side of her face. The girl could be thirteen or she could be seventeen. Her skin was so supple with youth, Harper was unable to peg her age.

She wore a beige outfit today, not the pure white she'd had on for the procession from the temple. She wore loosely-fitting pants of a simple weave and a shirt to match. The belt at her waist was the color that Harper now thought of as *temple brown*.

The church still had a claim staked here, as if the girl was a representative of the temple. Or belonged to it.

Not sure where to begin, Harper tried a small smile and was relieved when the girl stayed where she was. Harper put her hand against her own chest and patted twice. "Harper. My name is Harper."

Emi's face relaxed moderately, but she darted her eyes to the side as if searching for rescue. Then she looked again to the strange woman trying to speak with her. She moved one foot backward, scraping against gravel and leaves.

"It's okay," Harper held out both palms in an effort to demonstrate passive and welcoming body language. She nodded to the girl. "Is your name... Emi?"

Speaking the girl's name was like an auditory detonator. Emi's eyes flew wide open again, and she spun on her heels before bolting into the woods.

"Damn," Harper whispered with a slap on her thigh. "Wait!" Then, without a clue to her own motivation, Harper sprang into action and chased after her. She didn't stop to think. She only responded. "I'm not going to hurt you!"

She was probably breaking ten tenets of the *Shinto* religion dominating the village of Chuujitsu, but Harper wanted to set things right. Emi couldn't be as terrified of Harper as she acted, or else she wouldn't have returned once she knew the house was occupied.

Scrambling over ferns and low-lying shrubs, Harper finally made it to a trail and found better footing. She'd seen Emi turn this way and charged along the path in pursuit. The girl might be small, but she was spry.

Harper had a longer stride and hoped to make some ground without barreling up on the girl. She didn't want to scare her any more than she already had. A stray branch slapped her in the face, but since the blow glanced off her cheek, she pushed on.

The trail took a turn that led higher up the mountain and after a minute of racing without catching any sight of Emi, Harper began to accept her defeat. Especially when she came to the fork in the path. One way went higher up the mountainside, the other went down.

Stopping to catch her breath, Harper bent over and put her hands on her knees. Ragged pulls of air burned her lungs and all she could hear was the sound of her own gasps. She thought of endless hours on her butt in front of the computer. *I need to get more exercise.*

She stood and held herself still. Listening. What was that sound? Like footsteps on wood. To her left and upward. Harper found her second wind and took off, determined now to catch the girl. And she wasn't sure why.

Soon the path curved right and was easing along level ground, no longer leading her up such a steep angle. The trees spread out to reveal a wooden bridge spanning from one side of a ravine to the other. This was where she'd heard the tread of Emi's running feet.

The bridge was wide, at least six feet, and as Harper drew near, she peered over the edge to see a thin stream of water below. Not too far, thankfully, because she wasn't fond of heights.

Increasing her speed, she walked quickly over the bridge and found that the path on the other side was also wider. On each side of the passage were two lanterns—stone, like in her gardens, but of a different style.

These were taller with more levels, and the curve of their lines was somehow menacing. The lamps didn't invoke any sense of spirituality or harmony with nature. Not that she could feel.

She heard a rustle up ahead and saw a dark head whip back in hiding. "Emi, wait!" Harper ran, hoping the girl was having second thoughts about talking to her. She ducked into the opening in the hedge and found herself at the bottom of a long set of steps. The visual effect was amazing.

Gray stone slabs were set into the earth and rose in an eerily straight line up the mountainside. Moss grew in patches and gave the steps a mystical, organic quality. Despite the workmanship, she could tell the stone had been laid long ago.

The immediate area was maintained to keep the steps clear, but a few feet out, the brush returned to its naturally wild growth.

Emi was standing about ten steps above Harper. And she wasn't alone. A priest was with the girl, his hand clamped on her shoulder and dark eyes glaring at Harper. He pointed at her and spoke sharply in Japanese.

Boy, I have really done it now. She felt horrible about her stubborn pursuit of young Emi and hoped the girl wouldn't be in trouble as a result. Or even punished, if this man's face was any indication.

Harper held up her hand in attrition. "I'm so sorry. I chased her, and this is all my fault. I only wanted to ask her a question."

Again the priest berated her before turning his castigating tongue on Emi. The man was clearly furious, and Emi cowered under the onslaught of rage.

Harper was stunned to see the vindictive expression worn plainly on the priest's face as he pulled a thick, leather strap from his belt and raised it high overhead. He brought the strap down across Emi's back, and the *whack!* echoed in the quiet woods. The young girl cried out in pain, but buried her face in her hands to suppress the sound.

Harper recoiled. Her stomach heaved. "Stop! She didn't do anything." Thinking the best thing she could do now was take her eyes off of Emi—who must be a shrine maiden after all, if not some other important position—Harper waved her hands at the man and started to turn away.

She looked one last time into the young, brown eyes that now glistened with tears, and Emi did the least expected thing. She lunged away from the priest and held her arm out, reaching for Harper.

The priest started beating the girl on her back, shoulders, arms, legs, swinging wildly. Furiously.

"Don't touch her!" Harper bounded up the stairs to help the defenseless girl, but just as she came within reaching distance, Emi tore free from the man and ran farther up the steps. She was moving so quickly, Harper knew she'd never catch her.

That was fine with her, because the priest remained where he was. Near the bottom of the stairs and away from poor Emi, the girl who couldn't speak to defend herself.

The priest's face was red and he glared at Harper. Without warning, he charged down the few steps separating them, using his hands to land blows to both her shoulders before shoving her back until she stumbled and fell.

Imagining a neck-breaking tumble down all those stones, Harper tried to throw her weight toward the side, into the grass and bushes. She prayed they would lessen her impact.

The ground slammed against her hip when she landed, but after a brief roll, she was able to straighten her body out and slow the momentum. In one leap, she was back on her feet, ready to protect herself if necessary, but also to check on Emi.

The girl was at the top of the stairs now, and Harper's skin chilled when she saw two more priests flanking her. She made a move to go after Emi, but the priest raised his hand in warning. He blocked the stairs and held his arm out, straight as steel rod, to point a threatening finger at her.

He spoke again, words flying at her like daggers. Then he looked over his shoulder to the girl standing at the top of the stairway with two much larger men surrounding her.

The priest's eyes met Harper's again in a silent dare, and he lashed the leather strip against his own thigh. The message was clear.

If she came any closer, the situation would become worse for Emi. She nodded and bowed her head, feeling absolutely no embarrassment. She would grovel on her knees if that saved the girl from reprimand.

"I'm sorry," she said in a small voice. *Oh, why didn't I learn more of the language?*

With a sound caught somewhere between a grunt and a growl, the priest pivoted and stomped up the steps. Harper was shivering uncontrollably now. The chemical rush from the confrontation was wearing off, and the aftershocks were setting in.

Just as she took a step down the hill, she heard a light chiming sound. She looked up to see the two men with Emi. They were ringing bells, swinging them at her, as if dousing her with music.

While the men waved the bells over and over, Emi stood in the center of the pure, pleasant chorus. The peals should have been lovely as they echoed through the forest, but the vibrations were harsh to Harper's ears.

With guilt a greasy presence on her tongue and in her gut, she made the only choice possible. She left Emi in the custody of the priests.

But as she made her way back to the trail, Harper couldn't erase the image of Emi from her mind. She kept flashing to a disturbing picture of the girl standing still, golden bells ringing all around.

With her young face lowered in shame.

10

Harper reached for her cell phone again, but snatched her hand way as if burned. Just as she'd done on three previous attempts. She didn't know what to do about Emi and the priests but couldn't bring herself to call Saya or Reid for advice. The priest had clearly warned her to mind her own business. Not to cause any more trouble.

Now her instinct was to crawl into her own hole and stay there. Safe, secure, and more importantly, uninvolved.

She had no idea how Saya or Reid might respond. At this point, Harper's breach of protocol was minor, she hoped, and bringing further disruption to the church might backfire. Perhaps it was best to leave things alone and not get anyone else entangled in her mess.

Harper's concern wasn't for herself or even for her friends, but for the teenager currently at the mercy of temple priests. The kind who favored retribution for the slightest misdeed.

Lightning cracked outside, and she yelped before putting a hand to her chest and forcing out a breath. She took a moment to analyze her anxiety. She wasn't afraid of storms; in fact, she was mesmerized by the flash of lightning, the dark clouds that covered the earth and gave her a sense of insulation.

No, weather hadn't caused her increased heart rate, and gusting winds couldn't shake her foundations. Not like other things could. Not like people could.

People and the terrible acts they performed on each other.

"I know better. I should never have gone after her." Harper paced across the dark wood of the floor, growing more agitated with each step. "What do I know about the rules of a secluded temple in a Japanese village? Nothing."

But I know about suffering. Harper went to the kitchen counter and grabbed the edge, ignoring the pain when the sharp underside bit into her palms. *And I know about the fear and pain I saw in Emi's eyes.*

As a rule, she protected herself from the world at large, the crazy unpredictable domain of humans. But she hadn't always done so. Once upon a time, she had been fearless.

Now she was filled with dread. Her current life was built around trepidation and first-hand knowledge that just stepping out your front door could be perilous. That a literal walk in the park could...

"No! This is *not* the same thing." Harper put her hands to her temples and shook her head as if the motion could dispel unpleasant images. "There was nothing I could do. Nothing I could do."

The words weren't new to her lips. She'd recited the mantra hundreds of times, yet still, there were times when she forgot, when she had to make herself accept the truth again. She'd had no control and couldn't have prevented what happened.

She couldn't have saved her.

Harper let her hands slide down her face, her throat, before hugging herself to ward off the chill that racked her body. But this was a different situation altogether. Could she save Emi? Should she try?

Calmer now, Harper moved to the sink and went through the motions of making hot tea. She needed to do something with her hands, to break the monopoly that terror had on her mind and body.

If she could focus on measuring water and scooping the right amount of tea leaves, then she could break down her mental anguish in the same way. Step by step. Piece by piece.

The past wasn't the reason her breath was coming in uneven gasps or why her head was throbbing. She'd learned to deal with that agony, or to at least tuck it away for a period of time. No, the only new factor introduced to her today was Emi.

Well, that and the issue of Harper's attraction to Reid.

She frowned at herself in the window's reflection as she waited for the kettle to boil. Fine. She was attracted to him, but despite the fight or flight reaction he stirred within her, Reid Ellis and his pure green eyes didn't justify the level of distress she was experiencing.

And neither did seeing the young girl struck by the priest's belt. That alone would have caused righteous anger and perhaps pity, but there was more stirring inside Harper.

Past and present were colliding to raise long-buried emotions. Emi's predicament reminded Harper of another time when she might have helped someone. When she could have stopped something horrible. If only she'd known.

The kettle boiled too high, and water erupted from the spout to hiss and bubble across the glass-top stove. Harper was grateful for the distraction and moved the kettle before wiping up the spill.

She had no business getting involved with this girl and her church. If Emi didn't want to be part of the village's *Shinto* practice, then she or her family should make the change. Harper knew very little about the girl, the religion, or the people who lived here.

So she would do as the priest had apparently commanded with his raised voice and jabbing fingers. She would mind her own business and write the damn book.

Harper pulled her head to one side until her neck popped, sending a shiver of relief down her spine. She would have that bubble bath now, the one she'd delayed by rushing after the girl like a half-baked Charlie's Angel.

No more of that. From now on, she would stick to imagining and writing drama instead of looking for it in real life. Or causing it, like she may have done with today's crisis.

With her green tea steaming from the pretty pink-blossomed cup, Harper blew across the top and imagined releasing the last of her stress with the breath. She pictured tension flowing from her shoulders as she mentally erased her encounter with the wild teenage girl and semi-sadistic priest.

What she needed now was a long hot soak, and after that, a nap. She rarely allowed herself the luxury, but a rainy afternoon practically demanded the indulgence.

And when she woke up, Harper determined, she would feel much better.

悔
恨

Thunder crashed outside the house and jolted Harper from sleep. The room she lay in was devoid of light, and it took her a moment to recognize where she was. When lightning lit the room, she remembered cozying up in the theater to watch a DVD, then switching off the large television when her lids had started to sag.

She had no idea how long she'd slept, but jagged memories of a nightmare poked at her, prodded to be set free into her wakeful state. Then clarity reared up to assault her with images she would rather forget.

She'd dreamed of her sister. Of Haley. And the night that had changed Harper's life forever.

She immediately made the connection and knew why her sister was on her mind. Earlier she'd been comparing Haley to Emi. She'd been measuring past regrets against the possibility of new ones, and her subconscious mind had decided to work out the problem for her.

By shoving the hateful truth in her face.

"Damn it." Harper was wrapped in a blanket but whipped the fabric aside to free her legs. She leapt up and marched into the main part of the house, toward the kitchen. And straight for the *sake* the rental agency had left as a welcoming gift.

Harper didn't drink often, but when all else failed, she wasn't ashamed to turn to alcohol.

She picked up the bottle of frosted white glass to scrutinize the label. Most of the writing was in Japanese, but the words "Divine Drops" angled across the label in red script. She could use some divinity right about now.

She poured the rice wine straight into a cup, eschewing the rituals often involved with the consumption of *sake*. As soon as the chilled drink hit her tongue, she changed her mind and dug out two pots. One to heat water and a smaller one to immerse in the water to warm the *sake*.

Running a hand through her brown hair, still in the lovely style known as bed-head, Harper tapped her socked foot on the floor and willed the first pot to start boiling.

No matter how she tried, she couldn't stop worrying about Emi. The questions beating at her brain were familiar, and they all started with the dreaded *What if?*

She hated the inevitable process. Wondering what she could do, what not to do, and what she might have done better in the first place. She'd been through this before, but the answers had been too little, too late.

Tiny bubbles were barely forming at the bottom of the water when she added *sake* to the second pot and placed it in the first. She tried to count the bubbles, a senseless game with an impossible goal, but the task would keep her distracted.

Finally the drink was warm enough to be palatable, so she scooped a cup out and drank. When she'd downed the first, grimacing against the strong flavor and quick consumption, she scooped out a second cup and moved to one of the curved stools on the opposite side of the counter.

The images flashed, fresh and clear to her mind, and Harper was afraid no amount of alcohol would dim them tonight. Haley's smiling face always came first, like a shining prequel in stark contrast to the horror movie coming up next.

When Harper's mouth quivered, she clamped her lips together and closed her eyes. The scenes only became clearer. She saw herself in the dorm room, books and notes spread across the bed in what had been her college study habit.

She envisioned checking the clock on her desk, twice in fifteen minutes, and wondering what was taking Haley so long. Her sister had called to say she was leaving the library, and to ask if Harper wanted a late-night snack. Harper had declined, but that didn't mean Haley hadn't gone to pick up something for herself.

If only she'd called to make sure. If only...

"No!" Harper wrenched herself from the past and opened her eyes. She polished off the last of the warm drink in her mug and went back to the pot for more. At this rate, she'd be cross-eyed drunk before the *sake* even had time to cool. Great. Perfect. In fact, passing out would be a blessing.

Even as she got a ladle from the drawer, Harper could remember the chill running over her skin when her phone had rung that night. The shrill, robotic bell had echoed in the dorm room, and a glacially cold weight had settled on the nape of her bare neck. Heavy. Freezing with premonition.

Haley had called her that night. In her darkest moment, her sister had reached out to the one person who'd always been there for her. Who would always save her. But when Harper had answered the phone, the sounds she'd heard made no sense.

Muffled bumps and scrapes had crashed in her ear, and Harper had pressed the receiver into her cheek so hard she'd left a red mark. "Haley? Where are you?" A low rumble, possibly a male voice? Then a quick scream had broken through the phone line as if abruptly freed from containment.

Staring at the white wall of their shared dorm room, Harper had tried to make sense of what she was hearing, but her logic and her legs were paralyzed by fear. And the slow trickle of recognition. She'd known what she was hearing, but hadn't been able to react.

She'd listened to a few more scraping noises, sounds drowned out by crackling, as if the phone had been smothered by fabric. Then the panicked cry that had pierced her soul.

The last thing Harper ever heard from her sister's mouth was her own name. Pleading, calling for help.

Bile rose up to burn Harper's throat, the bitter acid breaking her focus on that night from so long ago. Though there would never be enough years to ease the pain. She turned on the tap and rinsed her cup with water before taking a long cool drink.

The nausea finally settled, but only because she refused to let her thoughts stray that way again. Instead, she started contemplating Emi and second-guessing her decision to leave well enough alone.

Feeling a bit light-headed now, she performed her own test of inebriation and clacked her teeth together. They were sufficiently numb, so she knew the *sake* was working.

Now she just needed to put herself at ease. If she solved her current problem, the ghosts from the past would stop picking at her. Yes. That made sense. Another opinion to back up her own. That was all she required.

She stared out the window over the sink, trying to make out the edges of the pond in the dark. After a few minutes, she cleared her throat and let her wobbly gaze track down to the pot of *sake*. There was about a cup left, give or take a few gulps. She might as well finish it off.

With drink in hand, she zeroed in on her neglected cell phone.

She'd been silly to be afraid of calling Reid. He was supposed to help her out, to clear up questions about the village, so what was she so worried about?

She dialed his number, belatedly checking the time to see if the hour was appropriate, then shrugged to see it was already nine o'clock. Not too late.

"Reid. I have a question," she said when he answered. *Be quick about it. Get it done.* "I was wondering if you'd heard anything today about a teenage girl in town. Her name is Emi?"

After a long pause, Reid asked, "*Should* I have heard anything?"

"I don't know. I mean, I'm not sure. Was there any trouble? Maybe at the temple?"

"What's this about, Harper?"

His voice was even and non-threatening. Nevertheless, she was overcome with the urge to start backpedaling. "Nothing. Never mind. I saw her with a priest today in the woods. After you left." She was babbling and digging in deeper by the second.

"Just forget I called, okay? I don't want any trouble." She hung up before he could respond, and realizing she'd made a fool of herself, Harper slammed her phone on the counter. Then she smoothed a hand over the surface to make sure she hadn't caused any damage.

"Stupid all around," she chided herself, pressing the heels of her hands against her closed eyes. The floor felt like it shifted beneath her, so she opened her eyes and formed a plan.

She needed food, but no noodles or rice. She needed substance—meat and cheese and real bread. For its absorbent qualities.

As Harper tried to gather the energy to make a sandwich, she thought of another time when her stomach had felt this way. Empty and contractive. When her gut had roiled at the thought of food. When friends and family had forced her to eat or drink, even resorting to those thick shakes in a can. The kind made for senior citizens.

And later, a time when she went without food by choice. A small penalty, perhaps, but one of many at her disposal. Harper had become a master at doling out her own punishment. Denying herself small pleasures in life.

Staring at the kitchen cabinets, then the refrigerator, she decided this was one of those times. Her stomach decided to reject the idea of food, and she couldn't bring herself to want anything. Instead, she would sit in one of the round chairs. She would finish her *sake* and look at the gardens.

She knew from practice there would be no easy peace. That the worst night of her life had come again to torment her, and all she could do was ride it out.

Sometimes misery was the only cure. No one would understand why she did this to herself. Why retreating into suffering actually helped.

What happened to her sister had ripped a piece from Harper's soul, but the guilt now filling that space was almost worse. If only she'd called Haley. If only she'd gone to meet her. But no matter how hard she wished for it, she couldn't go back in time and do things differently.

So she stared into the dark garden and allowed the past to ravage her. She might never find a way to forgive herself, but she could damn well be repentant.

11

Reid drove straight to Harper's house, knowing full well the unannounced visit would probably anger her. He'd deal with that if necessary, but he was going. He wouldn't rest until he could be sure she was all right, and the woman who'd just called in a babbling panic was anything but.

Her voice had been tight and distraught when she'd called, and her questions had made no sense. Had she gone back into the woods? What could have happened that involved a priest?

He arrived to find her gate unlocked, and that only confirmed his suspicion that something was wrong. Hurrying through the front garden, he pounded on the door to ensure she'd hear him from anywhere in the house.

He wasn't leaving until he laid eyes on her and spoke to her in person.

Soon after, he heard the lock turning, so at least she'd remembered to bolt the door. Harper poked her head around to squint at him, and he could see she was somewhat disheveled. Her hair was down and her face looked tired.

"What are you doing here?" she asked.

And now he could smell the alcohol.

"I was worried after your call." He stepped in and took off his shoes before she could deny him entry. "I saw your upstairs light through the trees and thought I'd check in."

"You can see my light through the trees?" She lurched

through the open door to glance around her yard and then back inside before slamming the door shut. "I don't want anyone to see my lights. It's none of their business!"

Reid stepped back as she turned and stomped past him toward the kitchen. Whoa. What was going on here? Was her drinking related to the questions she'd called to ask him? Something about a girl from the village. What exactly had happened after he'd left her today?

Reid followed and caught up with her just in time to see her pouring more *sake* from a pot on the stove. He should stop her. Drawing a deep breath he moved in swiftly, even though he knew her personal life was none of his business.

Just as her lights were apparently none of the town's business? He'd let that irrational statement slide for now, but he couldn't let her drink anymore. Swiping the cup from her hand just in time, he said, "This stuff is stronger than you realize." He smiled when she looked at him with a stunned expression.

Instead of getting angry like he'd expected, she shrugged. "That's becoming apparent." She stood there staring at him for several seconds, so he just watched her, waiting to see what would happen next.

When she started to sway, he caught her around the waist, startling her into awareness. "I'm fine," she told him, pushing at his arm with both hands.

"So drinking this much is normal for you?" He hadn't meant to sound so judgmental, but the question was out there floating between them now. And he found he wanted the answer.

"No," she snapped. "I've had a horrible day, and I needed to drown it all out. I don't drink much, but the last eight hours have been... exceptional." She leaned against the counter and seemed to steady herself.

Reid took the opportunity to empty her cup, as well as what was left in the pot. Both went straight into the sink. Very little remained, and he wondered how much *sake* she'd started with. "What girl were you asking about earlier, and why do you think she might be in trouble?"

"I never said anyone was," Harper replied stiffly, but her attempt to evade was unsuccessful.

"What happened after I left today? Because something did." He crossed his arms and stood firm, his posture clearly stating that he wasn't moving until she explained.

"Fine. A girl has been sneaking around my house. A teenager, I think. I described her to Saya, and she said her name was Emi. Possibly."

Reid frowned. I think. Possibly. He wasn't a fan of those words, and Harper seemed to have a lot of doubts about her own story. "Go on," he prompted.

"I've seen her out the window before, and today she came again. I went outside to confront her, but she ran." Here she stopped talking and rubbed her hands together. She stared at Reid, apparently hoping he'd be satisfied with what she'd told him.

He wasn't, so he returned her stare until she broke.

"I chased her, all right? She ran, and I didn't want her to be scared. I followed her through the woods and when I finally caught up with her, she was with a priest."

Reid's spine straightened. "What did you do then?" The priests of the temple were revered and the village had very strict guidelines when it came to communicating with them. Or anyone else who served the temple.

"He was really angry and started hitting her with a belt. I backed off and tried to tell him she hadn't done anything wrong, but he only spoke Japanese." Harper's eyes jumped back and forth as she relived the incident. "Emi finally ran up the steps to two other priests, and the one with the belt just yelled at me."

She caught her breath and seemed to deflate. "Then he left

and I left, but that's why I called. I was afraid I'd gotten her into trouble. I didn't know what to do."

"You shouldn't have chased her," he said. "And never try to talk to the priests or anyone else who looks like they might be affiliated with the temple." He ran a hand through his hair. "This is my fault. I should have told you, but interaction with *Shinto* leaders isn't usually an issue. They keep to themselves, and I assumed you wouldn't ever have a reason to come into contact with them."

"She came to my house. And she seemed so scared."

Reid smiled and tried to lighten the mood. "So you chased her? I'm sure that made her feel better."

Harper's cheeks flushed. "I know, but in my head, I only wanted to tell her I wouldn't hurt her. And to ask her why she kept coming here."

"I hate to sound cruel, but it sounds like this girl Emi broke some rules and was punished for her transgression." He didn't want to make Harper feel worse than she already did, but she needed to learn from today's mishap. "Next time, just let her go. Don't try to talk to her or let the priests see you with her. Though I doubt she'll stray again. Now that she's been caught."

Harper nodded but said nothing.

"I'm sure she's okay, but I'll keep my ears open for any news." He studied Harper and saw a hundred worries flash across her features. "Is that all that's bothering you?"

One of her shoulders lifted almost imperceptibly, a telltale sign that something else was going on. Then she said, "I had a nightmare about something from my past. The memories were with me when I woke up." She bit her bottom lip. "They wouldn't go away, and that's when I remembered the bottle of *sake…*"

"It's okay. You don't have to tell me." Reid moved to her and put his hand on her shoulder. She was getting more upset with every word, and he wanted to soothe her, not make things worse.

She lifted miserable gray eyes to his and said, "You are an attractive man, Reid, but that's not what worries me."

He was stunned by her random confession but couldn't help asking, "What does worry you?"

"Your smile." She sighed. "You actually seem to mean it."

He tried not to grin. The *sake* was obviously still in full effect.

"But that doesn't matter either," she said, "because you need to keep your distance. Like we talked about before." She smoothed a hand down her pajama top and flipped her hair over her shoulder. "I don't do relationships."

"I remember. So let me see if I've got this straight. You don't do permanent. And you don't do relationships. What *do* you do?"

She looked confused. "What do you mean?"

"You stay locked inside your house. That is, when you're not chasing wayward teenagers, and you do your best to avoid people." Reid pushed his advantage, telling himself it was for the good of their professional involvement. That if he understood her, he would do a better job helping her.

Bullshit. You just want to know what makes her hide. "What are you so afraid of, Harper? Do you worry you'll be physically hurt, or are you just terrified you might form an emotional attachment to another person?"

"Both. All of it. The world is unpredictable, and so are people." She rounded the counter and went to stare at the hearth with its cast iron kettle and fishy adornment.

"That's what makes life interesting," Reid challenged.

"No." She whirled to face him from across the room. "That's what makes it dangerous and cruel!"

Reid choked back any comment he might have made. There was something more going on here. Something deep and festering, and he told himself again to stop forcing her to talk.

"You wanted to know what I do?" she asked in defiance,

walking slowly back to meet his gaze. "I live inside my head, that's what I do. It's safer in there."

Safer from physical danger, Reid thought, but all that time in seclusion left plenty of room for the mental monsters to come out and play. To cause nightmares.

"You do the same thing," Harper accused suddenly, pointing an unsteady finger his way. "You sit back and observe other people, the lives they lead, food they eat, choices they make." She hiccupped. "Or pottery they make." Then she frowned. "I don't really know what an anthropologist does every day, but the point is, you watch and study but never get involved."

"I can't influence subjects, that's true, but I do have my own social life. I have friends." Reid stopped there, purposely avoiding the family portion of his rebuttal, because what Harper was saying stood precariously on the edge of his reality.

Observing was safer. "I enjoy getting out and meeting new people. Sure, I'm fascinated with cultures and the communities that thrive within each, but I take time to participate in my own life."

Moving to the silk screen at the end of the room, he stroked the curve of a gnarled tree branch as he gathered his thoughts. He wanted to address this head on, but without trampling her already-tender emotions.

He turned to her and spoke softly. "Look, Harper, I don't know what you've been through, what you've experienced, but how you view the world is ultimately a reflection of whatever's inside of you."

"So what do you believe is inside of me, Reid Ellis? Give me your scientific synopsis of what you've seen."

Pain. And the fear of going through more pain. But that's not what he told her. Instead, he offered advice. "We all have something that chases us wherever we go. All I know is that you don't have to let the past control the now."

Her face fell into a blank stare as she reflected on his

statement, or as much as she could through her *sake*-induced haze.

Because the air grew heavy with emotion, and because Harper looked like she was about to cry, Reid swiftly changed the subject. "Have you eaten anything recently?" he asked. "How about I make you something? You'll feel better." He tried for a smile. "After all, I am your assistant."

"No. You're my cultural specialist." Her mouth looked like it was trembling, but she blew out through her lips and wiped both hands down her face. "Thank you, but no. I have some... something I forgot the name of. The bag is in the fridge."

"Whatever it is won't do. You need some American comfort food tonight, and I know exactly what to make." He jerked his head to indicate she follow him to the kitchen.

"I don't have anything," she said, staying put like a child who was devising an excuse to dodge bedtime.

He hiked a brow. "You forget who does your shopping." That drew a slow grin from her, and Reid felt something in his chest kick hard. She seemed so vulnerable. Not like the put-together and independent woman he'd seen every other time they'd been together.

Harper was hurting inside, and Reid was glad he'd decided to come over. She was in a bad way, and whether she admitted it or not, she needed someone.

And he wanted that someone to be him. He held out his hand and opened his fingers.

Surprisingly, she reached for him and grabbed onto his hand before squeezing one quick time and letting go. "Okay," she said gently, coming to stand beside him as they moved in sync to the kitchen.

Reid had admired the sleek, contemporary room and had wished for a chance to play with its state-of-the-art gadgets. It was a shame the meal he had in mind hardly warranted such high-end appliances.

When she carefully slid one of the barstools out and climbed up on the seat, Reid turned to the stainless steel refrigerator and went straight for the drawer that held cold cuts and cheeses. He removed several choices, then opened another drawer and took out two plum tomatoes.

He spread the items on the counter in front of where Harper sat, so they could chat while he put things together. Next came sourdough bread, a cutting board, knife, and the butter he'd overlooked in the fridge before.

"Sandwiches?" she asked, crinkling her nose with no small amount of disdain.

"Don't be such a food snob. Sandwiches are the staple of American youth. Well, that and pizza." He moved to the sink to rinse the tomatoes and returned after he'd dried them. "More specifically, we're having grilled cheese and whatever-else-you-want-on-them sandwiches."

She twisted her lips and folded her hands primly in her lap. "Well then. *That* makes a difference."

He ignored her sarcasm and reminded himself she would probably blow a good point-three-oh on a breathalyzer right now. She put her hand to her hair as if to adjust her usual wild knot and seemed surprised to find the glossy brown flowing freely.

Reid glanced up again and tried hard not to think about how much he liked seeing her with her hair down, wearing nothing but pajamas. Stylish, black silk pajamas. Naturally.

Still, she was more approachable. Softer. And for the first time, he realized her glasses and constant hair fidgeting were just more means of self-defense. Small barriers between her and anyone who managed to slip past her gates—the real ones—not those made of stone and metal.

She'd probably shared more with him tonight than she'd ever meant to and had definitely been more relaxed. Open, and in a way, delicate. She was bruised inside, that much was obvious, and he wondered how she would feel in the morning when she woke and remembered what they'd talked about.

She sat quietly as he made her meal and remained introverted as she nibbled occasionally on the grilled ham, cheese, and tomato concoction.

Finally she stilled, and although her sandwich was only half-eaten, her eyelids were starting to droop. Reid should help her to bed while she could still get there on her own two feet. "Harper."

She jolted, her big, gray eyes popping open. "Hmmm?"

"I'll walk you upstairs to your bed."

"Okay." Her voice was small and sweet. Pliable. And Reid was suddenly very glad he had been in Chuujitsu when she'd shown up in need of assistance. He frowned at the idea of anyone else seeing her like this, or possibly taking advantage.

She leaned on him when they turned at the landing, so he slowed and let her feet find their way. He wanted to sweep her up and carry her, but the action seemed too much. It would cross a line.

"Why are you being so nice to me?" she murmured.

"That's my job," he said with humor, though she was still too out of it to notice.

Then he grew solemn, because helping her this way was *not* in his job description. Reid could sense a stirring in him that had nothing to do with pity for Harper, and everything to do with what she made him feel.

A bond was growing between them, on his part, if not hers. And she'd been right about him, to a degree. Normally he would scrutinize what went on between male and female and how cultural guidelines affected courtship, but the emotions jumbled up inside of him made no sense.

They were foreign and wouldn't fit into any particular category. He couldn't put them in a tidy outline to be expounded upon. And his inability to clearly define what was happening told him just how important the emotions were. They were new to him. Special.

For now, he told himself, if only to feel more in control, he would get her to bed and leave her in peace. He'd dissect his reaction to her later.

At the top of the stairs, Reid noticed a picture sitting on a shelf. In it, Harper was smiling like the cat who'd stolen an entire truck of milk, and better yet, she was standing with her arm wrapped around a girl who was obviously her sister. They both looked happy and wild, in the way that only the young can pull off.

"Hey," he said, grinning. "You have a twin."

Harper's lolling head snapped up. She stared at the photo before putting one hand on his chest to push away. "Had," she said, walking toward her bedroom alone. "I had a twin."

A chill settled beneath Reid's sternum, and so many things about Harper became suddenly clear. His little pep talk about forgetting the past now seemed trite and juvenile. *Way to be an ass.*

Some injuries stayed with a person for life, and it wasn't his place to lecture her on how to heal. Or how to move on.

Still, he followed her to the bedroom and helped her lift the sheet her fingers were fumbling to find beneath the pillows. She rolled inside with one fluid motion and closed her eyes.

After a moment, Reid started to rise, but her hand shot out to grab his wrist. "I'm going to be sick," she groaned. "Could you bring me a bottle of water from downstairs and leave it in the sitting room?"

"Do you want me to stay and help you?" he asked, pulling back the sheets she'd just crawled into.

Her eyes flared. "God, no." Then she went stumbling toward the bathroom, shoving the door closed behind her. He heard the faucet turn on and retreated downstairs to give her some privacy.

When he went back up to the sitting room, he did his best not to listen to the sound of retching, and left three bottles of water instead of one. Then he left as she'd requested, sparing her any further embarrassment.

He'd already seen and heard too much.

12

Several days had passed, and Harper was pleased to find herself back in an old and familiar rhythm. Waking up with a hangover after the *night of sake*, as the event had come to be known, she'd reflected on her time with Reid and the confidences she'd shared.

She'd spilled more secrets that night than the warm wine she'd been drinking, but in a strange way, her confessions had been cathartic. An unexpected result, but welcome nonetheless.

The candor that had existed between them had trickled over into the next day when he'd returned to see if she had survived the night. And he'd come again the next day, and the one after that.

He no longer needed an excuse to stop by, and both of them had accepted that was the way things were going to be from now on. Even Harper, who was normally so protective of her solitary lifestyle, felt no need to debate.

She didn't feel encroached upon when he was here. In fact, she was enjoying the company and the excuse to take a break when he showed up. She'd imposed a grueling writing schedule upon herself.

Since the strange and eventful night, she and Reid had become friends. Companions. And Harper fervently denied that any other level of intimacy might be developing. After all, she still didn't want or need a romance. The risk entailed in caring for another was just too great.

But she was enjoying the male camaraderie, and that was all she and Reid could ever have. No further discussion on the topic. No argument allowed.

She didn't feel imposed upon when he was here, and if she was caught up in work, he would do his thing. He'd find his way to the kitchen, check to see if she was running low on anything, and then he would slip back out.

When he left, however, the house felt emptier. He brought a level of comfortable yet sizzling energy with him. And he when he left, it evaporated.

No, she couldn't deny the attraction existed, but neither would she follow up on the sexual chemistry that simmered underneath their polite veneers. She couldn't take the chance that one of them would end up discarded and hurt.

Or that worse might happen. A tragedy to steal one of them away after true emotion had set in. Harper had already experienced enough loss for ten lifetimes, and she wasn't setting herself up for any more.

Forcing her attention back to the scene she was finishing, she let her fingers tap across the keyboard like a dancer with no choreography. She'd taught herself how to type, eschewing classes in defiance and claiming her fingers were too small to do it the "right" way. Thus her frenzied pecking that resulted in as many typos as readable words.

At least she was writing and had made good progress on the first draft, after Reid's visit and her explosion of truths.

Today, Harper had made a pot of coffee and thrown herself into the project. She'd filled a cork board with pictures of clothing, jewelry, and people she used for reference. Most details she could imagine, but it had been a long time since she'd witnessed any rippling abs up close and personal.

Besides, a few male models on the wall never hurt anyone.

And there was Reid again, popping into her mind. At times

like this, she wished she wrote mysteries with sweet grannies playing hero. No hot male bodies or steamy green eyes anywhere to be found.

Ugh! There he was again.

Saving the finished document to both her hard drive and a SIM card, Harper pushed her keyboard away and let her eyes fall to the drawer of the desk.

Reid wasn't the only thing popping into her head on a recurring basis.

She pulled open the drawer and removed the printout of the mysterious *kanji* symbol. After her run-in with Emi and the priest, she'd assigned herself the task of cleaning every glass surface in the house. And there had been a lot of glass.

Though she'd gotten her life back online and running smoothly, the oddity of the symbol's placement on every window and door still disturbed her. She couldn't let it go.

Reid wasn't an option if she had any more questions. He'd already told her everything he knew, and had reinforced his warning more than once. He'd told her to stay away from Emi. To stay away from priests. And to stop worrying about the *kanji* drawings she'd found in her home.

Not so easily done, she thought, tracing a finger over the flowing design. *I won't feel better until I know this symbol wasn't intended to menace or intimidate.* Because so far, that's all the strange drawings had accomplished.

Standing, she left her office and went in search of her purse. She had a plan and a place she thought might prove informative. And she wanted a second opinion. Okay, a third opinion.

With a conspiratorial smile, Harper decided she was ready for an excursion. She would get the answers she sought, then head straight home and fall back into a tight work schedule.

She wasn't exactly lying to Reid. She planned to tell him what she found. Just after the fact.

She wouldn't bother him this time and was glad she didn't have to. Spying her purse on the stairwell, she hurried over to dig for her phone.

After all, she did have another source.

悔
恨

There was no clanging bell to announce school was out, and no screaming, laughing children flooded from the doors in a colorful menagerie. The young students filed out in orderly fashion, so somber and demure they reminded Harper of a zombie movie.

Lifeless little people with eyes straight ahead.

She shook off the encroaching apprehension and studied the area around her. The streets were made of stones pressed into the ground like everywhere else, but the building was a bit more modern than the stores closer to the river.

The school's exterior was coffee-brown and was far from the clean sophistication found in Tokyo. She guessed flash and distraction weren't required, or even desired, in an educational setting.

Especially in Chuujitsu, where everything and everyone seemed to carry an extra layer of austerity. Even the blooming flowers now appeared to whisper slyly of great secrets. The things *outsiders* shouldn't be told.

Or maybe your writer's mind is running away with your good sense.

Harper looked again to the steady and controlled trickle of students exiting the school. A few children peeled off to enter homes along the street, while others marched on with packs on their backs and their shoulders hunched forward, as if settling in for a long walk. Perhaps they were farmers' kids with the greatest distance to travel.

While the students in their simple clothing had been rather non-descript, the same could not be said for Saya when she erupted from the doors with a style and vitality that no teacher's attire could disguise.

Her face brightened with a smile when she spied Harper, and she hurried over. "I'm so glad you called. I've been busy lately, but I meant it when I said we should get together again."

"Me, too," Harper said, a bubble of joy filling her chest. She'd been sincere as well and had been looking forward to spending time with the vibrant and talkative woman again, despite her original intention to avoid making friends.

First Reid. Now Saya. If she wasn't careful, she'd soon be a socialite.

"Now." Saya placed her hand on Harper's arm. "You have to tell me more about this covert operation and why I wasn't supposed to tell anyone what we were doing."

Harper would have felt ridiculous hearing her request framed in such a way, but in all honesty, this was a clandestine mission. "Remember that girl I asked you about when you came to dinner?"

Saya looked up as she searched her memory, then nodded. "Emi, right? What about her?"

Circling her arm through Saya's and looking down to admire her fashionable, wine-colored pumps, Harper propelled her forward. "Why don't I tell you on the way?"

After walking two blocks south, the two of them stopped outside their destination. Harper had explained everything to Saya about Emi's snooping, the awful encounter with the priest, and the symbol on all her windows.

"I know they might be unrelated, but with the girl's frequent visits to my house and her position with the temple—whatever that may be—I would feel better if I knew this symbol just meant 'prosperity,' or 'good health,' or even, 'don't break the glass.' You understand, don't you?" Harper asked, winding up her formal presentation.

"Of course. And you were right to come to me." Saya fished around in a burgundy clutch that was shiny and trendy, just like her shoes. She pulled out a pocketbook. "Because I happen to have a library card."

Standing in front of the building, Harper mused how little it resembled a library. The outside walls were the color of oatmeal, and the sharply-angled roof was covered in curved black shingles. At the top of the walls were vertical slats that might serve as windows.

Steeling herself for the undertaking and afraid of what she might discover, Harper touched her hair to ensure her tight twist still held. "Let's go."

Saya did a small dance. "I love a mystery."

Harper forced a smile and hoped they had reason for Saya to maintain her light-hearted attitude.

Once inside, she confirmed that the slats were indeed windows, and the narrow openings allowed sunlight to slant in from the top of one side of the sprawling room. The pale beams fell at a diagonal until they were cut off by floor, table, or bookshelf.

One large area constituted the library, and shelving units were centered in the middle with small desk cubicles all around the periphery. Each table had a small light with a pull-string, but only a few were in use. Harper smelled dust and an herbal overtone that reminded her of sage.

The shelves were constructed of thick wood and were bowed in some areas, declaring their age and years of use. They ran all the way to the ceiling, and a metal rolling stool was located near the lone librarian's desk.

The woman sat flipping pages in a book, and her eyes flicked up to scan Harper and Saya. There was no discrimination or offense in her glance, but there was no warm welcome there, either.

The woman returned to her perusal of the book lying open in front of her. She wore a navy dress with short sleeves and her hair tied back in a braid. A wooden bowl was on her desk, filled with some sort of greenery. Perhaps the sage Harper thought she'd identified.

Saya held a finger to her lips in the universal signal for quiet, but the cautionary motion was unnecessary. Harper didn't plan on making a peep.

Saya made her way to the very back and put her jacket, purse, and a larger bag with school supplies on the desk of the corner cubicle. She pulled out the chair there, as well as the one next to it.

"Stay here," she told Harper. "I'll be less conspicuous by myself." A grin spread across her lips, belying the seriousness of her tone.

With her legs fidgeting, Harper sat and waited as instructed, tossing the occasional glance toward the front of the library where Saya had disappeared. Her patience was rewarded when her friend returned with three books. One was the size of an American high school yearbook, but the cover was flimsy and looked aged.

The other two were smaller—one of medium size with a newly-bound cover of forest green, and the last looked to be approximately five by seven inches with a faded and torn red binding.

"There isn't much on the village's form of *kanji*, and of course, there's nothing about their *Shinto* religion, but I thought we might find a stray mention of something useful in these." Saya set the books down and slid the big one out from under the others.

The two women crowded together over the huge tome, but were disappointed to discover a timeline of the village's history. The photos inside were no older than the mid-1960s.

The only mention of more ancient times accompanied a

picture of the abandoned buildings where silver had once been processed. The caption, Saya translated, told how the mine had been closed down in the latter part of the eighteenth century, when the village had shifted from mining to farming as its primary financial means.

Since her arrival in Chuujitsu, Harper had learned that rice and potatoes were a major source of income, and exporting the goods to larger cities helped keep the village afloat.

With their little corner of the library shrouded in shadow, Harper considered turning on a couple of additional lamps. That might draw attention, as Saya had said, and they didn't want to be conspicuous.

Trying to ignore the creeping darkness and the cool, spooky fingers tickling at her back, Harper focused on their tiny light and its meager warmth.

They found nothing of use in the first book, so Saya closed its large cover and set it aside. Next she opened the green book, and while it appeared to be newer, the drawings and pictures inside spanned centuries.

Again, most of the information referred to the history of the village and held no hint of the current *Shinto* practices, but near the end of the book, they came to a section about village law and enforcement.

Surprisingly, several of the photos were gruesome and caused both of them to cringe at first sight. Remembering what Saya had told her about the absence of theft in the town, because people feared having their hands cut off, Harper instinctively tucked hers in her lap.

"I guess this section was included to remind locals not to step out of line," Saya said, gingerly picking the corner of the page up to flip to the next. She acted as if the book itself was bloody and stained.

Harper swallowed when she saw the image on the next page and understood when her friend removed her fingers entirely to rub them on her pants. Harper also felt the need to scrub off the grisly taint of what they were looking at.

A man—well, she believed it was a man, but couldn't be sure—had apparently been ripped apart, and villagers were standing in a semi-circle around his remains. Some were smiling in triumph.

Judging by the uneven and messy condition of his corpse, the unlucky man had been torn in two with the tear beginning at the right of his neck and shoulder area and extending down to his groin. Harper coughed against nausea just as Saya reached to shut the book.

Seizing the volume, Harper slapped her hand on the picture before she lost the page. "Wait. Look at that." Now that her initial revulsion was fading, she was able to take in the details of the scene. Her finger skated over the glossy page to settle on a portion of the man's split abdomen. "There. He has a symbol on his side."

Peering closely, Harper brought the book up to her nose and cursed herself for not thinking to bring the magnifying glass she had at the house. Finally the image came into focus, and she was able to make out the curves and lines of the drawing. "It's not the same symbol as the one on my windows, but the style is identical. I'm sure of it."

Nothing was written beneath the picture, so after tapping her foot in indecision, Saya finally retrieved the book from Harper. "There's only one way to find out." She stood and strode toward the front of the room.

"Wait," Harper said in a whisper, but Saya had already rounded the aisle. Harper's stomach ached again, but not with the threat of rising bile. The discomfort churning there now was generated by fear.

Saya had taken the book to the woman at the desk. She was going to ask the librarian about the symbol. Harper sat still, static in her ears as she waited without breathing. What was

Saya doing?

A sharp voice from the front answered that question, and Harper heard Saya answer back in a soft, conciliatory tone. The sound of an apology.

Harper shifted in her seat, unsure what she should do. Saya was familiar with the village and its inhabitants, so whatever had passed between the two women, Saya could handle it.

Harper had found another forbidden topic. The village was riddled with prohibited subjects, and the smallest infraction from an outsider, like her or Saya, infuriated the villagers.

She worried the books would be confiscated now. *I'll never find out what that symbol means.*

She let her eyes fall on the last book, the smaller one that was beaten and worn. Then she gazed back up the aisle. She couldn't see anyone, and the conversation between Saya and the librarian had calmed.

Still, the woman had been upset. There'd been no misinterpreting her loud, strident tone. Harper and Saya would obtain no more information here.

Without thinking of the consequences, Harper snatched the red book from the corner desktop and shoved it inside her purse. Her chest tightened as she thought about what she was doing. Stealing! In a place that rewarded thieves with amputation.

What was wrong with her? This place was making her crazy!

Saya emerged from between the tall shelves, and Harper's skull almost jumped from her spine. She clutched her purse to her chest. "You scared me. Is everything okay?"

Saya gave her a look and rolled her eyes. "Yes. I groveled sufficiently. A talent I've perfected since coming to this sacred and imperialistic village. I managed to keep my privileges, but we should go."

Saya stilled when she noticed there were only two books left on the table. Her deep brown eyes slid back to Harper. "She told me to leave the books here for her to put away." Her eyes narrowed shrewdly. "I didn't say how many we had."

She nodded her head a fraction of an inch, and Harper returned the gesture. Of one accord, they eased down between the long rows of shelves and passed quietly through the front section.

The woman at the desk was standing, and there was no mistaking her sentiment now. She was well and truly pissed off, but Saya bowed her head to the woman as they passed. One last act of contrition to pave their way out.

And they almost made it.

A man stepped into their path at the door, and Harper felt herself clutch up, afraid they'd been caught. But he simply stepped to the side, allowing them exit. He'd come in the door as they were going out. A harmless traffic jam.

Harper bowed slightly and smiled at him. Then she saw his tattoo.

He wasn't dressed like a priest, but wore a shirt of the same brown as their cloaks. A tattoo peeked from beneath his collar and appeared to circle from his chest to his back. Like the priest she and Reid had passed in the forest.

Harper met the man's glare and was chilled by the brutality she saw in his eyes. They were so dark, almost black, and burned with unidentifiable emotion. An intensity that might sear her soul if she looked too deeply.

Dropping her gaze, she grabbed onto Saya's elbow and stayed close on her friend's heels until they reached the street. Moving efficiently but without rushing, they strolled together down the streets of stone.

Saya hazarded a glance over her shoulder. "Looks like we're clear." Then she laughed, but the sound was as much a release of tension as mirth. "Girl, I always thought I was the one to shake things up, but you definitely bring excitement to town."

Harper shook her head. "I am so stupid, and Reid is *not* going to be happy about this."

"So don't tell him," Saya said. Then she leaned closer to Harper's ear. "Even if he has been coming to see you. Every. Single. Day."

Now Harper laughed and jabbed her friend lightly in the ribs with an elbow. "No. Nothing like that."

"Of course. Never think it." But it was clear by the dripping sarcasm and sly smile that Saya was thinking exactly that. "Well, look at it this way," she added with a toss of her raven hair. "If the very worst happens, at least we both have one to spare."

Harper's head was still wrapped up in Reid and his visits, so she felt like she'd missed something. "What do you mean? We have one to spare?"

Saya lifted her fingers and wiggled them in the air. "Hands."

13

Harper had ridden her bicycle to town, and by the time she made her way back home, the afternoon had grown late. The gray of mounting dusk was at the edge of the horizon.

She slipped off her shoes and went inside in bare feet, eager to open the red book and see what she could make of the riddles concealed within its yellowed pages. She and Saya had both been too terrified to open the book anywhere in town, so Saya had rushed her home saying, "Take the loot to your house and hide the damn thing. I just gave myself a manicure."

They managed to laugh about violating one of the village's most steadfast laws, but the humor was forced. The last look the women had shared was a mutual agreement to keep their mouths shut and pray they were never caught. Not until they were far, far from the long arm of Chuujitsu village law.

She doubted the archaic forms of punishment still existed, but were used instead as ghost stories. Tales to keep people in line and scare them into doing the right thing in case their consciences failed.

Harper could barely wait to delve into the book, but first she demanded comfortable clothing, a snack, and a kettle of hot green tea. Then she would cozy up in one of the round, cushioned chairs and read as the back garden fell under the veil of night.

Fifteen minutes later, with steaming cup in hand, her

garden-viewing fantasy was squelched. The only things she understood in the book were the drawings, and the horror in them made staring out into the darkness less appealing.

She felt vulnerable to the eyes of the woods, imagining the evil men from the book hiding amongst the trees, watching her as they planned to come inside and bind her. To right the wrong she'd committed this day by sawing off her hand.

Yes, sawing. The idea of chopping was bad enough, but if the sketches on the pages hinted at anything close to the village judiciary of today, Harper had been an utter fool to take the book.

Hopping up and closing the *shoji* screens against the night for good measure, Harper headed toward her office and the laptop resting there. One sleepy yellow light declared the computer inactive.

She couldn't read Japanese, so pictures were all she had to go by. Taking a pacifying sip of warm tea, she willed herself to calm down and do what her job demanded of her on any normal day. To research the unknown until she understood it.

With three different translation programs open on different Internet windows, she started with the first drawing that caught her attention and tried to figure out the written description below.

The process was slow and tedious. She had to compare the resulting translation of each program to decide which was most correct. Then she put her best guesses together to form a messy sentence structure. Even an exact translation would sound strange to the mind of an English speaker, but what she had written down was close to gibberish.

Soon a general meaning became clear, and to her chagrin, the image of the young boy having his hand removed was indeed a reference to the punishment reserved for thieves. She refused to acknowledge the absurdity of her situation as she flipped the pages of her *stolen* book, and resolved to move on to cheerier things.

Like the female wrapped in ropes and being burned over a pit of coals.

The smoldering skin was a horrendous touch, and Harper wondered if the artist had been a sociopath, relishing his job more than he should.

Then she reconsidered the characterization. If the sociology of the culture encouraged such cruel, tortuous acts, then the man who'd sketched the drawing would have been considered perfectly normal. Not the sociopath that Harper envisioned.

She shook her head and carried on with her work. She would leave the psychology of ancient peoples to Reid. Maybe he could make more sense of the acts of violence depicted in the book on her desk. But like Saya at the library, Harper was now loath to touch the cracked pages.

They felt tainted with evil.

Focusing on her task, she showed careful consideration for each Japanese symbol in the picture's description and took her time translating. The word *Shinto* popped up in two of the online translators, and the next symbol written was...

The tiny images blurred, so she reclined in her chair and put a hand to her forehead. The business of working with foreign words was hard enough. Starting off with *Kanji* then to Japanese then Japanese to English...well, the process was barely manageable.

But not impossible.

Harper knew from experience when she'd hit a mental wall. Just like a runner who could push no farther, she was in need of a break. With her tea gone cold, she went to the kitchen to pour the last swallow into the sink before refilling fresh from the kettle.

Back in her office, she noticed the deep purple leaves of the Japanese maple stirring from a light breeze. Did one call the tree a Japanese maple when they were, in fact, in Japan? She didn't know, nor did she care.

Her body and spirit were running on empty, but she wanted to give the book one last effort before retiring to bed. The clock on her computer read eight o'clock, but she called the laptop a liar. Surely it was at least midnight. That's what her tired mind believed.

Sliding open the glass door, she slipped outside to wander in the courtyard. The wind was brisk and refreshing and might do well to rejuvenate her brain. If only the stone pathway and lantern weren't so soothing, urging her to linger and relax.

Harper found herself following the curve around the end of her office and to the backyard. She passed the trim green ornamentals and strolled through the narrow pass between the house and the towering boundary wall.

Already she could hear the rhythmic sound of the pond's bamboo fountain, and as her eyes adjusted to the loss of her office light, she slowed her stride so as not to stumble.

She could make out the kitchen window, though the only bulb burning inside was the small one over the stove. A thin triangle of yellow cast from beneath the hood but didn't have the strength to reach outdoors.

The clean scent of cedar floated to Harper, pure and crisp, and she was grateful for the mountain location. Standing still now, she took in the amazing night. The stillness of the moon, gentle rustle of wind through the forest, and the reliable *plunk!* of the bamboo fountain. She closed her eyes and listened. She absorbed.

Absolute serenity.

Eventually she opened her eyes again.

And saw a man standing near the far corner of the house. His naked chest shone bluish-white beneath the moon.

There was no movement. No sound. Only the rush of blood inside her head.

She was trapped in that sickening, tingling moment when

the body sensed danger before the mind could fully comprehend. A sheath of cold velvet seemed to fall across her flesh. To shiver its way to her very core.

Finally she blinked, and the man was gone.

Terror squeezed her chest painfully before her lungs started working again, pulling in desperate draws of oxygen. Yet quietly. As silently as possible. So she could listen.

Sounds came back to her one at a time. The knock of bamboo, the caressing breeze, and a bird's cry. But that wasn't all.

She heard a scrape. Had it been a crunch of gravel or a foot scuffing across a path?

Harper strained to identify the source. She couldn't tell where the intruder was, what he was doing. Or if he was coming for her.

Panic burst inside her like a flash bang, urging her numb legs to run, back the way she'd come, back toward her office. She hit her shoulder on the corner of the house when she cut too close to step up onto the wooden walk.

Her ears were flooded again with heat and roaring static as she yanked open the glass door and pushed her way inside. With trembling hands, she slammed the door closed and threw the lock.

Chest heaving and mind alert with adrenaline, she closed the *shoji* screens and lunged for the light switch on the wall, plunging the room into darkness. A small voice inside revolted, insisting the shadows were even more menacing, but her rational self knew she had to become invisible.

Are all the other doors locked? Harper swallowed and tried to think. *Yes! I was nervous about the book. I checked them all.*

In the dark room, lit only by the tiny light on her laptop since the screen had gone to sleep again, she turned her head toward the upper floor. The terrace doors of her bedroom were open. She'd foolishly decided no one could scale the side of the house.

But if the man had gotten over the stone wall, he might find a way up to the balcony and the second floor.

He might already be inside.

After standing completely still for a few minutes, Harper's muscles ached. Bolstered by the lack of sound or movement inside the house, she edged to the doorway and peered around the corner. The hallway was empty, and the dark wood of the main room's floor glowed with a soft yellow. The kitchen light was still on.

Her phone was where she always kept it, in her purse, either on the kitchen counter or on the steps leading up to the sitting room. She had to get to her cell and call for help.

But her limbs were rigid and refused to move. She couldn't take a step down the hallway. What if he was inside? Waiting for her to give away her position?

Backing into a corner and crouching down, Harper went over her options. First, what might she use as a weapon? She thought of scissors, but the only pair was in the kitchen. She had pens on her desk, but that was all, unless she thought to hit him with her laptop.

Her laptop. Maybe she had a way to contact Reid after all. Her eyes sought out the slim case on top of the desk. The screen had gone dark, and once she touched it, the screen would light up with a bright white background. Her office would be awash in the glow.

What choice do I have? If the man comes for me, at least I'll be able to see him.

She definitely couldn't cower in the corner all night. She needed help.

Fueled by the thought of getting through to Reid, of knowing he was only minutes away, she lunged for the table and jiggled her mouse to wake up the computer. When the screen cast its white light over every object in the room, including her, she whirled around to check the hallway, sure she would hear footsteps at any moment.

And then what? She bent over the desk again and clicked her way to instant messaging as fast as her shaking hand would allow. A cool rivulet of sweat ran down the back of her neck, telling her just how hyped up she was.

No movie or book could ever accurately portray this feeling. Her heart was choking her throat, and her brain felt like it was on fire. No one should ever have to know what it was to have a stranger invade their home.

The one place Harper had always felt safe. Now even that was gone.

A sob rose at the revelation, but she bit it off, telling herself to stay silent and calm. She started typing as soon as the message box popped up. She knew Reid kept his computer on to receive emails and messages from his colleagues and the professor from his university.

She hoped he was home and would hear her IM come through. *Please hear me!* She kept it brief, so she could close the laptop again and cut off the light. [intruder in house help] Then she hit *send* and slapped the case closed.

She'd grabbed a pen when the light had been on, but as weapons went, the small click-top was laughable. Still, she would stab at his face if nothing else. As much of a coward as she might be, she would fight when cornered.

She almost laughed at the unintended pun, for she was just that. Cornered.

Minutes dragged by. Or were they only seconds? She heard nothing from inside or outside the house, and she jerked her arm when another drop of sweat made its way down the wet path of her nape. For a second, she'd thought a finger had come at her from behind.

A scratch on the far wall made her whimper, and she envisioned a hundred different scenarios to explain what might have made the sound. Had she ever heard it before? Was it normal?

Her rattled brain couldn't remember.

A low clatter came from the front of the main house, so low she started to convince herself she'd imagined it. A light whooshing noise followed afterward. Then footsteps. Oh, he was moving with stealth, but Harper heard him.

Instead of feeling galvanized and ready to defend herself, everything in her vision went white hot. Terror surrounded her, crushed down on her, so thick and heavy she felt like she would suffocate from the pressure.

"Harper?" Reid's voice cut through her panic, but still she remained immobile and waited for her heartbeat to slow to perceptible beats. She was still paralyzed. Still mute.

Then he was there, filling the doorway and flipping on the overhead light. Thank God she'd relented and given him back his keys to the house. She was frozen with fear and not sure she would have been able to respond if he'd pounded on the door.

His hands were on her shoulders, then her arms as he pulled her to her feet. "Are you hurt? Are you okay?"

Her head went to his chest as he wrapped her up in strong arms. Her hands slipped around his waist where she could cling to his back. Burying her face in the shirt he wore, she drew in a deep breath of him. Warm, male, and carrying the scent of cedar.

Stroking her back, he spoke low against the top of her head. "You're safe," he told her, over and over. He didn't ask any questions or push for explanations. He just assured her again, "You're safe now."

Harper finally found her voice and tried to release the tangle of nerves still in her stomach. "I'm sorry. I'm so sorry. I know better." She hugged him tighter. "I know better."

She knew she was babbling, not making any sense, but suddenly, nothing in her world did. Her life, her purpose here in Japan, even being in the house she loved. Nothing, nothing made sense anymore.

She held on to the one thing that was right. She clung to Reid as he enveloped her. As he whispered, "You're safe."

14

Flashlight in hand and with every light burning inside the house, Reid made his way through Harper's gardens. He checked every hidden trail, every shadowed corner, but no trace of a man could be found.

He didn't see any disturbances in the white gravel of the garden, but he searched the perimeter of the fence regardless. He looked for tracks an intruder might have made jumping down from the high stone wall. Or scrambling to find his way back up.

A motion caught his eye, but it was just Harper watching from her bedroom window upstairs. He shook his head in the negative, hoping it might relieve her mind. Her arms were still crossed across her midsection, a sign she was both consoling herself and trying to shore up.

She'd been rattled all right, but who wouldn't be? A strange house in a foreign country, and way out in the woods? He didn't doubt what she told him—well, not completely—because even if she hadn't really seen a man, she truly believed she had.

Making his way back around to the front, Reid stopped where Harper had indicated she'd been standing. He turned off his flashlight and let his eyes adjust. Then he closed them and waited, trying to put himself in her place, her frame of mind.

He opened his eyes and looked to the far corner where she'd seen the intruder. Nothing in the yard resembled a man, and the only pale color he noted were the leaves of a tree. The silvered undersides flickered when the wind kicked up, but Reid still couldn't make out the shape of body in any of the natural surroundings.

And despite Harper's well-developed imagination, he didn't think she'd seen leaves. He went to inspect the corner and paid close scrutiny to the ground. If the man had been startled by Harper, he might have left a mark in his haste to depart.

When he realized there was a flagstone path there, Reid sighed. No scratches or tracks would be apparent. No evidence of anything.

Yet, he believed her.

His gut burned, but he couldn't explain why. Nothing in his months spent in the village had ever given him pause. Sure, the people had been standoffish, but he'd never felt threatened. So why would anyone take such an interest in Harper?

First the girl creeping around, and now a man? Maybe she'd made some enemies the day she'd chased Emi and confronted the priest. Or maybe, he thought, feeling more certain with every step he took back toward the front door, maybe the girl had come back. That would explain why a priest might have been here as well.

The intruder could have followed the girl, trying to get her back where she belonged. If there was one thing the temple clergy hated, it was dealing with people who didn't share their religion.

Plus, the priest wouldn't have necessarily seen his visit as an intrusion. The mountain belonged to the villagers, after all, so if the temple decreed, deeds to houses were only meaningless pieces of paper.

And the girl? Reid had always heard she was different, that she was special somehow, so her mental state might be why she kept coming to Harper's house, despite the consequences.

Feeling more assured now, he went inside and took off his

shoes in the *genkan*. Harper was at the bottom of the stairs by the time he was done.

"Nothing?" she asked fearfully, but with hope. "I know what I saw," she insisted quickly when he shook his head. "There was a man there. I even noticed his hair was pulled back from his face."

Reid nodded. The priests often wore long ponytails or braids. "I don't doubt you saw someone, but I'm still not sure there's cause for worry."

Her mouth fell open.

"Let me explain," he said, moving to one of the couches near the square-shaped hearth. "I have a theory." When she came and sat slowly on the other sofa turned at a right angle to the one Reid was on, he hooked a thumb toward the large, iron square in the floor. "How about a fire? It's a good night for one."

"Yes," she agreed, gray eyes serious as she watched him make the preparations.

As he lit the coals beneath the large iron pot, he shared his idea about Emi and how she may have returned, only to be followed by one of her chaperones.

Harper frowned and stared into the flames as they took hold and started to burn brighter. "If she's mentally challenged, why would she be a temple maiden or serve any role in the religion?"

Reid shrugged and sat back against the brown leather. "Some cultures view things differently than we do in America. They might revere the mentally challenged. Consider them special or even blessed."

Harper tilted her head to the side, considering his logic, but quite convinced. "Special," she repeated. "I've heard that word every time someone talks about her. About Emi. I still think it's crazy that a grown man would climb over my wall to chase her instead of just coming to my door."

"And what would he say? You don't speak the language,

and priests aren't allowed to talk to strangers. He would have considered talking to you, or even bringing your attention to their presence, a much greater sin than simply following Emi into your gardens."

Reid could tell she didn't like that. She pressed her mouth tight, as she often did when tackling a problem in her head, but the movement only brought his attention to her lips. And he had no business wishing he could press his own mouth to hers. Now was not the time.

Hell, with Harper, there *never* seemed to be a time.

"There's something I haven't told you," she said, and after watching her pretty bow of a mouth form the words, Reid let their meaning sink in.

He looked up to meet her eyes. The gray seemed deeper than normal, the flecks of turquoise more brilliant. "What is it?"

She folded her hands in her lap and bit her bottom lip. "I went to the library today with Saya. We looked through some books and found a symbol similar to the one on all my windows. The same style."

She blew out an unsteady breath and said the next words in a rush. "The *kanji* symbol was on a dead man's body. He'd been ripped apart, so Saya asked the librarian about the symbol."

She stood abruptly, leaving Reid confused and concerned. He watched her stride to her purse on the stairs where she pulled something out of the bag. When she wrapped her hair up in a folded over ponytail that left the ends fanning out haphazardly, he realized she was armoring up. Harper style. *This must be bad.*

She put on the tortoiseshell glasses, and he knew then that *bad* wouldn't be an apt enough description. He stood to receive her news. "What happened?"

"The librarian got upset, but Saya managed to calm her down. We left straight away, so as not to keep things stirred up."

Judging by her stiff back, Reid felt sure she hadn't reached the climax of her story. He waited patiently.

"There was one book we hadn't gotten to, and we were afraid... no, *I* was afraid they wouldn't let us check it out." Dropping her hands to her sides, Harper left the room to go to her office. She returned shortly, bearing a small red book in her hands. "I haven't deciphered much. Translation is slow going to say the least."

Taking the book, Reid noticed Harper rubbing her fingers against the pale silver silk of her pajama pants. As if she were wiping away dirt. He opened the small book and was greeted by disturbing scenes of mutilation, torture, and murder.

He could see why she was upset but hoped to help put her mind at ease by translating some of the pages. "This isn't exactly bathtub reading," he started, trying for a light tone, "but I understand why it unsettled you."

"That's not the only reason. At the library..."

Reid frowned and shut the book with one hand. "If the library allowed you to take this out, the contents must be harmless."

"But if the information inside is supposed to be secret, they may not have." Harper pursed her lips and furrowed her brow. "Let us check it out, I mean."

A shocking revelation took hold of Reid. "*Did* you check out this book?"

"No."

"Did Saya check out this book?"

Harper pushed her glasses up so firmly he was afraid she'd leave an indentation. "Not in the manner you're thinking."

The truth of what she'd done blew through him. "Have the two of you gone insane?"

Clutching the book between both hands now, he paced back and forth across the dark wood, arguing with himself. "You've got to sneak it back in. No, they might catch you." He stopped moving. "I'll take it and put it back. They see me there all the time, so I wouldn't be suspect."

Harper edged over to stand in front of him, blocking him from his path of continued pacing. "No one's taking it back until I've had time to figure out what it says."

Feeling suddenly warm, Reid shoved his sleeves up to his elbows and went to the counter to set the book down. He made himself think rationally. The problem of the stolen text could be fixed, but first, he needed to make Harper understand what she was dealing with.

If she was so afraid of being hurt, by anything or anyone, why would she do something so reckless?

He turned to her, then took her hand and led her back to the couches. Together they sat, and he was glad for the warmth of the smoldering coals. "Harper, I know I've encouraged you to get out more and to not be afraid of the village or its people, but you've gone full swing in the other direction. You need to be more cautious of the rules here. The way of life."

Feeling a frantic clutch in his chest, Reid ran a hand through his hair. "Normally the world isn't as dangerous as you make it out to be, and this village could be a place of respite and tranquility for you. The haven you were looking for."

She nodded, but her shoulders stiffened defensively.

"But if you insist on kicking the hornet's nest, you are going to get stung. Badly." He shifted his weight, and something stuck him in the backside. Already irritated, he reached around and pulled his wallet from the back pocket of his jeans.

Harper picked it up when he tossed it down between them. "This thing has seen better days. Why do you keep it?"

"Sentimental attachment. And don't try to change the subject."

"Why sentimental?" she pressed.

Reid spit out the wallet's history just so he could appease her and get her back on track. "My grandfather gave this to me one year for my birthday. Satisfied?"

"That's not so unusual. Why are you attached?" He watched as she ran her finger along the edge and scrutinized the faded and worn leather. "The stitching has been redone. You've had this for years."

When she looked up and saw his face, she said, "Humor me, all right? Distract me with a story." Her mouth quirked to one side. "Take my mind off this night for a minute. Then you can go back to yelling at me."

"I was hardly yelling," he said, gently taking the wallet back from her. "My family isn't your typical Norman Rockwell scene. You could say they are... distant. From me and often from each other."

"But my grandfather," now he grinned as memories rushed in, "he married into the Ellis family. The Boston Ellises, if that paints a better picture for you."

"I don't know the name, but yes, I get the gist." She sat gazing at him and truly seemed interested in his background. "Then how is your last name Ellis?"

"My grandmother's father insisted she keep her maiden name. He almost made my grandfather take it too, but Hardy Boyd—that was my grandfather's name—he said he loved my grandmother enough to let her keep her surname for the sake of family peace, but damned if he was going to change his own." Reid had dearly loved his grandparents, and to this day, he wondered how his father had come from such down to earth people.

"My grandparents were somehow immune to the Ellis curse," he said. "They were decent people." When Harper said nothing, he added, "On my twelfth birthday, my grandfather Boyd gave me this wallet, but it's special because of what he told me. He said I was almost a man and would make my own way in the world."

Reid lifted his eyes to Harper. "He said I wasn't a product of the people I came from, and any shortcomings on their part had nothing to do with me. They were just who they were, and he expected me to be who I was."

"He was telling you it wasn't your fault," Harper said.

Reid nodded. "He was wise. He knew I was getting old enough to understand the lack of... emotion my parents felt toward me. So he gave me the most valuable gift ever."

Reid lifted the wallet and felt a pang of both loss and gratitude. "He gave me permission to let them go."

"So," he said with a sigh, "now that you've delayed the inevitable and managed to calm me down, which I'm betting was your real motive, why are you acting so out of character and putting yourself in danger? Courting it, in fact." Reid lifted one side of his mouth. "Did you like my use of author language there? Did you catch that?"

Harper's smile was slow but real, and her eyes crinkled a little at the corners. "And now you're trying to make me laugh. To make me feel better. But now we have to talk about what's really happening here."

"If anything outside the norm is happening," he pointed out. "Keep in mind that the villagers make their own societal guidelines, and what may seem strange or even scary to you is perfectly acceptable to them."

"I'm renting this property, so I make the rules." The smoldering flames in the hearth reflected against her glasses when she looked down again. "I know of very few societies that don't allow for personal space. A home and shelter that is not to be invaded."

Reid had to allow her point. "We'll go to the man responsible for enforcing laws tomorrow. You might think of him as a town sheriff, but even his position defers to the temple."

"Fine." Harper repositioned herself and bumped knees with Reid. She faltered, her bottom lip dropping slightly as if uttering a silent, "Oh," before she put her hand to her hair and moved away from him. The contact had disconcerted her.

The possibility that she held the same level of interest in him as he did her made him see her mannerisms differently. The small startled sigh, the way she touched her hair, and then there was the faint rosiness in her cheeks.

She'd blushed. She'd actually blushed, and Reid found the reaction endearing. Her heightened color had nothing to do with proximity to the fire.

"There are some stone steps in the woods," she said, breaking Reid from his pleasant reverie. The one where his mouth met the soft spot on the curve of Harper's neck.

He cleared his throat and assumed his best scholarly expression, hoping she hadn't picked up on his distraction. Or its cause.

"Steps?" he echoed, still forcing himself not to imagine how she'd taste right there. He'd bet she'd be sweet just below her ear, and spicy...

"A long line of steps leading up a hill. That's where I saw Emi with the priest that day. That's where they took her." Harper tapped a finger to the side of her glasses, a habit Reid hadn't noticed before. "I wonder what's up there?" she asked, more to herself than him.

And while he may never have seen the glasses-tap, he'd heard that tone before. The one she used when she was plotting. Only this time, he was certain she was planning for real life instead of fiction.

"Don't even think about it," he said, using another familiar tone. The one he reserved for wayward grad students who were disrupting his research more than helping. The one that warned they should choose their next action wisely.

"Fine," she snapped, reading him as easily as he had her. "Then you tell me what's up there."

"I don't know. It's forbidden to outsiders."

Harper scoffed. "How can you not know? You're an anthropologist here studying the village's culture, yet you've learned nothing about their *Shinto* practices? You've never taken a walk up there just to see?"

Okay, so she was still disturbed by tonight's escapade and maybe a little riled up, but he didn't appreciate the disdain creeping into her voice. "As an anthropologist, and also as a decent human being, I have respect for their privacy and practices."

"They have no respect for mine," she argued back.

Reid ignored her. "My job is to observe and learn as much as I can from their perspective, but I'm not going to force anyone to share what is most sacred to them. Especially if their religion prohibits them from doing so."

She opened her mouth to speak, but he raised a silencing finger. Another of his professor-in-training tricks. "Regardless, I'm not here to learn about their religion. My focus is the retention of younger generations to a rural setting and lifestyle in spite of modern advancements and opportunity."

"Spoken like a true academic," she groused. "But you're often forced to speculate, right? If you can't get the answers you need. If your subjects won't share concrete details or hard facts."

"Sometimes."

Now her eyes gleamed. "So what you do is really a soft science."

Grinning fiercely, Reid retaliated. "And you write soft porn."

"*Ouch.*"

"Mm-hm," was all he allowed, surprised and more than a little irritated by her sudden attack.

Sinking back into the sofa, Harper pulled off her glasses and rubbed the bridge of her nose. "I'm sorry. I don't know what's gotten into me."

"You're upset. It's understandable." Reid studied her as she struggled to come to grips with the drama invading her life. He knew the loss of privacy was especially hard for her, because she valued isolation so much.

On her terms, anyway. When she had an itch to find trouble, she did a damn fine job of doing so. And why was that? He watched as she let her head fall back to rest on the brown leather. What was pushing her to step outside her normal box? Her comfort zone?

Reid normally had the patience to wait a person out, to observe the tiny actions that revealed so much about who they were. And whether detrimental or helpful to that subject, or the community he was studying, he could stay removed. His personal feelings remained unaffected.

But Harper Gray was affecting him. The yearning to know her better was colliding with the need to protect her.

Something was churning inside her, and even if she was making more than was necessary out of this girl Emi and whatever role she served for the temple, the only thing that mattered was that Harper believed the girl was in trouble.

And now she felt threatened, too.

She had unresolved issues, and Reid suspected they revolved around her sister. Her twin, who he assumed was deceased. She hadn't said so, but her statement that she'd "had" a twin implied as much.

He glanced at her silver necklace and wondered why he hadn't made the connection before. Two knots on a single chain. Identical yet separated by a small space.

And Harper never took it off.

Whatever demons were being resurrected for her now, Reid would help her sift through her fears and do everything in his power to keep them from becoming real. He owed her at least that.

"Promise me you won't go to the steps again," he said, hearing the severity in his own words. "Promise me."

She sat up, startled. "You can't really ask me to—"

"I'm not asking. I'm telling. For your own sake, don't make

any more trouble." He reached out, his need to touch her overruling any reservations. Placing his hand below her jaw, he played his fingers lightly over the spot he'd wondered about before. "If you push the priests, they'll be forced to respond. Just leave it alone."

She put her hand to his wrist and tried to shove it away. "Why do you care?"

Instead of letting go, Reid ran his fingers up into the thickness of her hair and drew her in. "Hell if I know," he growled, pulling her to him to finally take that tempting mouth of hers. Suckling her upper lip and its fullness before plunging his tongue inside to stroke hers.

Harper made a soft sound in her throat, and he waited for her to jerk away. Maybe even slap him. But as good as she felt and tasted, the sting of her palm would be well worth the price.

Her upper body was stiff, unmoving, but he felt the slightest curl of her fingers as her nails sank lightly into his forearm. She was holding his hand in place now, lifting her mouth to his and leaning ever so slightly forward.

That was all the permission he needed.

His other hand went to the curve of her waist. The pajamas didn't flaunt her lithe figure, but couldn't hide her tiny waist either. And he'd been dying to see how his palm would fit on the gentle swell of hip.

When he stroked his way down to her thigh and deepened the kiss, he found another reason to like her pajamas. The material was slick and cool to the touch, but as his hand slid over the silk, he could sense the heat hidden beneath. Like mist gliding over fire.

Mechanical bells sounded somewhere in the house, muffled but persistent. The noise jarred Harper and she broke the kiss.

But still she held onto his arm. So that was something.

"My phone," she said in way of explanation. Her eyes were dazed. Pupils large. And the evidence of her arousal thoroughly pleased him.

"Go ahead," he told her, shifting away so she could stand without impedance. Then added in the same don't-bother-to-argue tone he'd used earlier, "I'm staying here tonight."

"Don't worry," he said when he saw the doubt enter her eyes. "I'll take one of the couches here or go to the theater. I don't want you to be alone after what happened."

Then he motioned toward the potentially dangerous red book. "Or after you've been looking at that."

Putting her hand to her lips as if recalling their shared kiss, Harper nodded. She turned to the stairs, picking up her purse on the bottom step. "I'm going to bed then, but you know where everything is. Make yourself comfortable."

She stopped mid-stride, and Reid watched as she got derailed by whatever was running through her mind. Him? The girl? The temple priests and her garden trespasser? Countless emotions flickered over a face that couldn't hide any of them.

"It's funny," she finally said. "Only a few weeks ago, I wouldn't let you have keys to my home. Now you're sleeping inside. And I actually feel safer."

It was a testament to how secluded she really was that accepting his presence was such a milestone. Or, as he hoped instead, a breakthrough.

Reid smiled at her, his ever-doubtful Harper. "I guess somewhere along the way you decided to trust me."

"Yes." Her brow wrinkled as if the idea were incomprehensible.

Reid didn't want to push his luck, so he dropped the subject. "Good night. And if you need anything…"

"I know," she finished for him. "You'll be here." Now she smiled and Reid's chest stirred. Like a compartment he'd carried inside his entire life had suddenly and decisively opened wide.

Ah. So this is what it feels like.

Now it was his turn to deal with an avalanche of emotion.

"Sleep well," he said as she continued upstairs. He plopped down on the couch to stare into the orange embers, rubbing his sternum and amazed by the bittersweet ache he felt there.

"Sleep well," he said to himself and the cast iron fish staring at him from the hearth. "Because I know I won't."

15

Though the tap on her bedroom door was light, Harper jolted from sleep and sat up. Her first instinct was to wonder who was in her home, but then she recognized Reid's voice calling her name. "Yes?"

"Sorry to wake you. I called Saya, and she can meet us at the Sheriff's office, but she has a class in a couple of hours." He spoke through the door, mindful of her privacy. "I thought it was a good idea to have her there for translation. She's meeting us in thirty minutes."

"I'll be right down." She went to the door and waited until she heard him go downstairs, then took a quick shower. She applied face powder and mascara but didn't want to glam up for today's meeting. The town lawman, who they just called the Sheriff, might be put off by too much show.

Then again, she thought with a grin, they would be there with Saya. Alongside the exotic and sharply-dressed beauty, Harper felt like a moth next to a butterfly.

But a butterfly she liked and admired.

Hurrying back to her closet, she scanned her hanging clothes. While she enjoyed sleek and chic black, she also adored color, so she pulled on a pair of emerald-green capris with a white blouse.

With her hair pulled back in a shoulder-length tail, she felt ready to face Reid and the awkwardness that would surely follow their impromptu kiss the night before. As ready as she could possibly be, she descended the stairs.

Reid didn't give her a chance to feel any discomfort, though, only pleasure when he looked her over from head to toe with an appraising gleam in his eye. "You look good," he said plainly. Then he locked one strong arm around her waist and pressed his lips to hers.

Her bones evaporated.

Letting her go almost as quickly, he stepped back and grinned while she struggled to see clearly again. "Just thought we should start the day off on a positive note," he said.

"Right. Good." Well, Harper thought, for a writer she was certainly a font of verbal eloquence this morning. If Reid didn't stop kissing her, she was going to be out of a job.

She watched as he strode to the couch where he'd slept and picked up a pillow and blanket. "Just let me put these back where they belong, and I'll be ready to go."

His long, strong legs ate up the floor as he walked. "Uh-huh," she heard herself mutter and grimaced. She was a real poet laureate this morning.

Why hadn't she appreciated his tall, rangy form and the tightly packed muscles before? Could she have missed how attractive he was, or had she just forced her female instincts to cower inside her body the same way she hid inside her home?

Last night had swept aside the last of her illusions. When he'd looked at her with irritation and concern all mixed up together, his eyes had burned like green fire. Then his mouth had been on hers, his hands on her body, and she'd barely controlled the urge to lie back and let him cover her.

Reid Ellis was like a thinly veiled snare. The second she'd gotten too close, desire had sprung up to grab her. Now, trapped like the fool she was, she would never look at him the same way again.

He met her in the front of the house as she slipped into her flats and he into his brown trail shoes. While he fastened his laces, she stole glances at him to study the masculine aspects she'd blindly ignored before.

In the weeks since they'd first met, his hair had grown out slightly, so the deep blonde fell haphazardly across his forehead. In the beginning, he'd been the clean-cut academic, but now he was a rugged yet refined field scientist. A mouth-watering combination.

His brains didn't make him any less attractive. Quite the opposite. She'd never known a man who was so handsome and smart, but still so easy-going. Unpretentious.

Finished with his shoes, he stood up and Harper studied him with a greedy gaze. She had to admit he was taller than she'd realized, made obvious when she actually let herself stand close enough to appreciate such things. When she didn't run to the other room like a coward.

Last night, with his arms snaking around to gather her close, she'd sensed the breadth and solidity of his chest, his arms. She'd smelled the clean soap on his male skin and had lost herself to the rough but slick feel of his tongue on hers when...

"Hey," he waved a hand in front of her face and she snapped her head back like a startled turtle. "Are you feeling all right? You look flushed."

"Yes," she said too quickly. "Let's go. We don't want to be late."

The car ride to the village was silent, and as they pulled into an alley to park, Reid filled her in on what to expect from the meeting. "Since the village is so rural and isolated, a residential police box was installed years ago. The building is called a *chuzaisho*, and the policeman, who we just refer to as the Sheriff, works out of the front office. He actually lives in the residential section attached to the back side."

"Do you think he'll help us?" she asked, slipping out her door to walk around the back of the car.

"I believe he'll be fair and listen, but he's originally from Chuujitsu, so we need to speak and act with the due amount of respect. He also practices the temple religion." They approached a building of white-painted concrete, and Reid held the glass door open for her to enter. Saya was already waiting in the lobby.

After a quick wave of greeting to Reid and Harper, Saya spoke to the woman sitting at the desk, who in turn went down a short hall and knocked on a door. She spoke to someone inside before returning and giving a nod to Saya.

Harper had already been told to let Saya lead, so there would be no misunderstanding in either language or gesture. Hand motions that are common in the States could easily be offensive to a native in Japan.

Silently, the three of them filed into the office, and Harper was surprised to find there was more than enough room. Durable blue carpet covered the floor, and despite a collection of framed photos and various memorabilia on the walls, the space was ruthlessly organized.

A bear of a man sat behind a black desk with his eyes focused on a piece of paper. While she and the others waited for his attention, Harper stifled a smile.

Other than the shortly-cropped black hair, the man would easily pass for a sumo wrestler. She could certainly understand why he was the law in the small village.

When he turned a beaming smile on them and spoke in a deep voice, she could see that he lived up to the common name of *omawari-san* which meant "dear patrol officer." A term of respect and gratitude for the person who served as both trusted friend and protector of the peace.

After niceties were exchanged, Saya indicated Harper and said her name. Then she spoke at length as the officer made affirmative noises and the occasional grunt. Once or twice, he shot a surveying look at Harper, but she had no idea what Saya had said just before each glance.

With a bow of her head Saya finished. The officer put the flat of his hands on his desk. He breathed deeply and nodded once to Harper. Then he began his own incomprehensible monologue. Luckily, Saya was on the receiving end this time and could translate.

"He said he would speak to the appropriate person, someone who is a spokesperson for the temple," Saya told her. "He'll make sure they know you are not comfortable with the trespassing."

Harper had a hard time believing anyone would want strangers sneaking around their homes, but she didn't say as much. She only smiled her thanks at the big man and said, "*Domo arigato*." That much Japanese even she knew.

"But," Saya added with a purse of her lips, "he reminds us not to engage the priests ourselves. That if you have any more trouble, you should come to him directly."

The man rumbled in his massive chest as he to spoke Harper. She paid polite attention while Saya translated at her side. "He says the village is proud to have an author such as yourself in residence and would like to ensure your comfort."

Again Harper smiled, and this time she did her best to imitate Saya's bow, though she felt strange and stiff. Unauthentic at best.

With hands pressed together in front of her like a praying child, Saya said something to the officer and began backing away.

Debating internally for only a moment, Harper decided she had more to ask. Though intimidating in size, the officer seemed like a kind man, so she blurted, "What about Emi? Shouldn't we mention what I've seen?"

She sensed Reid shifting his stance behind her, but he didn't say anything. Saya also looked nervous, but when the policeman made a noise that seemed to be a question, Saya had little choice but to repeat what Harper had said.

She spoke to the Sheriff again in a flow of words that ended with the girl's name.

Immediately the Sheriff drew himself up. He stared at Saya for a moment, then flicked his narrowed eyes at Harper. "Tsukada Emi?" he all but barked at them, using the girl's family name first, as was customary.

Then he surprised them all by waving both hands and saying, "No, no, no." He rattled out a spate of Japanese at Saya, and he didn't seem happy. His manner didn't convey anger, but nervousness. After a few more sharply delivered statements, the man nodded to Saya then Reid.

But this time, he wouldn't look at Harper.

Saya turned to Harper. "He says Emi Tsukada is a servant of the temple, and she should have no contact with anyone outside of her religion or family. Especially strangers." She hurried on to say, "He also said that Emi is protected. She comes from a very old and powerful Chuujitsu family."

With a few last words, the officer sat back down to stare at the paper on his desk, and Saya repeated the praying-hands motion before backing out swiftly, leaving Harper no choice but to go out as well.

Plus, Reid had his hand on her belt, pulling her back.

Feeling sure she'd just made a grievous error, Harper waited until they were on the street before she spoke. "I'm sorry. I messed up."

"No," Saya said evenly while Reid snapped, "Almost."

"I'm sorry. He just seemed so nice." Harper held up a hand to stop Reid from reminding her of their talk on the ride down. "I know I agreed to keep quiet. I wasn't thinking."

He ran a hand through his dense blonde hair and sighed. One hip cocked and hands on his waist, he gave her a begrudging smile. "Here I thought you were the quiet type, but you just keep racking up points for the unpredictable side."

"At least you won't be getting anymore late night visitors," Saya put in optimistically. "Probably not, anyway."

"And stay away from the priests," Harper said, anticipating their reminder.

"And Emi," Reid said. "If you see her, turn and go the other way."

"How about I make things easy for all of us?" Harper asked with a small smile. "I'll stay in the house and write for a while."

"Good idea." Reid's grass-green eyes studied her face and for a moment, she thought he might kiss her again. Instead, he dropped both hands and stood straight. "I have to go."

Harper felt a small slice of disappointment but chastised herself. It's not like she wanted him to kiss her. Especially here, on the early morning streets that were just coming to life with villagers.

Besides, for all she knew, kissing in public might be a punishable offense.

"I'm scheduled to sit in on a town meeting about the yearly harvest and who will be assigned what jobs. Everyone pitches in here, and they also reap some of the rewards." He exhaled as if dreading the time he would spend inside. "I'm not sure if I'll learn anything useful for my dissertation, but I won't know until I try."

He focused on Harper. "You need a ride back?"

Before she could respond, Saya stepped in. "I think I'll steal her for an hour, if you don't mind. This meeting was over quickly, and I don't have class for a while."

"Okay." Reid curled a finger softly under Harper's chin. "Just try not to commit any crimes before I see you again."

"No promises," she deadpanned, and his answering groan made her smile. With that, he headed toward the alley and his car.

Saya, who was much too observant, said bluntly, "You look tired."

Harper lifted a careless shoulder. "I didn't sleep well." She cast a half-smile toward Saya. "And I didn't have my morning coffee."

Saya lifted her elbow to tap Harper on the arm. "Well come with me, girl. I don't have coffee, but I'll introduce you to some tea that will make your cup of joe run screaming into the night."

With the rest of her smile finally emerging, Harper nodded to her friend. Saya had definitely cemented herself in that category. Harper was grateful for the levity. "You don't have to do that, you know."

"Do what?"

"Try to lighten the mood. I'm doing okay."

A shadow crossed behind Saya's deep brown eyes, but she shook her head and laughed. "How about I do it for myself, then, because to be honest, this whole ordeal is beginning to creep me out."

"I know what you mean," Harper said and sighed.

Together they walked the few blocks to Saya's apartment. As they turned to the outside staircase of metal, Saya spoke in Japanese to an older lady who was washing and shredding large green leaves. The woman grinned and nodded in a way that rocked her entire body.

"See?" Saya said at the top of the stairs as she unlocked her door. "There are plenty of nice people in Chuujitsu. They just have to warm up to you."

Inside, Harper stopped in the small square that served as the *genkan* and took a visual tour of the room. She noticed the scent of jasmine and the pleasing sound of silver wind chimes as they danced near an open window.

Saya's personality filled every available space. Bright and cheerful, yet tastefully done, the tiny apartment had been transformed into an oasis of contemporary opulence. "You should be a decorator," Harper said, the words popping out in unadulterated honesty and admiration.

Saya paused in the act of taking the lid off of her kettle, and an expression settled on her face. One Harper would have never expected from the confident woman. She looked insecure. Almost shy.

"Do you really think so?" she asked in a low voice. "I just play around. It's fun." She stepped forward and tilted her head as she looked across the room. "I enjoy the juxtaposition of everyday items mixed with extravagance."

Harper studied the design again and could see what Saya meant. On the wall behind a round table for two was a blown up photo of a green street sign. The sign was backlit by a sunset explosion of coral and violet. Urban fantasy.

Next to the table stood a floor lamp, but instead of a shade, the wooden tube was topped by a small chandelier. "Ooh. I love that lamp. Where did you get it?" she asked Saya.

"I made it," her friend said. Then she added, "And I took the picture as well."

Harper gaped. "Get out."

"No, I can't." With a wide grin Saya added, "I'm making you tea." The women fell into laughter, enjoying the ridiculousness of their banter and the ease that accompanied the teasing. Harper hadn't felt this comfortable with another female since... She looked to the floor so Saya wouldn't witness the rush of unanticipated tears.

The toes of her black flats went blurry as she stared at them and tried to blink away the evidence. The connection with Saya had been immediate the day they'd met, but Harper was suddenly struck by how much she'd missed female companionship.

She hadn't felt relaxed like this with anyone since her sister had died. Since Haley had been killed.

"You take sugar or the chemical stuff?" Saya's question and its phrasing made Harper smile through her tears, and she found she was no longer embarrassed. Wiping at her cheeks, she lifted her head and nodded.

Her friend stilled when she met Harper's eyes.

"Sorry. I'm not sad. Well, not only sad. I'm happy, too," Harper explained before heaving out a ragged breath. "I just haven't had any girlfriends in a long time."

Intelligent eyes twinkled at her with understanding. "I'm glad we're friends," Saya said with a somber tone leavened by a sympathetic smile. "And you can talk to me about anything. Any time."

With a wink, Saya turned back to the faucet and started filling the kettle, giving Harper a minute to gather herself. "Mind if I grab some tissue?" she asked her hostess.

"Sure. Bathroom's in the back."

After a minute of dabbing her eyes and blowing her nose, Harper was set to rights. She emerged with a bittersweet sense of loss paired with joy. Getting to know Saya had ripped open some places inside her that she'd tried to keep shut tight.

And while the first tear had been startling, there had been only a pinch of pain followed by gentle relief. Opening up again wasn't nearly as agonizing as she'd predicted. But then, it was hard to be miserable around Saya.

She emerged refreshed and ready to taste the delicious smelling tea that was permeating the apartment. "Is that raspberry?" she asked, joining Saya at the table against the wall. The Japanese woman had an authentic tea set out with deep blue leaves painted against a pale pink background.

"Raspberry with a kick," Saya said. "After this, you may never drink coffee again."

"Blasphemy," Harper joked. But when the dark tea with a hint of fruit slid over her tongue, she sighed. "This *is* good." She sipped again and let the warmth and sweetness rush through her. "Very good."

"So." Saya set her cup down and put one arm on the table to prop her chin. "When are you and Reid going to get down to business?"

"Wha—" Harper stuttered. She licked her lips. "I don't know what you mean."

"Please. I've seen the way you are with each other. You sneak a look at him. He sneaks a look at you." Saya waved her hand. "You two are like a couple of teenagers. From the 1950s. The way you both hem and haw around what's so obviously sitting right between you."

"Reid doesn't do as good a job as you, though," she continued with her eyes to the side in thought. Harper still sat stunned and silent, like someone who'd just been busted by the cops and was too afraid to speak. "Sometimes he can't help himself and looks at you with eyes that are all…" Saya paused then asked, "What is it you romance writers are always saying? Oh, yeah. *Molten with lust.*"

The laughter traveled up from Harper's gut and burst right out when Saya added a wiggle of brows to punctuate her words.

"Yeah. You know what I mean." Saya looked at her expectantly. "Well?"

Shaking her head and fighting a smile, Harper finally relented. "I don't know. All around me, things are turning upside down and sideways. I'm not working as much as I should be. All of this weird stuff is happening with the girl. Now strange men are in my back yard."

"But not in your bed."

"No," Harper murmured. "Just on the couch. For now."

The smirk that spread across Saya's slick red lips was sinful and satisfied. "A-ha. So you are considering taking things up a notch."

"I've been doing my best not to think about it at all." And when the confession spilled out, Harper realized just how true it was. She'd been more affected by Reid than she'd allowed herself to admit. Or even believe. She'd been shut away—and shut off—for so long, she practically viewed herself as on the shelf.

Put away for good due to uselessness.

"I'm not useless," she thought out loud.

"Of course you aren't." Saya popped straight up in her chair and gave one quick pat to Harper's hand. "What made you say that?"

"Oh, just comparing myself to a spinster of old and wondering how I let myself get this way."

Saya nodded. "We all go through that at one time or another."

Studying the spunky cut of Saya's black hair, her sculpted face and long, cat-like eyes, Harper shook her head. "I don't see you as being put on any shelf, or staying there if you ever were."

"And you shouldn't either," her friend shot back, making Harper feel as if she'd been somehow set up. "So why don't you dust yourself off with Reid? Even if things don't go long-term," she fanned herself as if she'd grown warm, "that man is hot."

Harper laughed. "Then why haven't you two hooked up? Not that I'm complaining," she added with a lift of her hand and a meaningful smile.

"He's too nice for me. Too smart. Loyal. Hardworking." Saya looked again to the side and bobbed her head. "And honest. Yep. That's all that's wrong with him."

"Then I guess you go for the quintessential bad boy?" Harper could see that with Saya. She could *so* see that.

"Big and bad," her friend said and rubbed her hands together. "Yum."

Sighing and letting her eyes drift, Harper looked out the window to two children throwing a ball in the street. Good. She'd been worried playing wasn't allowed in this town. "You're right. Reid is a major catch. I'm just not sure we're a match."

"I think you'd be great together. Interesting and challenging if nothing else." When Harper gave her a questioning look, Saya explained, "He's all science. He looks for explanations and reasons while you're the romantic. You go on emotion."

"That seems to be the case lately," Harper agreed. "But if I'm the romantic, why is he the one pursuing this, and I'm the one running?"

Leaning forward, Saya held her gaze. "That's an excellent question. Like I said, that man is *hot*."

Another round of laughs and raspberry green tea saw them through the next half hour, until Saya announced she had to leave to teach her class. "Listen," she said as they went back down the stairs and to the street. "Please be careful and don't do anything..."

"Foolish? Rash? Stupid?" Harper looked down the street, watching as people hurried around corners or inside homes. "I have a lot to get my mind wrapped around, and I could use a few days of hard work. Maybe get more pleasant images inside my head."

"Like hulking heroes with molten eyes?"

"Yes. Exactly like that."

Tossing a peacock-blue scarf around her neck, Saya lifted a hand and started edging backward. "I have a full schedule myself the next few days, but call if you want to get together for dinner." She grinned. "Unless you're too busy cleaning house or something."

Harper wrinkled her forehead in bafflement. "Huh?"

"You know," Saya said slyly. "If you're busy getting dusted."

16

After her second cup of morning coffee, Harper hummed with energy and just didn't have it in her to spend several hours sitting at her computer. Since sticking to her promise that she would stay home for a while, she'd immersed herself in work, making some much-needed progress.

But now she needed a change of scenery and graphic inspiration. She wanted to accurately depict the natural setting of the village and always did better with a visual reference. So it was time to get out and take some pictures.

Today was perfect for what she wanted. Clouds hung low over the mountains, and the forest sparkled after a drizzle of rain. She knew from having stepped out into her back garden that the air was thick with mists, cool and moist on her skin.

Remarkably, she'd been at peace the last few days, and even with Reid out of town, she'd been able to relax and enjoy her solitude. She'd had no more visits from Emi or her watchdog priests. She had to content herself with that.

After all, the Sheriff had told them Emi was well-protected and came from a powerful family. Considering all she'd learned, Harper felt foolish for believing she could, or should, do anything to affect the girl's situation.

She'd been operating off of fear and misconceptions, and in all honesty, letting go of the worry had been a tremendous relief. She'd come to Chuujitsu for a reason and would do well to focus on her writing.

If she really wanted to be scared, all she had to do was tell her editor she was going to miss her deadline. Now that was a terrifying thought.

Her steps were light and effortless as she climbed the stairs to get dressed. She slipped into some comfortable jeans and a long-sleeved T-shirt, and unpacked a light rain jacket with a hood. For now the mists were all that wet the air, but she'd been on the mountain long enough to know the rain could return without warning.

Downstairs she readied a small pack to carry. Camera. Water to drink. Cell phone. Snack bar. If she walked near town she might stop for lunch, but today wasn't a day for schedules or plans. Today was for following her curiosity, appreciating her surroundings, and going wherever the path took her.

With a smile, she put on her shoes. Reid was due back soon, and she'd actually missed seeing him. Maybe her brush with the unknown had shaken some of her fear loose, because she hadn't been trying quite as hard to deter his advances. Not since that kiss.

She shivered just remembering.

While Harper still had no intention of pursuing any sort of lasting romance, Saya might have had a point. Being safe didn't mean missing out on everything life had to offer. She wasn't too old to enjoy male companionship. Not yet. And taking advantage of Reid's interest didn't mean he would end up hurting her.

She just had to keep things in check. Know when to stop. When to get out.

Drawing a deep breath of the clean air, Harper exited the wrought-iron gate and made sure to secure the lock behind her. She wasn't giving up prudence or caution. She was simply trying to find a better balance.

She could take a bit of the joy, but not so greedily that she wound up being disappointed when the supply ran out. Clichés and adages were well-known for a reason. And all good things did come to an end.

Refusing to turn down the well-traveled road of heartache, Harper forced herself to see the potential happiness right in front of her. With Reid. For now, she'd take things slowly and see what developed. No expectations equaled no disillusions.

At least that's what she intended.

The path into the woods went in a westerly direction, down to the valley and toward the river. She'd never taken the trail toward Reid's house and was excited to explore.

The clouds and mists were really something, and she was sure to get some great shots. Then there was the river. On the far end of the village, the water returned to its natural state, and waves practically burst from aqueducts in a mad rush for freedom.

But first Harper had a hike to make, and she looked forward to whatever surprises she might find on the way.

Noticing every detail as she walked, she tried to come up with interesting descriptions. Low-lying plant life covered the dank floor. Mosses, ferns, and various other flora spread as far as she could see, interrupted by the occasional jutting rock.

Trees towered like petrified warriors frozen where they stood, some of whose roots had found their way up to twist aboveground. Harper stepped cautiously as the trail veered downhill.

Stuttering to a halt, she blinked twice to be sure she was seeing what she thought she was. A pale green snake was curled around the branches of a bush, blending perfectly with leaves of the same color. While most snakes in Japan were non-poisonous, she knew pit vipers and other venomous species were common.

Moving quickly and quietly farther down the trail, she tried not to startle the snake. It took several minutes for her heart to slow to an acceptable rate, and she doubled her efforts to watch where she was going.

When the path spread wider and led her out of the trees, she found herself overlooking the northern end of the valley. The river was closer but disappeared around the bend of the mountain. If she stayed on the same trail, she should come upon the waterway and, according to Reid's instructions, find a bridge to cross.

After taking a few pictures of the valley, so still and quiet in the settling fog, she quenched her thirst and emptied half a bottle of water. She wasn't anywhere near hungry, so she moved on, eager to see the river.

Once around the bend, the path swerved along the edge of the mountain with the rise on her right side, while the left descended to the valley. There was plenty of room to walk, but she didn't risk getting too close to the edge. The tumble would take her down a steep slope consisting mostly of exposed rock.

Soon she was back in the shelter of the forest, with a clearing visible in the distance. Wisps of dense fog swirled higher than she stood, so she couldn't see what lay beyond the cloister of trees. Tranquility embraced her as she walked, and a sixth sense whispered, telling her she was in a special place.

When a manmade walkway of round stones emerged, she saw the first granite marker and realized what she'd found. Few trees remained in the graveyard, and the ones there were monstrous with thick round trunks. Their green, brushy needles rode high into the sky.

Many of the headstones were tall, solid rectangles etched with writing. Most were weathered and aged. Among the graves were stacks of flat, round stones, with the largest on bottom and smallest on top, creating miniature pyramids.

Individually made pagodas, Harper told herself. Wishes and prayers belonging to those who had visited. Most likely blessings for the loved ones who had passed.

Out of respect, she stayed on the laid walkway and didn't stop to study any of the markers. Nor did she take any photos.

She didn't feel comfortable in graveyards. Not anymore. They always reminded her of the funeral she wished to forget. The one she should never have been forced to attend.

Harper had been young when her grandmother had died, but the older woman's death had been expected. She'd been ill for some time. So while Harper had mourned the loss, she hadn't been destroyed.

Unlike the second time she'd stood beside an open hole to bury a family member.

Her sister had been murdered, and Harper's life force had almost drained away with that of her twin's. It wasn't right for two halves to be separated. Not so early in life. Not so violently.

The day of the funeral had been bright and warm, a cruel contrast to the mournful ceremony. How could the blazing sun have dared to cast its light when Harper's world would forever be shrouded in darkness?

With the sacred burial ground behind her now, Harper picked up her pace. Returning to the dense forest was a welcome reprieve after the exposed and silent cemetery.

Two stone lanterns appeared on the right side of the trail, and when she stopped to look up, she saw wooden beams buried in the mountainside to create steps. At the top of the steps stood a *Shinto* gate, though not cared for like the red one at the village entrance.

The wood was splintered and rotting, with only thin patches of blue paint remaining. Apparently the gate was no longer in use, or was no longer important. So no one should take issue with her presence.

Jogging up the steps as if she might be caught, Harper made her way to the top, thankful the climb wasn't too high. Not like the stone steps where Emi had gone with the priests.

No. Not thinking about that. Not my concern. Resolute in her plan to have a good day, she positioned her camera and took a few pictures. The gate seemed lonely. Abandoned. And for a brief moment, she felt sorry for the neglected structure.

Wondering how old the site was and why the gate was derelict, she walked through to find herself in an open expanse. Only yellowed grasses thrived on this windy overlook, as if the entire area had been left to perish.

She walked to the edge of the clearing, and as expected, found herself looking down on the river. She couldn't see the village from here, but could watch the sparkling water below as it curved through the fields and disappeared between two mountains in the distance.

With little else to see, she took photos of the river and made her way back down the staircase. Returning to the trail she'd been previously traveling, she found the rest of the hike easy and without challenge. Near the bottom the way was clear, and it didn't take long before she came upon the river.

And then the bridge. Harper stopped and stared, shaking her head though no one was around to see.

Reid had failed to accurately describe the bridge. Or that the rope and wooden board construction would hang so high above the water.

No way was she going out on that rickety thing. She didn't ride in cable cars either, because if she was going to be fifty feet in the air, she wanted whatever was beneath her feet to be solid. Not swaying.

"Okay. So I'm a scaredy-cat," she told the creaking bridge. "At least I know my limits." And with that, she took a sharp left and continued her descent. She might have to walk all the way to the village whether she wanted to or not. At least there, she could find stone bridges.

Reid's home was across the river, and she'd hoped to get a look at it today. While he was gone and couldn't put too much value on the fact she wanted to know more about him and how he lived.

Harper soon realized she'd made a good decision. The ground leveled out quickly, and she found herself walking alongside the river. She came to a narrow section with a wooden bridge.

She paused to look downstream and snap off some shots with her camera before moving on. The trail started to rise again. Here, there were homes to be found, and what had once been a path was now a dirt road that went one way toward town and the other into a residential area.

Signs were posted near the end of each driveway, announcing the name of each family dwelling. The homes were spaced far apart, each on a large parcel of land and thick with vegetation. A few buildings were visible from the road while others were hidden completely.

Eventually she came upon a curving staircase. Wide wooden beams supported steps that were covered in gravel and led to a three-storied house of wood. The planks of the home were crimson, but time and moisture had left streaks of grimy black.

The steep roof was covered in thatch, a mixture of dying beige and newly-sprouted green. The incline on each side of the staircase was overrun by naturally-growing shrubs, but Harper could see placards in the yard near the top. The signs were spaced all around a structured garden, unlike anything she'd come across so far.

As she studied the strange collection, an old man crossed the top of the stairs. His gradual and uneven gait slowed before he came to a standstill. And turned his head to look down at Harper.

She sucked in a breath, mortified she'd broken another cardinal rule just by looking, but she couldn't pull her gaze away from his. Even from a distance, she could tell his eyes were lighter than normal, dull with the opacity of cataracts.

Yet he knew Harper was there, and as she took one step back toward the road, he lifted the cane he carried in one hand.

He held the staff out, tipping the end down toward her. Then he swung the cane around to point to his home. He smiled at her and began his leisurely trudge again.

He had gestured to her. He wanted her to come inside. Harper was sure of his meaning, but Reid's and Saya's warnings bounced inside her mind.

But this man wasn't a part of the church, and he'd explicitly invited her to join him. It would be rude to ignore his request, and as far as she knew, walking away might be a breach of decorum.

She couldn't afford to break anymore rules. That's what she told herself to justify her actions.

Her body started moving, legs taking one wide step at a time, as she accepted the inevitable. The man was the first villager who'd gone out of his way to welcome her, because Reid and Saya didn't count. They were outsiders like her.

She wasn't going to refuse this rare offer of hospitality.

When she reached the landing, she could see the upper area was well-manicured, just as most Japanese gardens were. Still, the odd signs were unique. The old man had left his front door open, so Harper moved that way. Until she saw a placard that stilled her pumping blood.

The symbol was here. Exactly like the one on her windows and doors.

Taking in the other placards, she saw there were more of the unique *kanji* symbols scattered about. Why did he have these here?

Then an idea struck and Harper started planning. Surely he would be able to tell her what the drawing meant. She would not mention the temple or anything about *Shinto* practices. Just a simple inquiry regarding a symbol found inside her own home.

A perfectly rational plan, right? Considering he posted the signs in his gardens for anyone to see, the old man shouldn't mind discussing the writing found on them.

With renewed purpose, she steadied herself and stepped into the small *genkan*. The inside of the home showed less wear than its exterior, and the wooden floors were shiny from waxing and care.

While slipping off her shoes, Harper heard the old man wheezing and grunting from a room to her left. The screen doors were open, so when she edged down the hallway, she saw him crouching down to sit at a low table. The simple act was taking a toll on his aged body.

With his back to an open window that framed the flowering trees in his yard, the man finally settled with a great exhalation. He narrowed his filmy eyes, deepening the wrinkles surrounding them, then shifted his gaze to a cushion on the floor. To the seat opposite his position at the table.

Harper took the gesture as a request to join him and bowed her head before sitting cross-legged on the thin, hard pillow. She waited, allowing her host to take the lead in case she'd assumed incorrectly.

Lifting his head, the old man called out in Japanese. Footsteps pattered through the house before a young boy—age twelve, she guessed—opened a side screen and entered. His brown eyes widened when they fell on Harper, but the old man spoke to the boy to draw his attention.

"*Hai*," the boy said with a rigid half-bow before he disappeared.

Harper figured she was in the clear now, despite the kid's shock at her presence.

However, minutes passed while the man across from her sat in silence, his partially-blind stare resting somewhere just above her head. She was about to pose her first question when the boy returned with a tea set on a bamboo tray.

The kettle was bulbous, rounder than the one at her house. The gleaming brown looked ceramic. Steam wafted from the high, curving spout as the boy served them tea. First Harper, then her host.

When the boy stepped back from the table, Harper looked up to smile her thanks. She was shocked by the disapproval on the young face. Though looking at her, he spoke to the old man. The elder answered and must have told the boy he was dismissed.

The boy almost ran from the room, and Harper felt the muscles in her back relax. The kid had been filled with animosity. Directed entirely at her.

Sipping tea, Harper and the man fell back into an unsettling silence. Strains of music suddenly floated from somewhere in the house. Low and soft, with the distinctive sharp and flat notes of an Asian tune.

"You are the American woman who writes stories," the old man said abruptly, startling her when he broke the peace.

"Yes," she answered, still being cautious.

"I keep records, of stories from the past." The corners of his mouth lifted slightly, as did his long white mustache. "Mine are all true."

"You are the historian." She didn't pose the words as a question.

He nodded.

Unable to take any more suspense, Harper said, "I've never come to this side of the river before. I took the trail down the mountain." She hoped the benign small talk would encourage him to tell her more.

He lifted one white eyebrow.

Since he was evidently giving her the lead, she carefully considered what she could talk about. The topic of their religion was off the table, including priests and any role Emi might play as a temple or shrine maiden.

But what about things the village no longer seemed to care about? "I passed an old gate on the way here." Might as well go for it. "A *Shinto* gate at the top of stone steps. The area seemed neglected, as if no one goes there or uses the place anymore."

He nodded. "The old place. No one worships the *kami* there. They have not for many years." He set aside his tea and placed both hands in his lap. His filmy eyes stared at the empty spot above her head again. "A faith divided is none at all. Once, the village was greedy, desiring too many blessings."

Harper held her breath, unwilling to disrupt the historian's speech.

He coughed and continued. "The people wanted too much and split their allegiance between the divine spirits." He gaze snapped back to Harper's face. "One *kami* became enraged, and the village suffered."

Doing a quick deduction in her head, Harper said, "The old *Shinto* gate was used in one of those practices?"

"*Hai*. The supreme being of the river was once venerated, and the people gathered high above to reflect on the power and beauty. The life-giving essence." He paused briefly, then lowered his voice. "But the water flowing away from this place was weak. The river had a rival, one much older and stronger. One that demanded retribution."

Impassioned by his story, the old man began using sharp hand gestures to punctuate his words. "A *kami* has two souls, one gentle, *nigi-matama*. And one assertive. *Ara-mitama*." The old man narrowed his whitened eyes on her. "When the *ara-mitama* awoke, crops withered, the silver veins disappeared, and disease spread among the children, stealing the young as payment."

Harper put her tea down now, afraid she might spill it. Her hands were shaking. *Payment. Retribution*. The meaning weighed heavily in her stomach and left a metallic taste on her tongue. *Stealing the young*.

"The mountain was filled with wrath!" His gnarled fist hit the table, rattling their cups and the tea service on its tray.

"Villagers turned all of their devotion to *Gekido-yama*. The angry mountain."

Then the locals had left the gate at the old place to fall into disrepair, Harper thought. Had buildings once stood there as well? A shrine? If so, the villagers had destroyed it all, leaving no trace behind that might insult the mountain *kami*.

"That was when the name of this place was changed." The historian's tone had quieted again. "*Chuujitsu*. It means the faithful. And for hundreds of years, we have been." He smiled. "You see our blessings, our bounty, in the flourishing crops. Our healthy young people."

Harper released her breath slowly. "The mountain is happy now."

Tilting his head, the old man frowned. "Not happy, but content. For now. Our people must continue to pay tribute."

Icy fingers clutched at Harper's heart, squeezing until each throb was painful. She ignored the fact that they had somehow strayed into forbidden territory. That she was not supposed to talk or ask about their religion. "How do you pay tribute?"

"We offer up. We give." He leaned forward abruptly and whispered near her face, his expulsion of breath carrying a stale, fetid odor. "*The penance stone.*"

With her face pinched in confusion, Harper held still, even though the man's close proximity was disturbing. "I don't understand. What is the penance stone?"

A commotion occurred at the front door, a shuffling of bodies as shoes were removed. Then hurried footsteps pounded down the hallway. "Harper," a male voice said sharply.

She turned to find Reid looking down at her, the boy who'd served her tea standing beside him. They were both furious.

"Reid," she said, clearing her voice when it cracked. "You're back."

17

Reid held the door open for Harper to enter his cabin but closed it soundly after he came in behind her. They'd walked the short distance from the aging historian's house to his place in silence, with Reid shaking his head in the negative each time she'd tried to explain.

He was simply too angry with her and didn't trust himself to speak. Not in the open where they might be heard. He wouldn't embarrass either of them with such a display.

Now that they were safely inside, he let loose. "I don't know what the hell is wrong with you. I really don't." His attack took Harper by surprise. Her eyes widened as she gasped.

"Don't speak," he said, lifting one hand. "Not yet. I thought I was ready, but I need a few more minutes."

He went to the kitchen, a single counter against one wall that was open to the living room. He wrenched open the black refrigerator door and pulled out a Coke. "You want something?" he asked, holding the can up.

He knew he was being hard on her, that his manner and tone were far from kind. But, damn it, the woman kept risking herself, so his previous acts of kindness and consideration obviously hadn't worked.

He needed to let his frustration show and not worry so much about her reaction. Maybe if he breathed a little fire, she'd remember where she was and how she should behave.

"You'll be lucky if the Sheriff isn't at your door tonight telling you to pack up and leave." He slammed the door of the fridge. "Is that what you want?"

"I didn't do anything wrong," Harper said, finding her own temper. She put her fists on her hips.

"You did everything wrong!" Reid knocked back his drink for fear of what might come out of his mouth, then decided *Screw it.* "You went into the home of a revered member of this community. The village historian. You questioned him about the one thing you've been repeatedly warned not to talk about."

Curling one hand against her chest, she said, "He invited me to come up." Her expression was both disappointed and indignant.

But Reid couldn't falter again. Or feel sorry for her for any reason. "He asked you to come in?"

"No. He used his walking stick to point at me and... I knew what he meant."

Reid shook his head and looked away.

"You don't believe me? You think I'm lying?"

"No." He picked up the can, but his fingers crunched into the soft metal. He moved to the trash can and threw the Coke away. Then he faced Harper. "I think you saw what you wanted to see. What you were looking for. Just like you did with that girl."

He moved closer to her, so swiftly that she flinched. "Damn it, Harper. You said you'd keep your distance from the temple and stay out of trouble."

"I did," she cried. "I haven't seen Emi or anyone else wearing that dreadful brown color."

"So instead, you go waltzing into the home of the village historian? Do you know how many hoops I had to jump through to get him to meet with me?"

She threw up her hands. "He wanted to talk to me. I don't know why, but he did."

Running a hand through his hair, he tried to channel restraint. Yelling at Harper only made her defensive. There had to be a rational reason behind her flagrant dismissal of village law, and he was beginning to think all of her problems were related.

Her preferred state of seclusion. The loss of her sister. Her fixation on the *Shinto* practices of Chuujitsu. And that kid, Emi. Why had the girl ever come around Harper's place? If she had just left Harper alone, none of this would have happened.

"Harper," he said in a tone he hoped sounded reasonable. "You're lucky the boy was there. The apprentice knew how bad your mere presence in that house really was."

"Is that why he ran and told you to come?" Harper was miffed.

"Absolutely. And I don't blame him. The historian holds many secrets."

"Then why did he tell me about the old *Shinto* and the new one? The angry mountain?" She flung a hand toward his window to indicate the soaring peaks of the Chugoku Range.

Reid squeezed the nape of his neck. "Because he's old and his faculties are failing. He may very well reveal things he shouldn't." He stepped closer and took her by the shoulders. "Both the old man and his apprentice could be severely punished for what happened today."

"Oh," Harper whispered, her face draining of color. "Oh, no."

Seeing her in distress made muscles clench in Reid's gut. He didn't want to scare her, but he had to get through that thick skull once and for all. When she bit her bottom lip, the look she gave him was pitiful.

Sighing with exasperation, Reid drew her to his chest. "It's okay. I'm not going to tell anyone, and neither is the boy. He was smart enough to come get me. And no one else."

He rubbed her back and felt shivers course through her. Stubborn woman. Why did she insist on causing her own suffering?

Reid pulled back and tipped her chin up. His gaze locked with hers. "Why do you keep doing these things?"

Her gray eyes swam with despair, but beneath her guilt was another emotion. The one that drove her.

Fear. Always fear.

She said in a shaky whisper, "Because something is wrong in this village."

For the first time, a line of unease snaked its way up Reid's spine.

Harper continued. "If they don't want me to know things or to be involved," she stopped long enough to swallow, "then why do they keep trying to communicate with me? They started all of this. Not me."

Though his impulse was to argue, Reid had to consider her point of view. The teenage girl *had* come to Harper's house, sneaking around more than once. And symbols had been left *inside* her home. More and more, Reid was suspecting they had been put there just for Harper's sake. But why?

And why had a man been in her back yard in the dark of night? Alone, the pieces made no sense. Individual occurrences. Unrelated. Purely coincidence.

But when they were lined up systematically, the pieces changed from a senseless, scrambled code to a message that was becoming clear. Even to Reid.

Had the old man truly manipulated Harper into coming inside?

"No," Reid thought aloud. "I'll agree that you've been received in a... strange way by some of the people here, but the historian couldn't have known you'd be passing his house today. He's an old, confused man."

"Maybe," Harper said with a frown. "But the fact remains that he gestured for me to come up to his house. And he did tell me things about their religion." Her brows shot up. "He said he knew who I was. The American woman who writes stories."

Reid didn't like the sound of that. He wanted to keep Harper away from all of the strange things going on, but somehow, she seemed to be the epicenter. "Look," he said, "the Sheriff told us he'd keep people from bothering you, and nothing has happened the last few days, right?"

Harper shrugged half-heartedly.

"Why don't we call today a near-miss and try to return the favor from now on? Try not to bother them, either." He let his hand slip from her shoulder into the glorious mass of warm brown hair. She'd taken the barrette out on their walk here, letting the thick tresses fall to her shoulders. "Try to keep your distance from people."

She laughed, but the sound was harsh. "When I first got here, you told me to get out more. To meet new people."

Reid let a wry smile slide across his face. She had him there. "Maybe I should defer to your judgment. You obviously know yourself better than I do. You're more familiar with the kind of havoc you wreak when unleashed on society."

She started to grin but shook her head instead. "No. It's the other way around."

Her hand was on his chest now, and Reid tried to ignore the flame her touch ignited. With the lightest caress, she made him want more.

"I'll try to mind my own business, but I'm still worried," she said. "About me and about Emi. I'm sorry, but my instincts tell me she's in danger."

"Let the Sheriff and the girl's family take care of her."

"What if they don't?" Harper withdrew from his arms. "You can see their *Shinto* takes priority over everything else. What if they intend to hurt her with the family's permission?"

"Whoa." Now her concerns were overflowing into paranoia. "What are you talking about, Harper? There's been nothing to indicate that."

"Other than a priest beating her with a belt, you mean?"

"Some schools still have corporal punishment in the States. I don't like it, either," he added when she scowled, "but that's why societies have laws. Each governs itself as their culture and history mandate."

"Fine, but what about what that man told me?" she challenged. Her eyes darkened, the gray transforming to thunder clouds. "What is the penance stone?"

"I don't know," he bit out. "I'm not *supposed* to know, and neither are you. It's part of their religion. Probably a cornerstone of their temple, literally a rock. Or it might be some type of idol. Even jewelry. Hell, for all we know, the stone could by symbolic and not even exist."

Harper slid wary eyes past Reid and toward the distant mountains. "Or the stone could be bigger. Like an altar."

"Exactly, an altar inside their—" Reid stopped speaking when she looked back to him and pressed her lips into a thin, pale line. "No way. Now you're pushing the limits, even for a writer with a big imagination. There is no sacrificial altar in this town, Harper."

He stepped closer to her. Got right up next to her so she would hear what he said. "Reel it in, Harper. Now. If you go around making crazy accusations like that, we could all get hurt. They might kick Saya and me out of town as well. Guilt by association."

She seemed to physically deflate before him. Then she rubbed her face with her hands. "Okay. You're right." She put her hand to her neck and spun away. "Can I have that drink now?"

"Sure." He let her walk away, giving her space to vent if that's what she needed.

And she did. After slamming the refrigerator the same way he had, Harper popped the top on her Coke. "I did a good job the last few days, you know. I stayed home and worked. I didn't go poking in anyone's trash or stealing anybody's chicken."

A smiled jerked at Reid's mouth but he tamped it down.

"Then I go for an innocent walk in the country," she said, "and a sweet old man points for me to come up and join him. He had tea served, for God's sake!"

She brushed a strand of hair back from her face with a vengeance. "Now I see I've fallen into another trap. Just like when I chased Emi. People come to me, they seek me out, and I'm the one who gets slapped in the face."

She pointed at him as she stalked closer. "Well no more. I'm not talking to anyone else, even if they come up to my front door." Her expression was animated. "Nope. I'll just call the Sheriff. Or... I'll call you or Saya, and one of you can call the Sheriff, since he wouldn't understand a word I said anyway."

"I can get behind this plan," Reid said, preferring her current ire over the previous remorse. Harper carried too much guilt on her shoulders, and he wanted to find out why.

If he understood the root of her pain, maybe he could help her.

Then as soon as he had the idea, he cursed himself for being an arrogant fool. He didn't know if he was in any position to help her or not. She might very well finish up the love story she was writing and leave him behind like she did everyone else.

Harper liked to go it alone.

Reid watched as she finished her drink and smacked her lips and knew he'd do anything to change her mind. He was determined to make her solitary soul yearn for a mate instead of a lonely bed every night. To make her desire him as much as he did her.

As a tidal wave of acceptance rolled through him, Reid was forced to admit the truth. *I'm halfway in love with her already. Now I just have to convince her to meet me there.*

With calm born of certainty, he crossed the floor to stand near her. He waited until she expended the last of her steam and deposited the crushed can into the trash.

Then he reached for her arm and pulled her to him. Their chests collided.

"What are you doing?" Her eyes danced with worry again, but this time her alarm was all because of him.

"I hope you stick to that plan," he told her, grasping the small of her back, amazed by how fragile she felt beneath his hands. "Because I can't sit by and watch you court disaster."

"Reid," she protested. "I'm all churned up."

"Good. Then you can direct that energy at me." Why couldn't she see what was right in front of her? Why did she always fight back? "I promise I can take it," he said, lowering his mouth to hers. Gently.

He whispered against her lips. "And I promise not to hurt you."

"I..." she breathed out, but Reid cut her off with another kiss. Then he took his mouth away, only to put a finger to hers. Slipping just the tip inside, he rubbed her bottom lip until her eyes fluttered closed and she moaned.

"I know you feel this thing between us. This heat. The pull." His words tickled across her neck as he tasted her there. Then he was next to her ear. "Tell me what you feel."

Fluid heat melded them together where they stood, and Harper could only hold on to Reid's thick arms as she fought to stay upright. Every natural instinct in her body wanted to drag him to the floor with her. To let him worship her the way his eyes promised he would.

She hadn't lied before. She was all churned up, but the irritation that had been riding her now sparked into something else. Her anger rolled straight into need, and for more than the delicious lust rampaging through her system.

Reid was offering more than sex, and she found herself longing to let him give it to her. All of it. He'd tucked her close and kissed her with his silken mouth, sheltering her with his strength and determination.

He always made her feel that way when he was near. Sheltered. Safe. Protected. The things she'd valued for so long, that she needed to live, he gave her with only his presence. And a few soft words.

She suddenly changed her opinion of Chuujitsu and all its dark secrets. Strange girls and creepy priests were the least of her troubles.

The man stealing her breath away was the greatest threat.

"I can't do this," she said, but her body revolted, pushing her breast forward to meet his seeking hand. She stood on her toes to kiss him again, a kiss that was far more demanding than his had been. And not nearly as sweet.

Reid's answering groan shot a thrill all the way down to her feet. He picked her up, arms wrapped around her waist to hoist her into the air, before leading them both to an old, green couch.

A hundred warning bells went off in her head but were ignored. Yes, she wanted this. Desire had been a stranger for far too long, and she welcomed the rush of pleasure. Then the raging desire as Reid sat and pulled her down to straddle him.

The thick length of his erection pressed against her core and arousal like she'd never known made her clasp her thighs around him. The throbbing sensation was so strong she couldn't tell if it came from her or Reid.

Wasn't that how it should be? Two people forged together, breathing and moving as one. Sharing the deepest, most personal act and the glorious satisfaction that resulted?

She pulled at the dark shirt he wore, long sleeves with no buttons. Grabbing the hem, she pulled it up and over his head in one smooth motion that left him with slightly tousled hair and a wickedly crooked grin. "I think I like you when you get churned up," he said.

Harper smiled back, but her attention drifted to his chiseled chest and abs. "That's utterly ridiculous," she told him. "No one should be this perfect." Her hands stroked down his golden skin. Her fingers feathered through the hair on his chest, darker blonde than on his head and just the right amount.

As if testing her reaction, Reid slid a hand under her shirt, smoothing his palm around her back, then down to slip inside the top of her pants. There he rested, the hint of what he might do sending Harper's body into overdrive.

She could imagine his hands in other places. She pictured how he would treat her, make love to her. Gently yet thoroughly, because that was his way.

Reid Ellis left nothing undone.

Harper's eyes popped open and her heart stuttered. No. He wouldn't leave anything unfinished. That included her, both physically and emotionally.

And Harper wasn't sure she was ready for that.

She'd been toying with the idea of taking Reid as a lover. And what a lover he would make. He'd level her with his eyes, pure green like no other's. He'd respect her body like he did her mind, her profession, and her neurotic need for privacy.

Suddenly panic was climbing like a poisonous vine, choking out the sexual energy, the pulsating need for release.

Reid was too good a man to be her lover. She already knew him as a colleague. As a friend. Her heart would crash right into his skillful hands if she let him get any closer. She wouldn't be able to stop it.

And then he would be able to hurt her. "We should think about this," she said, lifting herself up.

Reid latched onto her thighs and held her in place. "Over-thinking gets you in trouble, Harper. Every time." His face was a mask of disappointment, but he let her go and sat against the back of the couch.

Standing and patting her clothes and hair back into place, she feigned a dignity and distance she didn't feel.

With a resignation that made his entire body tense, Reid picked his shirt up and put it on. "You know, earlier I asked myself why you couldn't see something good when it was staring you right in the face." He stood and stared down at her from his towering height. "Now I know."

"What?" Harper demanded. His obvious annoyance made her insides roil. She felt cold and rejected, even though she'd been the one to retreat.

"Because your vision is filled with everything that might go wrong. You see every possible failure or mistake." His eyes flicked over her face, scrutinizing. "I can't help you with that. No one can."

"I didn't ask for anyone's help. And I'm just trying to be—"

"Cautious?" His laugh was harsh and bitter. "Your radar is backwards, Harper. You pick apart the things you should leave alone." He stepped around her and headed for the door. Then he opened it and turned to her. "But you hide from your own happiness."

Suddenly, all the aggravation seemed to fall away and he spoke to her in a flat tone. Defeated and weary. "Come on," he said, unwilling to meet her eyes. "I'll drive you home."

18

They hadn't been kicked out of town.

The realization that neither she nor her friends were going to be ousted from the village because of her chat with the historian should have put Harper's mind at ease. Just as her hot bubble baths should have relaxed her. And as sitting in the garden should have brought tranquility to her soul.

Yet the tried-and-true weren't working. Not since she'd let Reid stir up a wealth of unrest inside her with a killer combination of flaming green eyes and gently roaming hands.

Not to mention the way he'd spoken so low next to her ear, warm breath teasing her neck while his hands held her steady. *Tell me what you feel.*

Harper waved a hand in front of her face to dispel the heat permeating her body. If a memory of the man could cause a visceral reaction, she had to believe the live version would make her combust.

Too much. That's what she'd felt, and the way he'd wrapped her heart up in his strong hands had made her draw back, shut down, and run away.

Right back to her beautiful house in the hills where she had every luxury she could ever want and all the time she required to put in a decent day's worth of writing.

And where she was lonely.

Ooh! Impossible! Slapping her hands to her knees, Harper

set her electronic reader on the bench and stood to pace. Even the mystery book she'd been dying to get into had failed to keep her mind on something, *anything!* other than Reid.

She wasn't sure if she was angrier with him for making her miss him, or herself for giving him the ability to do so. Nothing had gone the way it was supposed to since the day she'd arrived in the village. Absolutely nothing.

Even her manuscript had an angle she hadn't originally plotted. The suspense had taken a hard turn toward horror, filled with dark woods and midnight noises. Creeping villains and surprise twists.

Well, considering the past six weeks, she was definitely writing what she knew and was on the verge of introducing a whole new subgenre. The scare-mance.

Harper sighed and kicked at the white pebbles surrounding the pond. One plopped into the water and she felt instant regret. "Why? There are no fish in there. Nothing is going to get hurt by the pebble." She looked to the clear, blue sky. "I've got a guilt complex."

Chastising herself was a new trick, too. She'd been using plenty of avoidance tactics since her unfortunate failure-to-launch with Reid, but nothing broke up the heavy clod of clay she seemed to be carrying around in her chest.

She missed him. That was the only answer. But acknowledging what was wrong with her didn't help. She only grew more frustrated.

He hadn't stopped coming by to see her each day or helping her with the duties he'd originally agreed to. And he was still the affable, solid, wise, and far too handsome Reid.

He just didn't look at her the same way anymore, and the absence of that warmth was gradually breaking her heart.

Physically he was present, but even when he stood right beside her, she found herself missing him. He was emotionally closed off, no longer sharing himself with her—not like he had been—and she couldn't blame him.

A small, brown bird fluttered its way through the bamboo stalks behind the pond. Then, finding nothing worth perusing or stealing, the animal winged its way into the air and was gone. Back to the forest and its home.

Home. She was beginning to reconsider that word and its definition. Dwelling. Residence. Abode. Quarters. None of those synonyms seemed to fit anymore. Not for her.

She'd found strength in her ability to stay detached from sentimentality. She relished the freedom to move from place to place, to meet new people. Or, if she were honest with herself, to run from the ones she already knew.

She couldn't let anyone become important to her. Oh, no. Attachment followed, emotion, and then the potential for hurt and loss. And Harper avoided pain if at all possible, cutting off the fresh growth of relationships before they ever had a chance to bud.

Let alone bloom.

Reid had been trying to plant himself in her life, and she had to decide what to do. Encourage him? Provide him with care and attention? Give him what he needed to thrive?

Or pull the whole thing up by the roots? Because he had taken hold, and clipping off the ends wouldn't work now.

She huffed and searched for distraction. Enough of that analogy. She was beginning to picture Reid with green skin.

Instead, she edged closer to the pond with its still water. The glimmer of rounded stones on the bottom was fascinating. Hues of umber, onyx, and several shades of gray provided décor and something pretty to look at in the absence of fish.

Short brush-like plants and large, flat stones framed the pond. An iron lantern sat on the ground, rust-colored and likely authentic. Harper tried to find some of the magic the gardens had first inspired, but the charm of the Saito house had faded.

Her peace and happiness had been shattered by worries over

her safety, both physical and mental. No matter how rational Reid and Saya were about the incidents with the villagers, she still felt a pervading sense of disquiet.

As if a huge breath had been sucked in and the atmosphere was just holding the air in. Waiting. Waiting.

Harper saw the white pebble she'd accidentally kicked into the pond. The white was bright and clear against the darker stones. Contrasting sharply. Screaming that it didn't belong.

Like Harper in the subdued village.

Needing to set her world to rights, even in this insignificant way, she reached into the cool liquid and grasped the smaller stone. She extracted the pebble and tossed it back in with the others on the ground.

With a shake of her arm to send droplets flying, she turned toward the front wall.

And saw Emi standing at the gate.

Thoughts flew into her head, collided and combated with each other. What should she do? Pretend she didn't see her or just run into the house without explanation? Perhaps she should let the girl know she wasn't welcome.

Of course that's what she should do. Any of the above. She'd promised Reid and Saya. And the Sheriff. Just look how her previous contact with any of the locals had turned out.

Lifting her hand as if to ward off Emi's existence, Harper started slowly shaking her head and retreating. "No. No, Emi."

The girl peered through the black bar, her head tilting like a confused puppy. She wore her ponytail today and appeared calm, with the usual flat and emotionless expression on her face. Then she stuck one hand through the gate and whimpered.

Damn. Harper stopped moving. She wouldn't leave any scared child alone, especially one that was reaching out to her for help. She would speak to the girl and make her understand. She'd make her go away.

She'd just do it gently.

Now her steps were precise and efficient as she went to the gate. "Emi. I can't help you." She shook her head. The denial sounded cruel, even as she told herself she had to send the girl away. "Go home. Go to your family." *Oh, what is the word for family? I still can't speak the basics.*

So she tried to shoo Emi away with her hand, and that made her feel even worse. The girl looked oddly at Harper's flapping arm then stuck her own hand through to clasp Harper's wrist. She whimpered again.

"Shit." She felt chagrined then remembered the girl wouldn't understand the curse word anyway. Emi continued to stare.

Before she could argue with herself, Harper pulled her keys from her pocket and unlocked the gate. She stepped back and swept her arm in a low arc to tell Emi to come in.

The girl leaped inside and closed the black wrought-iron gate before Harper had the chance, then stood with her arms hanging straight at her sides.

Putting a finger to her lips, Harper pantomimed being quiet. Keeping a secret. Because this time, their encounter had to remain between the two of them. No one else could know or they'd both be in trouble.

Hoping the girl would follow and come away from the bars, she walked quickly on the stone path toward the front corner of the garden. The path curved behind the pond, behind the soaring bamboo, and was enclosed on the other side by the high wall.

That was the most private, concealed place in the entire yard. Another bench was situated in the shadows as well, where Harper could take some time to converse with Emi. Or try to, considering her apparent lack of verbal skills.

Again Harper wondered what affected Emi. Possibly autism or mental retardation, but she knew there were vast differences between the two and many levels of cognition in both categories. However, she was not qualified to distinguish or identify any of them.

She would do what she could and use her natural feelings. Go back to the basics. She sat on the bench and patted the stone next to her, giving the girl what she hoped was an inviting and friendly smile.

Emi dropped down right away, amazing Harper by showing her a broad grin, as if they were playing a game.

Putting the flat of her palm to her chest, Harper patted her sternum and said, "Harper." *Pat. Pat. Pat.* "Harper."

Emi stared back. Then she patted her own chest, but without speaking.

Harper tried a different tactic, because she didn't want to touch the girl and risk scaring her away. She certainly couldn't reach over and knock on her chest. So she used her finger to point to her face. "Harper."

Then she pointed in the same way to Emi's face and said, "Emi." Another point to the girl. "Emi."

Then back to herself. "Harper."

Screwing up her face with an intense look of concentration, the young girl pushed her lips out, then opened her mouth wide before whispering, "Harper." She patted Harper's chest.

Laughing at Emi's surprising response, Harper nodded but tried to remain low key. Nothing too loud or vigorous. "Yes." She smiled and patted her chest. "Harper. *Hai.*"

Emi gave a short burst of giggles then focused her attention on the ground. With the bright smile still in place, she slid off the bench to kneel on the path. More of the white pebbles were scattered on both sides of the walkway and among the plants.

With her middle finger, Emi drew a symbol in the gravel. Then she pointed to herself and said, "Emi."

Deciding to see where this might lead, Harper joined her on the flat stone path and drew the same symbol. Well, she did her best, because *kanji* symbols were often difficult to copy, and the medium of pebbles on the ground made the process even harder.

When she'd drawn the sign, Harper repeated the girl's name and received three quick hand claps from the girl. Praise for performance.

While Emi sat there beaming, Harper tried to think of anything else she might draw. She had no idea how her name would be written with *kanji*, and she didn't know any other symbols.

She smiled to herself. She knew the one on the Japanese cereal box, the one she raided so often, but that wouldn't make sense to the girl.

There was really only one other symbol she knew well enough to draw, but voices rose up inside her to protest the idea. No one had told her what the mysterious symbols she'd found in her home meant. For all she knew, they could refer to something awful. Or forbidden.

Or they could simply mean *love*.

Harper bit her bottom lip as indecision raged, but the voices were falling silent. Emi could speak after all, even if only a few words, like her name.

So what could it hurt to draw the symbol in the pebbles? There was a good chance the young girl wouldn't even recognize the *kanji*.

Smiling for Emi's benefit and to settle her own nerves, Harper raked her hand over the gravel, erasing the symbol for Emi's name that she'd made before. Gesturing for Emi to watch, Harper painstakingly created the *kanji* symbol she'd been trying to decipher for weeks.

She wanted to do a good job, so the girl might understand.

When Harper finished, she shifted expectant eyes to Emi.

There was no question the young girl recognized the symbol. The drawing had affected her profoundly. Emi whimpered again and slapped her hands to her eyes, banishing the sight of what Harper had drawn.

"Oh, God." Harper jerked when Emi hit her own face again with her palms, hiding her eyes. "I'm sorry. I'm sorry." Harper scrubbed the symbol away and spoke softly to the girl. "There. It's gone. *Shhh.*"

"Emi," she lightly touched Emi's elbow, and when the girl peeked out, Harper showed her the ground. "It's gone. I'm sorry."

Emi's brown eyes welled with unspent tears as she stared at the spot where the symbol had been. Then she lifted a shaking arm and stretched it straight as a rod from her body. She pointed to the place where the symbol had been.

Then she patted her chest three times.

Harper felt as if the air stopped existing around her and all sound vanished. "What?" She had no idea how to ask the questions she wanted to ask. She and Emi were so limited in their form of communication.

She frowned and shook her head. Wondering how else she might tell Emi she was confused. Harper lifted both hands and shrugged.

Casting sad eyes at her, the girl stood, dragging one leg at a time in anguish. She sniffled and stared at Harper for what felt like minutes. She glanced again at the pebbles on the ground and blew out a breath with a hitch.

Suddenly, as if making a decision, Emi grabbed the side of her shirt and lifted the material. She dragged the waistband of her pants down to reveal her hip.

Harper gasped so hard she almost made herself cough, but she contained herself for the girl's sake. And condemned her own brutal insensitivity.

The young girl knew the symbol, all right. The very same *kanji* drawn on Harper's windows and doors. The secret writing style used only by the village of Chuujitsu.

The cursed sign might still be an enigma to Harper, but it was familiar to Emi. Very familiar.

Because it had been branded on her skin.

Harper put a trembling hand to her mouth. "Oh, God. What's happening? What does that mean?" Caught up in a flood of fears about the girl, the village, and once again, her own safety, she could only stare at the mark on the young, innocent flesh and quake as she knelt on the path.

Then a voice rang out in the forest. A man was nearby. He was calling Emi's name.

Though Harper and the girl didn't speak the same language, their eyes clashed in terror, brown to gray, both knowing they were about to be discovered.

And after discovery would come punishment.

The man's call was coming from the back side of her home, beyond the wall. She could get the girl out in time, but they had to hurry. "Go. Go." Harper's voice was a harsh whisper, filled with urgency but low to avoid detection.

Emi broke into a sprint, and only when she got to the gate did she stop to look back at Harper. One last plaintive plea for help.

Harper nodded. "Okay." She put her hand to her chest and hoped the girl understood she was making her a promise. She patted her chest three times.

Emi smiled against her flowing tears and said, "Harper." Then she leapt away like a young doe and was gone.

Harper listened to the girl barge downhill and into the woods, and after a tense few moments, she remembered the unlocked gate. She stumbled forward, gripping her keys tightly so they wouldn't clink and make noise.

After securing the wrought-iron lock, she crept back to the bench she'd been sitting on before Emi's appearance. She picked up her e-reader and turned it on, trying to slow her breathing and rapid pulse. Trying to act as if nothing out of the ordinary had occurred.

At one point she thought she heard someone walking near

the wall, but the noise was barely discernible. After several minutes, her brain started functioning, and she could think past the panic.

She could decide what to do.

If she was going to take this information to Reid and Saya, then she was going to go fully armed. She had to be able to back up her theories this time. And that would require proof.

Emi was in danger, and no one was going to convince Harper otherwise.

Yes, she was scared to death, and she had no idea what she could do to help the girl who was supposedly so well-protected. Harper was starting to wonder if Emi was only protected from outsiders. From those who might intervene on her behalf.

A stranger who didn't answer to the temple might try to save her. A stranger like Harper.

She stood and looked out over her stone wall, imagining the village in the valley below. The furtive actions and guarded religion of the village were beginning to reveals secrets. Such zealotry aroused suspicion.

Why did they fight so hard to hide their *Shinto*?

Harper slapped the e-reader against her thigh. *Maybe it's time I find out the truth.* She still had another kind of book in her possession. One Reid had never gotten around to helping her translate.

Without a care for bringing her outside shoes into the home, Harper marched across the dark wood of the floor and headed to her office. If she had to figure out what that book was about by herself, then that's what she would damn well do. Even if it took all day and all night.

That girl was in trouble, and for some reason, she had come to Harper.

Remembering another call and a cry for help that had gone unanswered, Harper forced aside the sadness and regret. The agony of knowing the past could never be undone.

She pulled the small red book from its hiding place under a cushion. Sitting down to the computer, she stared at her reflection in the black screen.

This time she would heed the warnings. She would listen to her intuition. This time, Harper promised herself, she would do something before it was too late.

19

So this was the old mining compound. Harper looked through the chain-link fence and studied the run-down buildings. Wood was rotted, the stonework cracked and crumbling. Long vines had reclaimed what they could with their creeping limbs, scavenging what humans had left behind to decay.

She remembered what the aging historian had told her, that the silver mining and production had been stopped centuries ago. When harvests had been ruined and silver had become scarce. When *Gekido-yama* had supposedly wrought devastation on the village for lack of devotion.

Gekido-yama. The mountain of wrath.

Harper had spent hours the night before deciphering what she could of the little red book of horrors. That's how she thought of it. Torture, mutilation, and death. All to keep people in line.

She was more convinced than ever that the symbol she'd seen in her house—and yesterday on Emi's skin—was the same style as the ones in the book. The fluidity and style of the *kanji* were identical, and her scrutiny of every page, under a magnifying glass, had revealed plenty of symbols in the book.

Just not the one she'd been searching for.

What did it all mean? The unidentified drawing. Emi's brand and the way she was guarded by priests. The village's secret *Shinto*. The symbols and their relation to the horrendous acts in the book.

Everything was related. Fringes touched to form a circle, but still lacked the centerpiece.

And Harper believed that missing piece was the infamous penance stone. If she could figure out what the old man had been talking about, she might make the final connection.

Because she had to be sure. She needed to be right. Especially if she was going to help Emi.

Her rescue plan still had a few kinks to be worked out, but in the back of her mind, the strategy was pretty basic. Take the girl and get the hell out of this village.

She would deal with kidnapping charges later.

Pushing away from the fence, Harper told herself that wouldn't happen. The Japanese courts would intervene if they found out what was going on here, in this quiet country hamlet. They would have to. While no expert on their federal laws, she knew the Japanese government would condemn unsanctioned death penalties.

Now all she had to do was prove that was happening. Or had happened. Or might happen?

She wasn't sure, but after yet another heart-wrenching experience with Emi, Harper intended to do what she could to prevent harm from coming to the young girl. Because that was the one thing she was positively sure of. Emi was in danger.

The mining area was behind her now as she strolled back toward the center of the village. She was taking her time, walking at a leisurely pace, and checking every home or business for *kanji* symbols written in that special type of script.

She kept a vigilant eye out for the unique style that belonged only to the hush-hush religion of the village. The secret *Shinto*.

Sketchbook in hand, she was prepared to note any location she discovered the writing and draw a quick replica of the *kanji*. So far the only examples were in the book, and none of them corresponded with anything good.

Each picture in the book had referenced a *kanji*, and she'd eventually picked up on a pattern. There was a sign for the act of tearing a person in two, and another for removing the hand of a thief. So if the symbols still existed anywhere in the village, Harper reasoned, then so did their corresponding punishments.

After combing the eastern side of town closer to the mines, she made a left and headed south. Soon she was in the residential district, where most of the family homes were located. The midday sun was high, but no children were anywhere to be found. Still at school, she imagined, and waiting to be dismissed for lunch.

Saya was teaching an English class today, so Harper didn't have to worry about bumping into her. She didn't want to involve her friend unless she absolutely had to.

Saya had a life here. Students she cared about. So until Harper knew more, she wouldn't risk her friend's status in the village.

She, on the other hand, had nothing to lose. Save the trouble of lost rent and the time she'd need to relocate.

By the time she reached the far end of the village, she was beginning to second-guess her plan. She had yet to see any of the strange symbols and had already reached the southern edge.

A three-story building—the second tallest in Chuujitsu after the *Shinto* temple—rose above her in pristine white. The size of the medical clinic and services it provided were surprising in such a small village. Harper guessed the necessity was due to location.

Chuujitsu was far and away from any other city, and a critically injured patient probably wouldn't last the two-hour drive. She spent a moment pondering life-flights and whether the clinic had a helipad before shaking herself to set her mind back on task.

No symbols aside from the regular Japanese *kanji* were on or around the clinic, so there was no reason to linger.

After performing the same crisscross pattern, and over two hours on her now-aching feet, Harper had covered almost all of the newer section of town. Having bought a bag of fried vegetable chips, she leaned against a low wall and contemplated the far side of the village.

The arched bridges would lead her across the river. And take her back in time.

While finishing her snack and bottled water, she used the time to people-watch. She studied their faces, dress, and any objects they might be carrying. While a few villagers wore brown robes or belts to signify their association with the temple, many more appeared to be regular citizens.

If they were allowed to visit the older area, why couldn't she? No one had warned her it was off limits. And if the symbols were going to be found anywhere in Chuujitsu, she would put the archaic western side of the village at the top of her list.

Shoving her empty chip bag inside her purse, she removed her sketch pad again and set off. Two others were crossing the nearest bridge, one hauling laundry baskets and the other a brown sack. Harper didn't concern herself with their destinations but took the opportunity to follow.

She fell in behind the one with the large basket and kept her face down, eyes on her pad. To anyone looking, she would appear to be a woman with a to-do list. Nothing more.

And she prayed no one would recognize her as the troublesome American who was a magnet for temple priests and scared young girls. Girls she was forbidden to talk to.

The woman with the laundry went one way and the man with the sack the opposite. As they peeled off, Harper was left standing in front of a mansion of gray stone. The same color found throughout the village in streets, walls, and bridges.

Looking up, she saw a high terrace on what may have been

the third floor. From across the river the homes had seemed large. Now they were monstrous, casting long shadows on the streets.

Harper rubbed her arms, wishing for a jacket. The sun didn't reach the ground here and couldn't heat the heavy stone slabs of the homes and streets. This section of the village was obviously more ancient, but it was also colder. And darker.

The writer in her appreciated the symbolism, but the beating heart inside her chest constricted with unease. Animal instinct made her hairs stand on end, her pupils widen. Intuition whispered in the most primal portion of her brain. *Don't go in there. Stay away.*

And like any good heroine in a suspense novel, she also had to do the right thing. Which somehow never, ever seemed to be the *smart* thing.

Veering toward one corner of the mansion, Harper smoothly made her way to the side street. Surreptitiously, so as not to draw undue attention. The temple was a few blocks farther back in the old sector and one street toward the center.

She could see the tower. It seemed to pierce the sky. And though her primitive impulses still screamed their refusal, Harper stayed true to her path. To her destination.

She would enter the soul of this malevolent place. Where she would finally find the truth.

Inside the temple.

Reid is going to be so angry. And Saya. But Harper rather liked the idea of witnessing Reid's fury. That would mean she'd made it out alive. *Oh, stop with the dramatics. Worst case scenario, I'll get booted out. Yelled at. Possibly taken to the Sheriff.*

Then she would be forced to leave Chuujitsu. And so be it. She'd go to a higher level of government and tell them what she'd found. If she managed to dig up anything worth telling.

And if she didn't? Then she'd be intensely happy to have

been proven wrong. And that would be the end of it.

When she rounded the last building and came upon the temple, she stalled just long enough to muster up the last bit of courage she possessed. She scoped out the most optimal position for observing the front doors. If anyone saw her enter, they'd report her immediately. Or come kick her out themselves.

With one glance, the villagers would see she didn't belong.

Inspiration struck when she studied the side alleys. The shadowed passages would serve her well. Once she was in the concealing darkness, she would have a better chance of moving undetected.

The stretch of shadows led up to one corner of the steps. A quick jog and she would be inside the temple. Which may or may not be empty.

Casting caution aside, Harper sauntered toward the side street as if taking a casual walk through the neighborhood, but as soon as she hit the darkened pathway, she crept closer to the outer wall of the temple.

She eased to the bottom of the steps, gave a cursory look around for onlookers, then darted up the steps. She had to pause long enough to push her way through the massive doors.

The entrance was painted in red lacquer and was at least twelve feet high. The doors didn't squeak but gave a soft sigh as air was displaced, and as soon as she could slip through the crack, Harper closed them behind her.

Her skin was on fire and her head buzzed. Reality had taken hold of her senses and adrenaline was kicking in. She was inside the temple. The temple! *Slow, deep breaths. For God's sake, don't pass out!*

Heeding her self-instruction, Harper leveled out her respirations and shot her gaze to every corner of the room. She was all alone, as far as she could tell, and the silence hung over the cavernous space like a heavy cloud. The inner sanctum was completely cut off from outside activity and sound.

Standing stuck to the wall is a waste of time. She wiped the moisture from her brow. Pure panic-induced sweat. *Just get what you came for. Move!*

Similar to Buddhist temples Harper had seen, the main worship area had expansive marble floors, but the ones she walked over now were the color of soot. No bright gold or white in this grand hall. No cheery turquoise or drapes with delicate patterns.

The mood here was somber. Taking light steps to avoid making noise, Harper eased down the center aisle, partitioned on both sides by great, round pillars. Her arms wouldn't be able wrap around their girth, so they must be supportive as well as decorative. They were smooth, polished to a sheen, and were the deep, rich color of spilled Merlot.

Flickering lights caught Harper's attention. A shrine was in the front of the room. Silver goblets were stacked on a square table and on shelves that flanked both sides. The center of the wall was recessed, set deeper into the stone like one large shadow box.

Candles burned on holders, their flames highlighting a sculpture resting inside. It was a miniature landscape of mountains. Harper moved closer, observing the zigzag of ridges and peaks, certain she recognized that particular range.

Then she remembered staring through the fence earlier near the abandoned mine shacks. She'd noticed how lovely the mountains on the east side of the village looked with the sun beaming down. The intricate model in the wall was identical.

The historian had said the modern *Shinto* revered the mountain, and here was more evidence.

Whump. A soft sound carried to her from an opening on the far side of the room, as if stairs were just beyond and someone above had closed a door. Now Harper's scalp tingled from fear of being discovered.

Her widened eyes bounced nervously around the huge, open

space. There was nowhere to hide if anyone entered the room. And she still hadn't made any solid connection between this temple and the atrocities she'd seen in her stolen book.

Raking her gaze over every object in the hall, she searched for *kanji* symbols. There were none. No placards or paintings of any sort. How could that be?

Backing toward one of the pillars, Harper put her hand out as she made one more visual sweep for the writing. She pressed against the wood, so she'd be hidden from the side of the room where the noise had originated. She turned to mold her front to the pillar and look around.

Her palm moved across the smooth surface of the wood. Her hand stilled as she slid over a patch that wasn't smooth at all. Indentations bumped under her fingers, so she stood back for a better look.

She found herself staring at an engraving. Grooves had been carved in the wood well before the pillar had been stained and erected as part of the building. Maybe centuries before.

When she took yet another step back, the full picture came into focus and Harper gasped. She'd finally found a symbol, and it was engraved on one of the mammoth pillars.

Quickly she pulled her sketch pad out and rendered a copy of the symbol, though she recognized the *kanji* as one from the book. The one associated with the man who'd been ripped in two pieces.

From what she'd gathered, the punishment had something to do with infidelity. Her translations weren't perfect, and she needed Reid to help her with the rest of the book. If his offer still stood after finding out what she'd done.

Since no one had entered the room yet, Harper rushed to the next pillar and sketched the symbol there. They all faced the front doors where she'd entered from the streets, as if to remind worshippers of the *Shinto* laws.

She'd copied four of the engravings when she realized the

table with silver goblets was empty in the middle, as if the cups weren't allowed there. Intuition made her surge forward to examine the center of the table. The large square that held such a place of honor.

She almost dropped her pad when her eyes landed on the detailed carving. Here was the most important symbol. The one she'd been searching for since the night she'd found the *kanji* in her house. The same one that had been branded on Emi's hip.

There was no need to draw this symbol. By now she knew the lines by sight and could sketch them from memory. The meaning of this *kanji* had to be the most significant, because it was the only one featured on the table and centered directly beneath the mountain sculpture.

Still frozen, she couldn't tear her eyes away from the table. From the terrible symbol that adorned the massive piece of furniture.

Until male voices echoed down the stairwell.

Harper whirled to face the side door. She held her breath and listened. Light scuffs were barely discernible. Footsteps? Possibly.

The men spoke again and this time she was sure. They were coming closer, heading toward the main room.

Without a second thought, she bolted for the front doors. She tried to move stealthily, but speed was more critical. Her hands slammed against the heavy front doors, and she shoved her way out, already planning to duck into the alley's shadows again.

She prayed no one saw her fleeing the temple like a thief. Or the intruder that she was.

The return of daytime noises flooded her ears. Only mild sounds really, like an unhurried bicycle rolling on the street, and two women laughing from a lofty balcony, but compared to the tomb-like silence of the temple, the gentle intrusions were thunderous.

And the day was bright. Too bright. Her veil of shadows had been consumed by the sun, leaving her no place to hide.

So she just kept moving, ducking into the alley and walking at a fast clip until she came to the next block. There, she turned and continued north, never taking time to look back. To see if she had been spotted or if a mob of angry priests was giving chase.

No, she stayed true to her northerly direction and didn't intend to stop until she was behind locked doors. She would head down to the river and follow the waterway, all the way to a cabin in the woods.

Whether he was ready to deal with her or not, Harper was going back to Reid's.

20

At least an hour passed before Reid made an appearance. Harper was sitting in one of his deck chairs, knees jittery and mind anxious, waiting to share her latest discovery. She saw a clear connection between the clues she'd found, but doubted her cynical assistant-turned-make-out-partner would be as easily convinced.

Reid was walking with his eyes on the ground, in no apparent hurry. When he looked up and spotted Harper, he stopped, staring at her quizzically and probably wondering why she was here.

In the space of a few seconds, she saw surprise, curiosity, and alarm flash across his features. And then finally, a dash of hope.

Her insides felt suddenly hollow and light. He was more than her assistant, and "making out" hardly described what passed between them when their bodies came together. Sexual sparks sizzled for sure, but not only that.

What really worried Harper and compelled her to run, was the sweet, lingering sensation of being touched on a deeper level. A tender connection that surpassed the physical thrill, and delved into the heart of who she really was.

And that bond gave Harper one more thing to be afraid of.

Fixing a stoic expression in place, Reid strode forward and hiked one blonde brow. Half inquiry, half-dismissal. "What brings you out this far?" He noticed the sketchbook clutched in her hands. "Or do I really want to know?"

"Probably not," she said, swallowing against the guilt rising in her throat. She'd promised herself she wouldn't bring him or Saya into this, but she needed a touchstone. A sane opinion to either back her up or shut her down.

And like it or not, she trusted Reid more than she'd trusted anyone besides her parents in a very long time.

He carried a sack filled with groceries and went straight for the kitchen area to set the bag on the counter. Placing both hands on the edge, his shoulders lifted and fell with a heavy sigh. "What have you done, Harper?" He seemed to dread hearing her answer.

"I went to the temple. I went inside and saw…" she stopped when he lifted a hand, fingers splayed, a clear sign of his building frustration.

"You're going to have to give me a minute to process that," he said.

Shaking his head and looking briefly to the ceiling as if searching out a deity to give him strength, Reid looked back at her. No. He glared. "I would ask why you keep doing these kinds of things, but that would be a waste of breath. I know you won't answer."

His movements were jerky and short as he unpacked the bag, revealing his agitation more clearly than even his clipped words. "I need to put these things away. Then we'll talk. Or we'll evade talking about anything that really matters, which seems to be way things usually go."

Harper bit her bottom lip. No doubt about it. Reid was angry, and she couldn't blame him. Half of the time, she felt her choices were absurd, and he apparently agreed.

Moving away from him, Harper hid her telltale face under the guise of studying the view from the picture window. Unlike her, Reid faced the open world while he worked, unafraid of distraction or the temptation to step outside.

Yes. He was different from her.

Her desk faced the wall. She liked the feeling of being closed off from everything out there. But if the rest of the world was shut out, that also meant she was shut in. Trapped and closed off from society, with all its beauty. And its peril.

It meant she was all alone.

So yes, she hid her face from Reid, afraid he would see too much. He had asked her why she was breaking from character. Why she, who was so worried about running into danger, was now chasing after it at every turn.

Maybe a part of her had been sparked back to life by meeting him. Some piece of her psyche wanted to embrace joy, even knowing the eventual result could be grief. Part of Harper was fighting for a return to the light. To life. And to love.

But that still didn't explain her obsession with the symbol and her stubborn belief that a sinister force was operating in the sleepy country village. Was there more to her pursuit of the truth? Did her tenacity spring from another source entirely?

She was afraid Reid would see what she couldn't. That was his job, after all.

He might be able to pick apart her behavior, her actions. He would consider psychological and historical factors, as any good anthropologist would. With his analytical and practical mind, Reid would assign reason and motivation to her relentless quest for answers.

And what would his conclusion be? Would he make a connection between her current fixation and her tragic past? The similarities between Emi and Haley?

In Harper's mind, one had been in need of rescue, and the other still was. Where she had failed her sister, she was now driven to succeed with Emi. Her sense of injustice, no doubt fueled by guilt, wouldn't allow her to make the same mistake again.

She had to help Emi. She wanted to rescue her.

She needed to.

Harper tensed when she smelled mountain cedar mixed with sultry male. Reid was behind her, having moved with surprising silence. Or perhaps she'd just been lost in her own mind.

When she turned to him, he held her steady in his sights. He was both at ease and focused at once. "Go ahead," he said, gesturing to the pad she held.

"I had a good reason..." She trailed off, telling herself she would not start off by defending herself or making excuses. No emotion. Just facts. "I'll start with what I found in the temple. She reached in her purse and felt around, clasping onto the little red book when she found its familiar shape.

Extracting the book, she turned to one of the pages she'd marked with a sticky note while waiting for Reid to get home. "The *kanji* in this book are also engraved on pillars inside the temple. They are still in use today. Still valued."

Reid studied the sketch she showed him. "That temple was built two centuries ago, at least. You don't know they still enforce these archaic laws." He took the book from her and flipped until he found the *kanji* drawing on one of the pages.

The picture was of a woman whose face had been disfigured, her wounds still healing. "This is barbaric," he said, "but I don't know of anyone who's been punished for adultery like this. Not in the last century."

"Not that you know of," Harper said, throwing his words back at him. "And they *are* still enforcing these laws. I found the symbol that was drawn inside my house. It was on a table in a place of honor." She drew herself up. "But that's not the only place I saw this *kanji*."

His eyes narrowed but remained silent.

"Emi came to see me again." When he stepped back and opened his mouth, probably to yell, Harper rushed ahead. "She has the symbol on her hip. It was *branded* there."

She quirked a brow and couldn't stop the I-told-you-so from showing on her face. "Emi is only a teenager, so they *have* used that symbol recently. All because of the mountain they worship."

Reid shook his head. "This is all getting out of control," he said, "and I'm not blaming you. At least, not completely." He rubbed his jaw, then took a few steps away from her. "I don't understand why that girl won't leave you alone."

"Because I'm an outsider. She knows I'm not part of the village church. That I might actually help her."

Reid whirled back around. "Help her what, Harper? Escape? You said yourself that she can't even speak. For all we know, that mark just means she truly is special. That she's mentally disabled and, therefore, is to be worshipped."

He threw up his hands. "The Sheriff said she's protected and maybe that's why. You still have no idea what the symbol actually stands for."

He shot her a sideways look. "Do you?"

Harper cleared her throat. "No. But she's terrified of those priests. I know she is. And I find it hard to believe that this symbol is harmless when it was found in the same place as these others." She tossed the book on his desk, and it fell open to the page of a man torn asunder.

"Tell me what that means," she said, pointing to the picture. "All I could make out was some type of infidelity. If they cut a woman's face, why tear a man in two?"

Reluctantly, Reid picked up the tattered book. After a moment of reading, he spoke. "This punishment wasn't for marital infidelity."

He pressed his lips together as if he didn't want to tell her the rest. But he told her anyway. "They tied this man to two different trees that had been pulled down and fastened. Then they cut the ropes and let the trees right themselves, pulling apart."

Harper gulped. "And the man with them."

"He wasn't unfaithful to his wife." Reid's stare burned into her. "He was unfaithful to the church. He revealed information of the village *Shinto* to those he shouldn't have."

"To outsiders." The room seemed to plummet to freezing temperatures, and Harper rubbed her arms. "Outsiders like me."

"Harper, I don't know what to tell you. This isn't a game, and the village takes the sanctity of their religion very seriously." He put the book on his desk and came to her. He spoke softly. "I know you want to help that girl, but we have got to tread carefully. We need to be certain before any attempt to intervene."

Harper's head jerked up. "We?"

"Yeah." He frowned and still seemed upset that she'd been so reckless again, but when Harper looked closer, she saw more than simple anger in his emerald eyes. More than fear for her safety or confusion over her irrational behavior.

Just before his gaze dropped and his brow furrowed, she caught a glimpse of an emotion she knew all too well. Reid was vulnerable. His heart and pride hanging out there to be battered by anyone careless enough to do so.

He was wearing a brave face, though he'd already been hurt, and an undeniable feeling came over Harper.

Contrition. Because Reid had been wounded. And she was to blame.

"Reid, I'm sorry. You don't deserve this." Harper put a hesitant finger on his hand, as if unsure she should touch him. Or if he'd want her to. "You don't deserve any of this."

"Neither do you," he said. When her eyes shadowed over, he suspected she was thinking about more than *Shinto* customs and the trouble they were causing.

There was so much he wanted to say to her. To ask her.

Yet Harper carried more on her mind than the problems of a Japanese village. His desire to be close to her warred with the instinct to defend her. From everything. Including himself.

Dredging up old memories might make things worse, but Reid couldn't know how to proceed if he didn't know what Harper was dealing with. He could only speculate, but he felt sure that her past was haunting her, that it was affecting her judgment.

A terrible tragedy had to responsible for her reclusive way of life. Her automatic lack of trust and her reticence to let him get too close.

Reid felt he was doing a damn fine job of hiding his bruised ego, even though the last week had been torture. Every time he'd seen Harper, he'd wanted to grab her and kiss some sense into her. To force her to let him in.

And to stop taking such brazen chances with herself. To stop daring fate.

Hiding how much he cared about her was becoming more difficult by the day. He was also having a hard time coming up with excuses for her behavior.

And for her rejection of him.

Not since his parents had he longed so badly for someone else's acceptance. He'd given up on them a long time ago, though, and had learned to deal with carefree, short-term relationships.

In fact, with his lifestyle and the constant relocating, he'd preferred his unattached state. Living the free-and-easy life was what made him happy.

Until Harper Gray had come along with her unusual eyes, sharp mind, and a terrible knack for the Japanese language. He knew the woman behind those endearing traits now, and he found himself needing that acceptance again. From her.

His mother and father would never love him as parents were meant to. He'd gotten used to that reality. But now he yearned for Harper to look at him and see him for who he was.

He wanted her by his side for all the good and bad times. Just as he would be there for her. From the first day they'd met, he'd wanted to swoop in and take care of her.

He'd just had no idea what a little troublemaker she could be.

"Why are you grinning?" she asked, snapping Reid out of his musings and back to the present.

"Huh? Oh, it's nothing. Just thinking." No, he told himself. Why not just be honest? It was bad enough to have one of them keeping secrets. Reid needed Harper to know how he felt.

If she ended up walking out and right across his heart, then that's what would happen, but he would at least know he'd done all he could to hold onto her. "Actually, I was thinking about your eyes."

"My eyes? Now's not the most appropriate time, Reid."

He palmed her cheek. "There's never a good time, but here it is. I care about you, Harper. I care. And that's the cleanest, least alarming way I know how to tell you."

Biting her bottom lip, she reached up with one tentative hand, then dropped it. She lifted it again and put it to the back of his hand where it still rested against her face. She sighed. "I don't know what to do about you. I'm used to being alone and handling everything by myself. Now I find myself running to you all the time."

"I don't mind."

The smile she gave him was a little sad. "I know. You're such a good friend."

A good friend? Reid stiffened and expelled a breath. "Quite possibly the cruelest words in the English language."

"No." Harper pulled his hand from her cheek and grabbed for his other to clasp them in her own. "They're the most important ones. I needed a friend, and you were there. No matter how irrational I've been, you never shut me out. At least, not totally."

She was reminding Reid of the last several days and how distant he'd been.

"I know you don't understand why I do some of the things I do," she said, "but when I sensed you closing yourself off..." Her gaze fell to their joined hands before she said in a soft voice, "I didn't like it."

The ache in his side began to recede. "Are you telling me you're feeling some of the same things I am?"

"Like what?" she asked, tracking her way slowly back up to look at him.

"Like the heat flowing between our linked hands right now."

She only nodded, the gray of her stare warming and blending with the turquoise flecks.

"Like when I think of you," he continued, "I get a strange pressure right here," he tapped the middle of his chest. "And then I realize I'm not breathing, because I'm so caught up remembering your smile. Or the way you put your glasses on when you suddenly get an idea, then run to scratch the words on any handy piece of paper."

A smile teased the edges of her lips. "No. I never feel like that."

His heart stumbled and fell. "What?"

With a wicked smile she whispered, "You don't wear glasses."

"Enough." Reid smothered the laughter that threatened by bringing her into his arms and kissing the side of her mouth where it turned up. "I want to stop right where we are and enjoy knowing you think about me that way." He kissed the other side. "At least on occasion."

Then he lengthened the kiss as her hands slipped to his shoulders. He deepened the penetration while she clung to him and angled her body closer to his.

Reid sensed her complete surrender but was still aware of her vulnerable state. So when she was fully relaxed and giving him her trust, he eased away and let her go.

Trailing a finger down her neck, he murmured softly, "Thank you."

Her eyes were glazed, hazy with desire. "For what?"

"For coming back to me and giving me another chance." Guiding her to his sofa, his hold on her slid from arm to wrist to hand. "But I'm not going to rush you. Not now when you've got so much bubbling up inside, ready to spill over."

"I... that makes sense. I guess."

"I want to help you, Harper. I want to be there for you." He paused and waited for clarity to return to her lovely eyes. "But to do that, you need to tell me everything."

She shook her head. "I have. You know as much as I do."

"No." He saw her jolt at his abrupt denial. Saw the reluctance push its way back to the forefront. "I don't know nearly as much as I should. And if only half of your suspicions are true, we have a big problem."

"We do. I've been trying to tell you that." She seemed affronted, but Reid knew she was simply gathering up her defenses. Ready to cut him off before he made his way past any more of her resistance.

"I need to know why you're so determined to put yourself in danger for a person you hardly know, who can't even tell you for sure that she *is* in danger. Why you feel like she's in trouble. Or that she needs your help."

Harper's bottom lip fell and she stared at him as if he'd started speaking another language. One she pretended not to understand. But Reid had to press his advantage if he was truly going to help her.

In his mind, Harper needed saving far more than the teenage girl who was running around making trouble for everyone.

"Are you sure this is really about Emi?" he asked, holding tighter to her hand when she would have jerked away. He took a deep breath. "Or is this about your sister?"

"I don't know what you mean. One thing has nothing to do with the other."

"Then talk to me. Tell me what happened to her."

Rearing her head back, Harper sat up straight and froze. "I never talk about that. I don't even want to remember, so why would I ever actually..."

A sob broke from her throat and she clamped her eyes shut. After a struggle for control, eyes still closed, she asked him in a hoarse whisper, "Why would you bring this up?"

Reid didn't hug her or stroke her arm. He held firm and steady, afraid any show of sympathy would break her. "Because I think you need to talk to someone. Your fear is almost palpable. It's in everything you do. The decisions you make. Where to live. How to interact with other people."

She finally looked at him, her body shaking and tight with suppressed emotion. "I can handle it."

Reid gentled his voice, his expression. "Oh, baby. I don't think so."

Shaking her head, Harper stifled more choking sobs. "I can't talk about it. I just can't." She threw herself at Reid, burying her face against his chest. "I have been thinking about my sister. I have. And I can't tell anymore if my worry over Emi is affecting my memories or if it's the other way around."

Reid held her trembling body and tried to console her. She felt so small huddled against him. Pressing his face to the top of her head, he rubbed his hand over her back.

"I don't know how this happened. When I lost control." Eventually she leaned back enough to look up at him, and the dread she normally tried to conceal was evident on her pale, distraught face. "Reid, I can't make sense of what's happening, and I want to do the right thing."

She sucked in a breath. "But... I'm just so scared."

"I know," he said, at a loss for anything more. "I know." Sitting against the back cushion, he cradled her against his side, determined to hold her until she made him stop. Until her stubborn resiliency returned, then together they could decide what to do next.

"I don't want to go home tonight," she said, letting the words float in the air.

"Then you'll stay with me." Reid was relieved to know she'd be there with him, and not just because he wanted to spend every possible minute with her. The things she'd told him today, the symbols she'd uncovered and deductions she'd made... they were starting to get to him, too.

If anyone found out what Harper had been up to... Hell, he wasn't sure what would happen. So he'd be smart to find out what was really going on in the village. Harper had become his responsibility, and he couldn't afford to make assumptions.

While she rested on his chest, Reid watched twilight creep over the valley. He let himself consider the possibilities. Was the girl in danger? Was Harper?

With narrowed eyes, he studied the darkening cedars and knew what he had to do. Soon she would fall asleep.

And Reid had a phone call to make.

21

Together Harper and Reid walked down the corridor of the high-rise building in Oda City. The drive had taken them over two hours, but Reid had insisted they make the trip. He'd woken her this morning with a steaming cup of coffee and a new plan.

Harper had slept in his bed all night, peacefully and without nightmares. And she'd slept alone. Reid's ingrained chivalry had dictated he take the couch for the night. Though she'd been somewhat disappointed, she'd also been charmed.

Now they were in the city, and as he'd explained on the ride over, they were meeting an acquaintance of his. A man who'd been born in Chuujitsu but had permanently relocated.

Reid had met Mr. Nishimura while researching his dissertation and felt the man would be a great resource for them now. Given his severed connection to the village and their strict regulations, Mr. Nishimura might be willing to give them the information they needed.

Now as Reid knocked on the condominium door, Harper's stomach fluttered with anticipation. What would this man be able to tell them?

With everything she'd been through, and all the turmoil she'd brought to Reid's once-peaceful life, she discovered a secret hope that the man would prove her wrong.

The door swung wide to reveal an exuberant man she

guessed to be in his late thirties or early forties. His hair was thinning in front, and he wore rimless glasses with casual business attire. He seemed delighted to see Reid.

"Ah, Reid." He shook Reid's hand with vigor. "I was happy to hear from you. More questions about why I left the village for life in the big city?"

The man stepped back to let Reid pass before noticing Harper was there. "You are Ms. Gray," he said, equally amicably. He opened his arms and waved them both inside. "Come in. Come in."

"Thank you," Harper said before slipping out of her shoes. While Reid unlaced his, she appraised Mr. Nishimura's home. The open floor plan was modern and allowed natural light to spill in from a row of windows. Most of the walls were white, but the living area had one accent wall painted to look like butter.

The design was Spartan at best, but the man evidently enjoyed his spots of color. Among the clean lines of metal and leather furniture, Harper noticed a plant in a glazed indigo pot, and a red paper lantern hanging from the ceiling. The bright ball brought a taste of whimsy to the space, and for some reason, it endeared her to the man who lived here.

Reid touched her shoulder and gestured for her to follow him. He led her to a set of two white sofas near the kitchen. The couches were identical and faced each other with a round glass table between them.

Mr. Nishimura had turned a corner and disappeared, but soon he returned bearing a large tray. By now, Harper should have anticipated the offer of hot tea, but she was pleasantly surprised by the addition of a fruit plate and a platter of various small cookies.

Either Mr. Nishimura didn't have visitors often, or he really liked Reid.

Glancing aside at her handsome companion, Harper felt a

slow, warm pull in her belly. She was betting on the latter.

There was no question Reid was striking with his dark blonde hair and green eyes, and that was enough to have any woman looking twice. But it was the intelligent and kind man beneath the exterior that made her heart sigh.

And he was considerate of most people, not just her. She shouldn't be surprised the Japanese man was so affable with them both. Reid was well-received in Mr. Nishimura's home, and in turn, so was Harper.

"Please," Mr. Nishimura said, holding his palm upright to indicate the beverage and snacks. He poured the tea while Harper and Reid took small white plates and filled them with food.

The three of them made small talk as they ate, but Harper only nibbled a cookie. She was enjoying the pleasant exchange, but was worried their visit might turn sour when Reid confessed the reason they'd come.

They were here to pump him for information about his home village and to ask if his childhood religion was evil.

When the conversation lulled, Harper felt Reid's hesitancy. She glanced over to find his jaw set and eyes serious. He was about to broach the subject she'd been dreading. Yet the one she desperately needed to discuss.

"Mr. Nishimura," Reid began, "I brought Harper along today, because we need your help."

"Oh?" The man dusted his fingertips and set his plate down.

Deciding she'd take over, since this was essentially her problem, Harper spoke to the friendly man. "*I* need your help." She gave him a small smile. "Since I moved to Chuujitsu, some strange things have been happening. Incidents involving members of the *Shinto* temple."

"Oh," he said again, but this time, the single sound held a wealth of concern.

"Do you mind if I show you some pictures from a book I have?

I'll warn you that they are gruesome."

"Gruesome?" he echoed as if not familiar with the word.

"Violent," Reid supplied. "We need to know if you've ever encountered anything like this in the village when you were growing up. Or if you ever heard any stories."

Now Mr. Nishimura scrunched his face and pushed his glasses up on his nose. He leaned forward to look when Harper extracted the red book from her purse and opened to the page with the woman whose face had been cleaved as punishment for adultery.

Pursing his mouth tightly, he shook his head. "This is a very old custom. I heard of it in years past, but not in my time." He sat back and picked up his tea, but he couldn't hide his disquiet.

Harper flipped to the page of the man ripped apart by the two trees. "Or this?" she asked, silently cursing herself for having to expose the friendly man to such awful pictures.

He glanced at the photo and stared. His face drained of color. Then he took the book from her and closed it softly, but with finality. "I am familiar with the old teachings. They don't exist anymore."

"How can you be certain?" Harper asked.

Dividing his attention between his two guests, Mr. Nishimura finally said with dismissal, "I haven't been to Chuujitsu in many years. I live here now and follow the rules of this society."

Harper felt the rebuff. "I apologize if these photos are disturbing, but we can't ask anyone in the village, as I'm sure you understand."

He nodded.

"You decided to leave the village," she said. When he only dipped his chin in assent, she added, "Is there a reason you didn't go back?"

Rolling his lips in for a moment as if weighing his response, the man looked once more to Reid, then back to Harper. His eyes dimmed ever-so-slightly when he said, "Chuujitsu no longer has hold on me. All of my family is gone. Dead."

Harper frowned at the strange phrasing of his words. No hold on him?

He made a show of pouring himself more tea, but Harper suspected he was performing the ritual to give himself some time. To recover his outward appearance and the pretense of disinterest. But Harper could see he was affected by their conversation.

They'd dredged up the past for this man, and she understood his desire to forget anything that may have been painful. She didn't know what his childhood had been like, so she couldn't guess what experiences he might have endured in the distant village. Or if they still influenced his behavior today.

Suddenly an imaginary light went on in the back of Harper's mind, an elusive switch that had finally been discovered. She found herself relating to Reid's predicament.

He didn't know what she'd been through, either. He couldn't begin to imagine.

No wonder he was at a loss and unsure about Harper's theory. Her reasons for pursuing answers, even to the point of jeopardy.

Her face flushed with warmth and regret. Keeping Reid involved without full disclosure wasn't fair, and it was well past time to remedy that.

Finally Mr. Nishimura looked at them again, but he wore an overly-large smile. He was trying too hard.

Harper wouldn't ask about his family or his reasons for moving to the city. She had no right to cause this poor man any more discomfort. After years of protecting her own privacy so voraciously, she was now trampling all over his.

"Mr. Nishimura," she said politely, hoping he would see she meant no disrespect, "the real reason we came today is out of concern for someone in the village. A young girl has been contacting me. She doesn't speak much, but she's made it clear that she's afraid of something."

Harper bit the inside of her cheek as she studied the man's face and his lack of response. She continued. "Her name is Emi Tsukada. I said it backwards, so her name would be—"

"Tsukada?" the man asked. It wasn't an overt change in his expression that told Harper the name meant something, rather the way his features froze, as if guarding his reaction. "You say she has come to you?" Three wrinkles formed in his forehead. "That is very strange."

"Do you know her?" Reid asked.

"No. But I know of her family." The Japanese man set his cup on the table gently before meeting Harper's gaze. "If this girl has anything to do with the temple, then you must stay away from her. Tsukada is one of the first names of the village. Very old. Very powerful. They and several other families have been there since the beginning."

"But if the girl is in trouble, shouldn't someone do something?" Harper couldn't believe they'd driven all this way just to have another person tell them the same thing. *Stay away from the girl.* "Besides, she was the one who searched me out."

"That does not matter. Do not let her foolish actions bring you trouble." Mr. Nishimura widened his eyes slightly, ensuring Harper paid heed to his words. "Perhaps this girl is reckless and impetuous. She would not be the first young person of Chuujitsu who tried to refuse family duty. But she will come around."

His eyes grew dark. "They always do."

"But—"

The man cut Harper off by waving his hand, then softened the affront with another smile. "You should not worry yourself with church business. Or a spoiled child. I promise you, if she is of the older families, she will be taken care of."

Though he continued to smile, his face tensed at the edges.

"The older families are the law in Chuujitsu."

Harper let out an exasperated breath. Could he be right? Was Emi just playing some sort of twisted game with the unsuspecting American? For fun? Or was this some adolescent act of rebellion against her parents and the temple?

"I just don't understand," she finally said, staring out the window to the surrounding buildings. The shining white concrete and silver window frames seemed so foreign to her now. She'd become accustomed to deep green forests and clean-scented mountains.

And dark, secret-filled places.

"Has anyone else from the temple come to you?" he asked.

"A man came into her garden one night," Reid said, and Harper could have kissed him. He didn't say, Harper *thought* there was man, or Harper saw *something* in her yard. He stated the intruder's presence as fact.

"Do you know of any reason he might have been there?" Mr. Nishimura blithely took a cookie from the tray.

"No, but we assumed he had come for Emi." Harper shrugged. "We spoke to the local police the next day, but nothing ever came of it."

"The intruder never came back?" He chewed the cookie.

"No." Harper added nothing else to her answer. What else was there? The more she tried to convince this stranger that some diabolical plot was being hatched in the village, the less she believed it herself. "But the girl, Emi, she had a brand on her hip."

Sending a questioning look to Reid, Harper reached for her purse. When Reid nodded, she took out her pad and showed their host the drawing of the unidentified symbol. "This was on her hip and in the temple."

"You went to the temple?" The man sat forward suddenly. "You must not."

She bobbed her head. "Yes. I know, and I won't go back. No

one saw me," she said, rushing to allay his worry. "Please look again at the drawing." She held the pad closer to him. "Do you know what this *kanji* means?"

"Hmm. The lines do resemble the secret language, but no, I don't recognize this symbol. Very few people in the village are privy to the upper tiers of church affairs. Only some are chosen to be taught. To carry on the tradition."

"And to enforce the laws," Reid said, his blonde brows drawn together.

"Yes," Mr. Nishimura said. "They may seem foreign to you, and even some of us born there decide to follow a different path." He gave Harper a fatherly look. "I do not know why this girl has sought you out, but you would be well-advised to block her attempts. I do not believe she means you well."

Harper hadn't considered this angle before, but the more she thought things over, the more they made sense. No one in the village had threatened her. Not overtly. The only real problems had arisen after she'd seen Emi.

Every time, the teenager had come looking for Harper. "There is a chance the girl is," she looked to Reid, "mentally challenged?"

Reid nodded to her, then translated for Mr. Nishimura.

"Ah, yes. That may explain her irrational behavior." Now the Japanese man seemed more at ease, his previous strain having disappeared entirely. "Ms. Gray," he said with empathy, "if you do not feel safe in the village, you should leave. My country has many other beautiful places for you to see. To stay."

He moved to the edge of his seat and surprised Harper by taking her hand between his. His dark eyes locked on hers. "Safety is the most important thing, yes? You must be at ease."

Harper nodded. "I suppose so." She was beginning to feel like she'd been conned. All of her suspicions about the temple, the priests, and the book might have been purposely provoked.

As awful as the ancient laws were, those photos *had* been

taken decades ago, maybe more than a century. And Reid was right about the pillars in the temple. They could have been made even farther back in history.

Frustrated once again, Harper let her mind roam to other subjects. While Reid and the man fell into another round of small talk, she thought of Mr. Nishimura's last question.

Was security still her first priority? Was it better to be in a constant state of lock-down now that she knew what she'd been depriving herself of?

Since she'd taken a chance on other people, she'd met the funny and high-spirited Saya. A friend to make her laugh and tease her about men. About Reid.

And what would she be missing if she'd never met him? Reid was steadfast and true. He made every day that much brighter just by being there. She could rely on him.

She wanted to take a chance with Reid. To let him in, where he would see all her faults and weaknesses. Would he choose to share her burdens? Accept her frailties and phobias?

Their time together would eventually come to an end. Would it be an amicable parting with little sadness? Or would losing Reid be devastating?

Harper wasn't a fan of risk, and she'd vowed years ago to avoid any venture that might bring her pain, especially when it involved people and relationships. Those fragile, unpredictable bonds. Almost as breakable as the human body.

Or the heart.

Reid laughed at something their host said, and the warm, rich sound drew Harper's attention. His expression was so open and inviting. His friendship genuine.

And in that moment, when his smile hung crooked and his green eyes crinkled, Harper knew she had her answer. Heartache and loss might be waiting around the corner for her, but she could no longer keep Reid in the dark.

If she cared for him, truly cared for him, then she'd tell

him all about her past and the loss that had changed her life forever. She'd explain why she preferred to stay indoors and why she feared strangers.

She'd tell him what happened to Haley.

22

Dusk was crawling toward the valley when Harper and Reid returned to her house. The drive back had been quiet and for Harper, full of self-reflection. So many conflicting emotions and rationalizations had run through her head as she'd watched the countryside pass. As city blocks turned to open fields, then again to sky-high mountains.

Mr. Nishimura had given her a new perspective to consider. All of Harper's unrest had essentially been caused by Emi, and whether the girl had done so on purpose remained to be seen. Her impaired social skills may excuse her actions, but if the teenager had simply been playing a game, she must not have understood the repercussions.

At least, Harper preferred to think that way. She didn't want to believe Emi could be so cruel.

Despite his dismissal of any diabolical scheme to hurt the girl, Mr. Nishimura's parting words had been filled with warning. "Don't speak of this to anyone, and don't tell others you were here." He had looked pointedly at Reid and Harper then, flashing cool brown eyes between them. "If you choose to remain in the village, trust no one."

The implication had rocked Harper. His rampant cynicism was contagious, and now she doubted everyone except Reid. And Saya.

Tossing her purse to its place on the bottom of the stairs,

Harper turned back to Reid. "You trust Saya, don't you?"

With a slow pace, he moved to join her. "Of course, but I don't think we should involve her in any more of this if we can help it. The best course of action now is to go about business as usual. Well," he added with a grin, "business as it should be. No more sleuthing and sneaking onto church property."

A cool rush traveled down Harper's back and through her legs. She almost didn't recognize the feeling for what it was. Relief. "I plan to embrace normalcy and boredom for a while."

Reid gave her a narrow-eyed look. "I think I've heard that somewhere before."

She laughed and grinned guiltily. "This time I mean it." Then she grew somber. "I want to make changes, Reid. Big changes."

He studied her. "Go on."

"I want to tell you my story. It's true. I am affected by my past, but now..." She inhaled for courage. "Now it's affecting you. Us. And I don't want to make a mistake."

"Do you want to sit down?" Hands in his pockets, Reid angled his body to indicate the couches.

"Yes." Harper was about to put her worst experience into words, and though she would forego details, the picture would still be crystalline in her mind. Images she'd never forget would rise up and blind her. Burn her eyes, clog her throat, and twist her lungs into a suffocating knot of grief.

The sorrow would never leave her, but she'd finally found a reason to fight through the pain. Sharing her tragedy with Reid might not take the hurt away, but it was a step toward recovery. To allowing some happiness into her world.

Even if it didn't last.

When they sat together on the couch, Reid took her hand in his. At first, Harper considered pulling back. That had always been her way, especially when she opened the gates of her memories to let that horrible night rush back in.

Cutting herself off from human contact didn't make her forget, but she'd pretended it somehow protected her. Reid had shown her differently. She'd isolated herself and missed out on meaningful experiences, but the love stirring inside her for this man was too important. Too special.

If they were going to move forward, if there was a chance they might find the real thing—actual, lasting love—then Harper had to reveal herself to him. Scars and all.

Or he would never truly know her.

"You've probably figured out that my sister is dead," she said, hating the clinical sound of her voice. She had to be as removed as possible, or she wouldn't make it through this. When Reid nodded, she said, "Her name was Haley, and she was my twin."

Reid already knew that, but saying the words out loud gave them a kind of power. Harper needed to remind the world that her other half had existed. And that her sister had meant everything to her.

"What you don't know is how she died, and when you do, I think," she paused and bit her lip, "I *hope* you'll understand me better. Why it is so hard for me to expose myself, either physically or emotionally."

She didn't want to go back to that night, but Harper forced herself to recall the specifics. The way she'd been sprawled across her bed studying. The way the ringing phone had annoyed her, disrupting her focus on the textbook that had seemed so important at the time.

"We were in college. Our senior year. A lot of people wondered how we could stand to go to the same university and even room together." A sad smile touched her lips. "They thought we should be sick of each other, but Haley and I weren't like that."

"I mean, we didn't dress the same or anything, but being together gave us strength. We balanced each other and shared ideas, encouragement." She sighed. "Sometimes without even saying a word."

As she recalled their secret language, how they could convey thoughts with barely a glance, Harper felt the familiar shame encroaching. Wrapping around the back of her neck and squeezing. Punishing. "That's why I should have known she was in trouble. I should have sensed it. Felt it before it was too late."

Impulsively, she ripped her hand from Reid's grip, tucking both palms against her ribs, under her arms. Retreating and hiding in the only way she could. "I'll never forgive myself for that or stop wondering why our connection wasn't there."

Harper cleared her throat when she felt like letting go. Like crying. "Why I couldn't feel her on the one night I needed to."

She must have fallen silent, lost in her own remorse, because soon she heard Reid call her name. Then he asked, "What happened that night?"

Wiping away the threat of tears, she clamped down on the roiling emotions inside and spoke again in that cold, steady voice. "She had gone to the library to find some books she needed. No big deal, right?"

With accusing eyes, she stared at nothing in particular, showing her contempt for the callous turn of fate that had brought her sister to that place. On that night. At the wrong time. "We lived on the college campus. There were call boxes everywhere." She looked to the ceiling. "Haley cut through a park area. It should have been safe."

"But it wasn't," Reid said, already anticipating what would come next. Such a familiar story, and a reflection of societies all around the globe. As much as things changed and got better, certain human depravities persisted.

He couldn't stand to watch Harper shake and clench her fists, like her body was fighting off a raging illness. Taking her hand again, even though she didn't notice, he imagined what she was going through was far worse than being sick. That reliving the loss of her twin sister was physically painful.

As much as he wanted to stop her, to ease her suffering if he could, Reid understood that she needed to do this. Catharsis didn't always come easy and rarely felt good while it was happening.

He would be here for her, waiting on the other end when she emerged from the dark, from the hateful past. He would hold her and soothe her.

And love her all the more for her strength.

"Two men were in the park," Harper said, speaking quickly, spitting the words out as if they tainted her mouth. "They were drunk, and Haley was a pretty girl walking alone."

She raised tortured gray eyes to stare at Reid. "She called me on her cell phone when she got scared. Just before they attacked her."

Reid's gut seemed filled with lead, heavy and sickening. "Did you have a chance to talk to her?"

Harper couldn't hold her tears back any longer. She shook her head. "No. I tried but it was too late." She sobbed in a breath. "But I heard her scream my name. I heard the struggle." She clapped her hands to her ears, trying to block out sounds that would always echo in her head. To remind her.

Reid clenched his own fists now. He wanted to pound on something. Or someone. Anything to keep Harper from having to live through this agony.

And the real fury came from knowing he couldn't. That these memories would stalk her for the rest of her life. They would hide away and wait for the right time to lunge back into her mind, shredding her peacefulness over and over again.

Reid couldn't help it. He brushed her warm brown hair from her eyes and willed the anguish away. He wouldn't say he was sorry. Empty, useless words. Instead, he would stay with her and let her guide him.

He would learn what she needed, because she belonged with him. As a scientist, he shouldn't believe in fate. In destiny. But sitting here now and watching Harper's agony, he knew he would give anything or give up anything to help her.

"Harper, do you want to stop now?" he coaxed softly.

She shook her head back, sniffed hard, and swiped at her eyes. "No, I need to finish this." She took a deep, shuddering breath, gathering herself as she continued. "The short story is that they raped her. When she tried to scream, one of them wrapped his hands around her throat and didn't let go until she was unconscious. When they were... finished, they decided to strangle her again. So she couldn't identify them."

Rising to pace, Harper scrubbed at her face, then went to the kitchen where she grabbed a paper napkin to use instead. "They were drunk, so they were sloppy. It didn't take long for the police to identify them."

She looked at him from across the room, her eyes empty. "When asked why they did it, one of the guys said, 'Because she was there.' Just like that. No planning of the act. No consideration of the horror they were inflicting on her. Or the destruction left behind for her family and friends."

Harper shrugged and tossed the napkin in the trash. "No meaning at all. She was just there."

"You never mention your parents," Reid said, still sitting on the couch. He turned so he could see her. "Do you still have a relationship with them?"

Harper smiled. "They're the only two people I *do* have a relationship with." Then she bit her bottom lip again. She looked nervous. Scared. "Until you. Now I'm feeling all these things. Wanting things I thought I'd shut out for good."

"I won't hurt you, Harper." The promise sprang from somewhere deep inside, and his chest vibrated with the truth of it.

"I'm beginning to believe that." With small steps, she made her way back to him. "After Haley was killed, I moved back home to live with my parents. We thought shared misery would help us all." She shook her head. "But we were wrong."

"One day," she put her hand to her chest, "I had my hair loose, like my sister had usually worn hers. I walked into the kitchen and my mother looked up from where she sat at the table. She looked so surprised. She smiled and stood up with this expression of wonder and happiness. Right before she called me Haley."

Latching onto his arm, Harper kept talking, her brow furrowed. "God help me, Reid. I almost said, 'Yes, Mom. It's me.' I wanted to give her that so badly. Just a moment of relief. But I knew how devastating that would be in the end."

Coming around the end of the couch, Harper sat next to Reid again, and he could see the worst was over. She almost had control of herself again. "I moved out after that," she said. "And that was the first time I ran. That I hid."

She faced him. "I've been hiding ever since. Writing from home, for magazines or newspapers. Doing whatever I had to do to stay cocooned in my safe little world."

"You can't regret it all," he told her. "You have your writing because of it."

"I know. I burrowed selfishly inside myself, seeing only to my own needs. And I guess I still am."

This time, Harper was the one who reached out. She feathered a finger over his lips, his jaw. "I'm trying to do better now, and maybe all this running around, chasing imaginary bad guys will be a good thing in the end. I discovered bravery I didn't know I had."

She moved closer. "I want to use my courage for something else now. To pursue another selfish need." She put her lips to his, like a whisper of faith, of communion, and promise.

"What do you need, Harper?" He held his hands tight against the leather of the couch, refusing to touch her until invited. The feelings between them now were so raw, newly exposed, and throbbing with the pain she'd just shared.

His thoughts echoed the very thing she'd said earlier. *I don't want to make a mistake.*

Instead of deepening the kiss, Harper sat back and pierced him with eyes that were clear and purposeful. The rims were still slightly red from crying, but she was focused. "I need you, Reid. More than anything."

23

Moonlight flooded the upper floor, beaming through the wall of glass like pure, unfiltered magic. Harper let the thrill of the night soak in as she held onto Reid's hand and led him to her bedroom.

She wouldn't lie to herself. She was still afraid. But along with her intent to overcome that fear, to take hold of this wonderful man who'd dropped into her life, there came a trembling sense of empowerment. As if a piece of herself she'd buried years ago was awake again and ready to live.

She was grateful for the view through the floor to ceiling windows, and the glass doors that opened to the balcony. Letting go of Reid for a moment, and only a moment, she opened the doors to let the fresh spring air sweep inside. Trees had turned silver in the moon's illumination, and their shivering leaves reflected Harper's own quivering anticipation.

She went back to Reid and lifted his hand. She guided his palm to the opening of her shirt and pressed his warmth against her heart.

"Are you sure?" he asked, his voice deep, hushed with reverence and respect for the emotional wound she'd just laid bare to him.

Now she put his fingers on her top button. "More than." Pulling the clamp to release her hair, she shook it free and lifted her face to his. She watched the mountain green of his eyes darken with desire as he teased her shirt apart and revealed her body inch by teasingly slow inch.

She swore she could feel his eyes on her, searing her skin wherever his gaze landed. She felt like the most exquisite treasure, being unveiled by a man who knew its value.

Her top was finally undone and slid from her arms to the floor. Reid skimmed a hand over her shoulder and down her back where he unclasped her bra with deft fingers. That earned him an impish smile. "Had some practice with that move, have you?"

His answering grin was sinful. "No. I'm just good with my hands."

"We shall see," Harper whispered, so aroused the clothing she still wore seemed too heavy on her skin. She tingled and ached for more of Reid's careful exploration but didn't know how much longer she could stand still and take it.

He must have shared the sentiment, because in one quick move, he ripped his own shirt over his head and tossed it aside. Locking his arms around her waist, Reid lifted her so his naked chest was in full contact with hers. He groaned and plunged his tongue into her mouth, swallowing Harper's answering gasp of pleasure.

The connection between them burned away any lingering doubts, leaving absolutely no room for fear. The heat was unimaginable. Scalding. Like falling into the sun.

Her body responded with a long, liquid pull in her core. A healthy, natural yearning that had been suppressed for far too long. *But I'm so glad I waited for you.*

Now Reid's hands were slipping along the arch of her lower back and inside her pants to cup her backside. He held her in place as he thrust one thigh between her legs and moved against her.

His unapologetic possession made her tear her lips from his to cry out.

She'd been with men before her self-imposed isolation, but she couldn't recall anything that had felt this good. This *intense*.

Pleasure coiled inside her, a hot spring that twisted tighter and tighter. "Reid," she sunk her hands into his thick, tawny hair. "It's too much. I want you inside me."

Her plan for letting him undress her was tossed aside as they both worked on buttons and zippers, pulling and pushing at elastic and cloth barriers before falling to the bed together. Glimpses of long, muscular legs and wide shoulders gave her an even greater appreciation for his physique. And she wanted to cherish every bit of him.

Later. After she'd had the release that was clawing its way through her straining body.

When Reid settled his hips between her thighs, he stilled long enough for her to feel him. Hot against her core, so close to filling her.

"Harper." As he said her name, he captured the side of her face with one hand. "Look at me."

Look at you? Harper shuddered on a breath. She wasn't simply looking at Reid. She was *seeing* him. She was surrounded by his tenderness and potent, unwavering will.

She was drowning in lust and love so thick she couldn't tell where one left off and the other began.

With his smoldering eyes fastened on hers, Reid pushed his length inside her, claiming her with his stare just as he did with his body. She wanted to keep looking at him, to stay lost in that pure green gaze, but he'd started moving inside her.

Her head fell back as she gave herself up.

Reid saw the pleasure rip through Harper when her eyes closed. When a ripple of tension rolled through her and left her lean, curvy body limp beneath his hands. He couldn't take everything in, divided between watching her face as she climaxed and devouring her perfect pale skin with his gaze.

She was lovelier than he'd imagined, and the most beautiful thing about her was the faith he'd glimpsed in her gray eyes. The trust she had placed in him. All doors had been thrown open for him tonight, and he wouldn't squander the gift.

Here was the uninhibited woman she'd kept trapped inside for so long. The Harper Gray that wrote about love, because in her darkest, most private moments, she yearned to find it for herself.

Reid could finally admit his own fear. Falling so hard, so fast for her, had left him vulnerable and unsure. He'd always been the one to hold the cards. To decide what move came next.

But with Harper, all he'd been able to do was stay close and hope that one day she would meet him on common ground.

He'd put his heart out there time and again, and now he was grateful his instincts had been right. He knew she would take good care of the love he offered.

Now that she'd chosen to accept it.

When she drew one last ragged breath and melted into the mattress, Reid decided to change his pace. He'd been holding a steady rhythm to ensure her release, but now he was ready to break the chains.

One full, deep stroke had her clasping her arms around his hips. She urged him on, fingers curling into his muscles as she rose to meet his new tempo. Measure for measure.

She moaned when he snaked one arm under her thigh and hooked her leg over his shoulder. And again when he drove deeper.

He and Harper had experienced a meeting of the minds weeks ago. Then slowly, after much patience and persistence, her heart had finally caught up with his. Now they were at the final stage. The physical connection fulfilled.

And Reid had never been more satisfied.

When she breathed out his name, he knew she was riding that crest again, and this time, he would go with her. He reveled in the perfection of their union, and had to stop himself from telling her.

Not now, when ecstasy and emotion were blending together, swirling into one overwhelming sensation. He wanted to say he loved her when there was nothing between them but tenderness.

And maybe a few moonbeams.

Now his name was on her lips again. The sound of passion and triumph.

Inside, Reid echoed the sentiment.

After they'd both spent themselves, he collapsed to her side but made it clear he wasn't ready for her to slip away. He took her fingers and raised them to his mouth for a kiss. Then dropped her hand on his stomach from sheer exhaustion.

Harper nuzzled his neck, then kissed his chest. "You put a lot into that." The woman speaking now was a minx. Playful and seductive.

He smiled into the moonlit shadows. "I've been saving it all up. Just for you."

"Maybe we should abstain again for a few weeks." She swirled a finger around his belly button, then down the trail of hair that led to his sheet-covered hips.

He captured her wrist. "Not possible. Especially if you keep that up." He rolled on top of her, suddenly fueled by a newfound energy. "Besides, I've got too many other things to show you." He kissed her lips. Then her neck. "Things I've been imagining doing to you since the day we met."

Stretching her arms above her head and bowing her back, she purred with contentment. "Since we met? I had no idea."

"I know." He eased her legs apart. "Believe me I know. Waiting for you has tested my endurance." He felt himself stir again as he kissed her breast. "And has increased my water bill."

Her brows raised in question.

"Because of all the cold showers." He slipped inside her then, taking pride in her sudden gasp. Seeing her bite her lip aroused him even more, because the gesture had nothing to do with indecision and everything to do with bliss.

Now that he knew what her full lips felt like, he wanted to feel them again. He grasped her chin to hold her steady for another delving kiss. Another slow taste.

She smelled like roses and something spicy.

She felt like paradise.

It was Harper's turn to take the lead, and she did so by wrapping her legs around his hips and urging him to roll onto his back. She sat up and let her head fall back, like a nymph announcing her conquest.

So Reid did as any good captive male would do. He gave way and let her ride.

And later, much later, he thanked the stars that Harper wrote love stories.

Because she had a wicked imagination.

悔
恨

Harper's inner clock told her it was early morning when she woke. That eerily still hour before light came back to the land.

Reid was on his stomach but had one leg stretched out to mingle with hers. Invading her bed and her territory in ways no one had since... well, ever. She'd always liked her personal space, even when she'd had boyfriends.

The comfort of having him so close was a shock, but one softened by taking one look at his sleeping face. He was so damn handsome.

She would have slept peacefully the rest of the night and had only woken when she heard that other womanly call. For the bathroom.

Gently disengaging her legs, she eased out and padded on her toes to the restroom. Smiling to herself the whole way.

When she came back to bed, she didn't go directly to her pillow but crawled onto the bottom and kneeled near the edge. He'd rolled onto his back in her absence, so she could see his strong visage.

Watching Reid sleep, she mused over her destiny and how it had taken another unexpected turn. Though this twist was certainly welcome.

She was still getting used to that.

"Reid?" she said, not too loud, but not too soft. Testing to see if he was awake, she tried again. "Can you hear me?"

He slept on, the easy rise and fall of his chest proof that he still slumbered. That he wouldn't hear her or remember what she said.

Harper knew she was still being a coward of sorts, but personality faults couldn't be changed in a day, or even a month. She still had obstacles to overcome. But with his help, she had a fighting chance.

"Reid?" Now she whispered, a secret shared between her and the coming dawn. When he still didn't stir, she said, "I think I might love you."

His dark blonde hair had fallen across his forehead and one arm sprawled above his head, resting on the pillows. Deciding to take the open spot for herself, she lay down next to him and rested her head on his shoulder.

He sighed and moved his hand to her waist, still sleeping but seeking out her warmth.

Harper would tell him how she felt another time, when the sun was high and his eyes were open. But until then, she would own this small victory. Her one brave admission.

Tonight she would be content to sleep in his arms. And feel safe.

24

This was the fourth night in a row that Reid had retired to Harper's house at the end of the work day, and he was still buzzing with just how easy their relationship had become. They'd skirted the last few obstacles with skill and grace, each marveling at how naturally they'd fallen into sync with the other.

He'd always heard he'd know when he found the right person, because things would be... easy. Simple. And although they certainly hadn't started off that way, the last week had made up for the early hardships. Mostly.

Her conservative nature paired nicely with his hang-it-all-out-there attitude. She was proactive where he procrastinated. And in turn, he was stable when old terrors tried to push their way back into her life. Her mind.

She would never forget her sister, of course she wouldn't, but at least she was finally allowing herself to breathe freely. To laugh without guilt. Smile without a shadow in her eyes.

And love?

Well, maybe there was still one last barrier, since neither of them had worked up to actual vocalization yet. They hadn't said the words, but they lived them every day.

While Harper pulled canned diet drinks from the refrigerator, Reid took carry-out containers from a paper bag. He wished he could have brought her the ham and pineapple pizza she'd been craving, but some things just couldn't be found in the village.

Maybe they'd venture out to the city again when she finished her book, or at least came to a good stopping point. Given the fervor with which she'd hit her laptop every morning, he hoped that day would come sometime soon.

Moving to take down some plates, Reid gave her back a light rub before opening the cabinet. He seemed to be doing more of that lately. Trailing his fingers down her arm. Stroking her hair. The things a man did when he couldn't stop touching a woman. When he craved the simplicity of being near her.

"What did you bring?" she asked, and it took Reid a moment to remember their earlier discussion of DVDs. Harper wanted a movie night, thus the desire for pizza, but she had no interest in the Japanese films she'd found in the TV room.

"All I had were action flicks." He gestured to the cases he'd set on the counter. "High adrenaline and moderate level of violence. No." He reconsidered. "High level of violence, too."

The import of his words bounced back at him and landed squarely on his shoulders. "Harper, I'm sorry. I didn't think..."

She tossed him a quizzical look before understanding dawned and put her at ease. She smiled in appreciation. "It's fine. I love movies, even scary ones. I don't know why they've never bothered me like the real world does, but fake gore and explosions just don't affect me."

She walked to him and planted a kiss on his cheek. "But thank you for worrying."

He'd gotten good at that, Reid noticed. Despite the strides Harper had made since their visit to Mr. Nishimura—and after their talk about what had happened to her sister—Reid was still in the habit of checking on her. Her moods, her anxiety, and whether or not she still worried about Emi and the village *Shinto* practices.

She'd been acting as if nothing abnormal had ever happened in the secluded village. As if she'd never been obsessed with ritualistic torture and murder.

Reid was more than happy to do the same, but that didn't mean he didn't keep an eye out for warning signs. He liked seeing Harper laugh. He loved hearing it.

And he never wanted to see that debilitating fear ever again.

With their plates, drinks, and napkins set up on trays in the theater, Reid turned on the huge television and inserted the DVD she'd chosen. Espionage and a woman who worked best with knives.

He grinned. Harper just kept surprising him.

Halfway through the movie, her cell phone rang out a digital rendition of "Ode to Joy." The ringtone was part of her head-to-toe attitude makeover. "It's Saya," she said. "She's leaving tomorrow, so I should answer it."

Mouth busy drinking his soda, Reid lifted his brows in acknowledgment.

On Harper's end, he heard her say, "No. I'm sure. I need to work, but thanks for the offer." Then a laugh. "Maybe when I leave the village." Harper sighed. "I might be ready for real-life shopping by then. Busy stores and crowded streets." She cringed. "Maybe."

When she hung up, Reid noticed the wrinkle on her forehead. "Saya heading home?"

"Yes." Harper nodded but looked glum. "Now is the only time the school could grant her vacation days. There's some sort of holiday this week. She asked me to come with her, but I really need to stay here."

A chilly needle of concern pierced Reid's chest. "I'll be gone, too. She probably didn't want you to be here alone." *And neither did he.* There hadn't been any issues with Emi or the temple lately, but if Harper was alone and the girl came back...

"I can rearrange my trip," he said.

"No, you can't." Neither Harper's expression nor her tone brooked any refusal. "You're too close to finishing your dissertation, and I've heard you say twenty times how hard it is to schedule a meeting with this professor. You need his final input," she told him. "And you aren't going to mess up all you've worked for just because I tend to jump at shadows."

"I'll just lock myself in—you know I'm good at that—and I won't come up for air until you get back." She leaned over and kissed him, this time on the mouth, and her lips lingered with promise. "Besides, you've stocked the house with enough groceries and supplies for a small apocalypse. I'll be fine."

"Yeah. I'm sure you will be." Reid didn't want to feel like an overbearing father, but his insides twisted up at the thought of being so far away from her.

Especially when Saya wouldn't be around in case of emergency. Harper's Japanese was still awful, so she would have a hard time communicating with someone if she needed to.

"Stop worrying," she said, shaking his arm. "Or you'll make me worry, too."

"Done," he said with false cheer. "Looks like we've traded places. Now you're the one making me feel better."

Harper picked up the remote control and got ready to start the movie again. "Then I'll call that progress." She winked, and Reid had to bite his tongue. That familiar warmth was rising in his chest again, but he refused to declare his love over the smell of *yakiniku* barbecue.

Instead, he settled back in his seat to watch as the spandex-clad assassin prepared to make her kill. *Harper will be fine. Nothing to worry about,* he chanted silently as blood spurted across the screen.

Nothing at all.

悔
恨

Bohm. Bohm. Silence. A long pause, then Harper heard it again. *Bohm. Bohm.*

Sleep held her in its tight embrace, but her eyes were straining to open. When she finally looked at her surroundings, she saw a large blue rectangle. *What the...?*

She bolted upright, then smiled once she got her bearings. *Just the television.* Not a huge blue void coming to suck her in.

Sliding out from beneath the blanket she and Reid had tossed over their legs, she stood to turn off the TV and flicked the hall light on in its place.

She and Reid had opted for a second movie, and apparently, both of them had nodded off. With a small frown, she realized this was the first night they'd fallen asleep without making love.

Gazing at Reid's tousled hair and the way his shirt stretched tight across his chest, she tilted her head with a lurid smile. *Well, the night's not over yet.*

She moved closer with the intention of kissing him awake, but stilled just above his face when she heard a strange noise. *Bohm. Bohm.*

Recognition rushed back to her and made her heart thud heavily in her chest. She'd heard that sound in her sleep. It was why she'd woken up. Now that she was lucid and could pay attention, she stood silently and waited for the pounding to come again.

A minute or more passed, then... *Bohm. Bohm.*

Drums. Those were drums.

Harper almost jumped in Reid's lap before she got a grip on the panic. Visions of priests with knives and ropes came at her in a flurry of gruesome images, but she forced herself to breathe in and out, counting until she felt the lightheadedness fade.

But that didn't change the reality of what she'd heard. Gently shaking Reid's shoulders, she whispered his name once. Twice.

After a few seconds of grogginess, he opened his eyes and focused on her face. He jolted awake, reaching for her. "Harper. What's wrong?"

"I heard drums." Saying the words out loud made her feel suddenly foolish, but the sound was ominous in the stillness of the night. "It may be nothing, but I know I heard them."

She didn't waste any time trying to figure it out, because there might be a simple explanation. One Reid was already be aware of. So she waited for his reaction.

Then the drums rolled through the night again, and his brows furrowed with confusion. "I don't know what that is. Let's go up to the balcony and see what we can see."

Good. Harper agreed and wasn't ashamed to admit she felt comforted by Reid's presence. What if she'd heard this when she was alone?

No. She couldn't think that way. Reid *had* to leave. But, just to be safe, if she started falling back into her fearful ways, she could always just accept Saya's offer and go with her friend to her parents' place in the city. She could take her laptop and still get her work done. Problem solved.

As she hurried up the stairs behind Reid, she felt her stomach turn over. She didn't want to be scared again. She was just getting used to the lightness in her heart. The ability to venture outside her walls and feel secure, even if Reid wasn't around.

Somehow, just knowing he would return to her was worth more than any amount of psychotherapy she could have undergone. She was grateful for the wondrous changes Reid had made in her life. She didn't want to backslide now.

Once they were in her bedroom, they went straight for the open glass door and out to the walkway. They moved slowly, following the sound of the drums until they had circled to the opposite side of the house.

They were facing east. Facing the mountain with the silver

mine, the stone steps that led to a mystery, and the direction Harper had chased Emi that day.

Her encounter with the girl and the priest seemed so far removed now. Long ago and distant, as if her subconscious had padded the memory with cotton for her own protection.

"What do you think they're doing?" she asked. Beside him, she gripped the rail until her knuckles stung. Easing off, she focused instead on the peaceful nighttime forest and the breeze that ruffled her hair.

"Probably just a ceremony of some kind." Reid's hand found hers, and his warmth infused her with calm. As did the simple fact that he knew she might need the contact. That she would be unsettled by eerie midnight drums.

Harper quirked her mouth. *Seriously, who wouldn't be?* She didn't have to be a scaredy-cat to be creeped out by the echoing percussion, but cowardice certainly sped the process along.

More pounding bounced off the mountainside and Harper felt as if her breath was trying to crawl back into her lungs. She couldn't listen to that all night, lying awake and wondering what was happening.

Reid could be right in his assumption. If Saya had been given the week off for a village holiday, it made sense that the people would have rites to observe the occasion.

Or... there might be priests in the woods with a knife poised above the chest of some poor, innocent person. This season's sacrifice for health and prosperity.

Ridiculous! *Stop the insanity, Harper.* She snarled to herself in annoyance, upset with the path her mind was trying to take. But no matter how crazy the idea seemed, she'd been spot on about one thing.

She wouldn't sleep until she knew what was going on.

"Let's go," she said hurriedly.

Reid glanced at her, then did a double-take. "Go where?" He looked at her as if she were as crazy as... well, as crazy as she felt. "Go out there? Stumbling around in the dark to see who or what is beating drums?"

He sighed. "We don't need to stir that back up, Harper. Not now. Not when I have to leave you here by yourself."

"All the more reason to find out what it is, so we can both breathe easier. We'll be quiet. We won't get close enough for them to see us, and we won't interfere, but I need to know what's happening." She turned a mutinous face on Reid. "I have to know there's no danger out there. I have to."

As if to contradict Reid's concerns, fire flamed to life higher on the mountain. Harper lifted a hand toward the sight. "See? Practically an invitation."

"Let's just go back inside and go to bed."

"I won't be able to sleep. This will drive me to distraction."

He rounded on her and slipped an arm around her back. "How about I drive you to distraction instead?"

She stood on her tiptoes and kissed him. "Absolutely." She lowered herself again. "As soon as we see who's out there and make sure no one's being butchered."

She couldn't tell in the dark, but she thought she felt him roll his eyes before he said, "This newer, braver version of you scares me a little."

She spoke softly. "I'm not brave. I just can't stand the thought of sitting here. Listening. Not knowing."

He stroked her cheek and started tugging her back along the balcony. "Fine, but we do not, I repeat, we do *not* make our presence known. No sounds at all."

"No matter what they're doing?"

He whirled and took her by the shoulders, the ferocity of his grip belying the softness of his voice. "No matter what. If we see something that needs to be brought to the attention of the sheriff, then we will go straight to him. We'll hunt him down in his living quarters if we have to."

Reid still hadn't let go of her. "Promise me, Harper." Not a question but a demand. "We aren't running in to save the day."

"You're right. I promise." She went back inside with him, walking silently as if already in stealth mode. Luckily they were still dressed, so they quickly slipped on their shoes, but not before Reid had retrieved a small flashlight. And a big kitchen knife.

"I thought you said we wouldn't make ourselves known."

He thinned his lips. "Expect the unexpected."

His words kept repeating in her mind as they eased silently out the front gate, then followed the trail that would lead them uphill.

Doing their best to keep the burning orange flames in sight, they made various twists and turns when the path diverged, judging which one would take them closer to the fire and drums.

Fire and drums. Harper quaked in her tennis shoes. What madness had overcome her good sense? And now she'd infected Reid. "Maybe this wasn't—" she started to voice her changed opinion, but the drums suddenly beat louder and faster. A rapid burst of eight or nine strikes.

Then they fell silent.

"I'm sorry," she whispered to Reid, but now she was too terrified to utter any other explanation. She'd better get her pulse back under control before she passed out.

"Shhh," Reid hushed her. "Let's just keep moving. We're almost there. The fire is on the other side of those trees."

Around them, the woods were beautiful, majestic and thick with spring greenery. Where the moonlight didn't reach the ground, though, darkness flourished. Crawling into every covered space. Every hidden crevice.

Up ahead, the trunks and leaves were cast in a yellow glow. As fascinated now as she was nervous, Harper crept closer with her hand still clutching Reid's. Her reckless curiosity was back with a vengeance, and intrigue ruled her brain. She had to find out what the priests were doing.

She knew the people gathered here were part of the temple, even before they came into view. Because after the drums had ceased, a different sound began to penetrate the forest. Low voices were chanting. A monotone sound that didn't fluctuate but droned on steadily.

The quintessential song of a murderous cult.

When they found a break in the tree line, Reid and Harper squatted down to watch. The chanting was coming from men dressed in brown robes. Temple priests.

Approximately twenty of them stood within a large oval outlined by torches. The fire burned at the tops of poles that had been anchored in the ground.

Harper shifted back and forth, looking between the men for any sign of a boulder or granite altar. If ever there was an appropriate time and place for the penance stone, this was it.

She only saw the priests though, chanting inside the burning spires.

Then the male voices stopped as one, and another sound erupted. She recognized the sweet yet chilling music immediately. Bells.

The same bells that the priests had surrounded Emi with at the top of the stone steps. The steps Harper had never climbed, because she was forbidden. Because she was an outsider.

What she saw next made her heart stutter. She squeezed Reid's hand so hard he pulled his fingers free and rested soothing hands on her shoulders. "Stay calm," he whispered. "We still can't be sure of anything."

Emi had entered the ring of flames, guided by a man and woman dressed in white robes with ornately embroidered belts of black, red, and temple brown. When the woman let go of Emi's hand and turned, Harper caught a glimpse of her face. She so resembled Emi that she could only be her mother.

Harper swallowed, but her throat was parched. What the hell were she and Reid watching? *Please let Emi be safe.*

The teenage girl was dressed in a white robe, silk or satin, judging by the gleam of its long folds. Around her tiny waist was a red band. The same bloody hue as the flowers in her hair.

Don't think of blood!

Without her usual ponytail, Emi looked slightly more mature, but the hopeless expression on her features was still so youthful. So innocent.

And absolutely terrified.

Though her manner was composed, her dark eyes darted in an unanswered plea to the faces encircling her. Watching her.

The bells continued to chime and peal throughout the darkened forest as more priests filed in after Emi's parents. They were swinging the golden instruments at the girl just as they had the day she'd run from Harper.

"What are they doing with the bells?" Harper whispered to Reid.

"I can't be sure, but in many cultures, the vibrations and sound are used for cleansing rituals. Sometimes to guide spirits to upper realms." He shrugged. "Or because they sound nice. Music and ceremony go hand-in-hand all over the world."

"Regardless," he continued, "you were obviously right about Emi. She's been chosen for this ceremony, and this might explain what people meant when they called her special. They may not have been referring to her being mentally challenged or different. Maybe they meant she'd been selected for this because of her innocence. Her purity."

Harper said nothing, nodding in the dark.

"I don't see anything to cause alarm," he said. "No knife or rope, not even a sash that could be used to strangle."

"Ugh," Harper choked out.

"I'm just trying to be practical and up front here. I want your mind to be at ease." He leaned closer to her in their hiding spot. "Once and for all."

Exhaling a breath filled with more distress than she cared

to admit, Harper leaned her head on his shoulder. "Me, too. I've been enjoying our time together. No village bogeymen or trespassers."

When the bells started ringing more furiously, Harper's head snapped back up. The chimes were synchronized now, and the men were closing in on Emi.

They packed so tightly around the girl that Harper lost sight of her completely. "Reid," her voice caught on an anxious hitch.

"Hold on. Just wait a minute."

The bells fell silent as abruptly as the chanting had before. The priests with bells could be seen walking back the way they'd come in a single-file line. The man and woman Harper had guessed were Emi's parents left next.

Then, walking freely and unscathed, was Emi, moving gracefully with her head held high. She seemed transformed, as if she'd been replenished and reenergized by the rites of the ceremony.

A pent-up sigh erupted from Harper's gut. Relief so immense it departed her body by physical expulsion. "She looks okay," she said in awe.

It was then she realized her hand was back in Reid's again, and that her grip had ratcheted back up to vise-worthy. She let his fingers go. "Sorry."

With a low chuckle, he said, "It's okay. I'm just so glad we can put this all behind us now." Together they stood and slunk back into the trees, away from the ritual site and toward the trail that would lead them back.

"We can put this to rest now, right?" He leveled her with a stare that half begged, half threatened.

The laughter that tickled her throat was elated. A fresh wind of reprieve. Liberation from the strain and suspicion that had dogged her since she'd arrived in Chuujitsu.

"Oh, yes," she confirmed. "Now you and Saya can leave without issue, and I can enjoy my solitude again."

When he made an insulted sound, she bumped into him on purpose and added, "You know what I mean. I can be alone and not be afraid."

Then she lamented, "I am going to miss you, but in a way, it will be good to get back to my old routine. I'd like to fight off the monsters on my own for a while."

"Just like the old days," he said, but there was an undertone in his voice.

Harper stopped and grabbed his elbow. When he paused beside her, she placed her hands on both sides of his face. "Danger or not, I fully expect you to keep coming around."

She let her eyes hold his, gray clashing with green, and hoped the words she couldn't quite say were at least evident in her gaze.

"I don't want to go back to the old days, Reid." She swallowed and revealed only some of what was in her heart. "Because the old days didn't have you."

With a soft kiss and tight embrace, Reid showed her how much he appreciated her admission. "I don't want to go back, either." Then he grabbed her butt. "Well, unless you mean back to bed. That's one ritual I could get used to."

"I don't have any drums or silk robes, but there are plenty of candles in storage."

With a growl that made her stomach swirl and her pulse surge, he started walking again, pulling her with him.

Feeling stronger than she had in years, Harper hurried down the path in the woods, holding onto her man and picturing what they'd be doing for the rest of the night.

And in her heart, she would swear she heard the ringing of clear, perfect bells.

25

Harper rolled her bicycle up to the rack and parked. She'd ridden into to the village with the hope of scoring her favorite local treat—small, round artery-clogging pastries. The little balls of bread dough were deep-fried and then rolled in a mixture of sugar and various spices.

Completely unhealthy, but the strength of her craving had driven her out of her home and into town in search of the delectable confection.

When she turned the corner toward the restaurant, she found the storefront dark and quiet. Dismayed, she studied the sign hanging in the window, and while she couldn't read the writing, there was no doubt the store was closed.

"So much for that idea," she grumped, looking down the street and noticing for the first time how peacefully quiet the area was. Usually this section of town was hectic this time of day, but as she listened for the familiar noise of pedestrians and merchants, the only answer was silence.

Deciding to enjoy a quiet stroll, Harper scented the fragrant spring breeze and realized how different everything was. She could smell distant flowers, because none of the restaurants were in operation to drown out nature with spice and soy.

Many of the windows were shuttered, on commercial buildings as well as residential. As she ambled to the next block, her search for human life became somewhat of a game.

She'd been told many villagers would leave the area for the week, but nothing had prepared her for the ghost town she now found herself exploring.

She wondered where the locals had gone and why they would leave in the first place. Wouldn't a village celebration require people to be...*in* the village?

The tune from "The Twilight Zone" danced in her ears, and she had to smile. Now, more than ever, she was grateful for what she and Reid had witnessed two nights earlier in the woods. Emi's participation in the seemingly benevolent ritual had vanquished the last of Harper's concern.

Now that the young girl had fulfilled her purpose, Harper could stop worrying. And since a mass of clouds had just floated across the valley to blot out the late afternoon sun, she was even happier to have thoughts of evil priests and cruel deeds out of her mind.

The desolate village was scary enough as it was.

Though she knew Saya had also fled the area for a happy vacation, Harper still found herself turning down the street that would take her past her friend's apartment. Here, on the side of town with more family homes, she finally spied other people.

A white hatchback was parked on the street, and a woman was standing near the passenger side door holding the hand of a toddler. The little girl wore a pink dress, and Harper was encouraged by the semblance of normalcy. She waved to the child and smiled.

The little girl chattered in Japanese and waved back, drawing the mother's attention first to her child, and then to Harper. Panic flared in the woman's eyes momentarily before she masked her reaction and spoke sharply to her daughter.

She picked her little girl up and loaded her into the back seat of the car, just as a man emerged from the house. He tossed Harper a blank look, locked the door of his home, and climbed into the car without a word of greeting. Once the woman was safely inside as well, the man cranked the car and drove them all away.

That was strange, Harper thought. Then she lifted an eyebrow to dismiss the occurrence. Frankly, almost every experience she'd had in this place had been weird in one way or another, and apparently, today would be no different.

She shoved her hands in her pockets, though the spring weather was pleasant, and let her mind drift to Reid. He wasn't due back until the next day, and Harper wasn't used to feeling lonely. She hadn't adjusted to the longing that filled her chest whenever he was gone.

Missing him was a physical sensation. She ached without him, yet the romance of having him to miss was somehow sweet. She felt effervescent inside, stopping more times in the day than she would like just to picture his amazing eyes or the way he kissed her.

The irony struck Harper dead center. She'd come to Chuujitsu for the isolation the village offered. Now here she was, wandering empty streets looking for signs of life and pining for the company of a man.

Her parents would be thrilled to hear about Reid, but she hadn't broached the subject with them yet. After all, her and Reid's relationship was a recent discovery, and they hadn't discussed life after the village. He would return to the university in the States to complete his doctorate, but that was the only absolute.

Harper hadn't made any arrangements to move on. She purposely avoided the topic, because what would she say if he asked her? Was she ready to take their relationship to the next level? To make any type of promise or commitment?

She sighed and glanced up at the sky, still shrouded by clouds. She would feel a whole lot better if she were certain of Reid's feelings. While they both did a good job of communicating their affection without actually saying the words, it was the words that Harper needed.

And eventually, someone would have to break. She bit her bottom lip. *Please let it be him.*

A sudden flash of color had her head jerking up to locate the source. She caught just a glimpse of a girl running, and her first impression was one of recognition. *Emi.*

Of all people to be left in town. My little stalker. Harper flushed with remorse as soon as she had the thought. She shouldn't be so unkind, but the stress of the previous incidents with the girl had left a cloak of dread on her shoulders. She was still apprehensive about seeing Emi and having the girl defy more temple rules.

As selfish as it might be, Harper just didn't want to be involved in any more drama. She'd had enough *Shinto* to last a few lifetimes.

Loud male voices thundered from the far end of the street just before two priests rushed past. They weren't running, but the two men were definitely in a hurry. And moving in the same direction Emi had gone.

You don't even know if that was her. Harper stubbornly rooted herself in place. She would not go in that direction. She would not see what was going on. She and Reid had already been relieved of conspiracy-theory duty, and she did not want to get mired down in it again.

She's probably just run off again. No real trouble. But no amount of arguing with herself could convince Harper not to at least take a peek around the corner of the last building. All the commotion was on the very southern tip of town, so of course, that's where she headed.

The gray stones of the street were cool beneath her feet, and now the sky had darkened even more. Pewter clouds overpowered white, brewing and swirling with turbulence. A scrap of paper whipped by Harper's face, driven by a sudden gust.

The red *Shinto* gate loomed up ahead, so she knew she was nearing the southernmost area of the village. When she made the final turn, Harper looked left in search of the fleeing girl and the priests who'd pursued her. She saw no one.

Every building appeared empty and lifeless. No lights shone in windows. No voices carried from inside. Everyone had gone from Chuujitsu. Everyone but a troublesome girl and those who served the temple.

And Harper.

She was beginning to ask herself why she'd left the sanctuary of her home when a dull thud caught her ear. She looked quickly toward the noise. It came again, and this time she saw the front door of the medical clinic shake as if struck from the other side.

Had Emi gone to the clinic? Was she hurt or sick? She sure hadn't moved like a person suffering illness or injury.

With a more determined stride, Harper made her way down the street and straight up the wide cement steps painted white. She reached for the door handle and pulled. It was locked, and the closure of the only medical care for miles told Harper just how forsaken Chuujitsu really was.

I should just go home. And she would, Harper promised herself, just as soon as she peeked inside to see what had made the noise.

She didn't see anything right away, just an empty waiting room and a long, dark corridor. Light spilled in halfway down the hallway. From windows or maybe another entrance?

The steady light was suddenly disrupted by shadows. Jerky, erratic movement that suggested several people were blocking the light.

And they appeared to be struggling.

Just when she'd begun to think she was imagining things, Emi darted into the long hallway and ran toward the back of the building. A priest was right behind her.

Panic flared, causing Harper's eyes to go wide and her mind to search for any rational reason for what she was witnessing. When another priest stepped out to block Emi's escape, the torment and suspicion of the last two months came flooding back.

She'd been right all along. Emi was being held against her will. But if the religious ceremony was over, why was the girl still trying to run? And what could they possibly still want with her?

Harper felt sick to her stomach. She'd abandoned Emi, along with her own screaming instincts. The ones that had told her something insidious was happening in the village. Something that centered on that poor girl.

Emi was crippled by her own inability to speak. She couldn't tell anyone how much danger she was in, or that she was afraid. Her actions and beseeching eyes had spoken volumes to Harper, but she'd forced herself to ignore the girl.

Harper's first reaction was to lift her fists and bang on the door, but that would only alert the priests to her presence. And she was all alone. No assistance. No weapon. And no one who might take her side.

The temple ruled in this forgotten place, so she needed to come up with a better plan. Maybe she could get in through the side door. If she confronted the men, what next? As she hurried around the building and along the side, she decided to make one move at a time.

First, she had to get into the building. And if she did that, she could find a weapon. Anything that would help even the odds. If she could surprise the priests, then she and Emi would run. The mountain forest was extensive.

They would simply hide until Reid could come and get them. He was only a couple of hours away. *I can do this. I just have to get her out of here. Surely she will realize I'm trying to help.*

She'll come with me. She has to!

Harper gasped when the side door swung open beneath her hand. She'd expected it to be locked like the front. Terror clutched at her from every angle, trying to freeze her mind, lungs, and muscles.

Then the shock lost its grip on her and she moved inside, closing the door behind her slowly and quietly. She was in a short hallway with a metal door on her right that led to stairs. She needed to stay on this level, though. That's where she'd last seen Emi.

There was nothing here but wall and floor. Nothing to use as a weapon, not even a fire extinguisher. She could only hope she passed a treatment room or office space with more options to choose from.

Edging her head around the doorjamb, she got one eye clear and was able to see down the corridor. The spot where Emi had run into her captors was empty, with no sign of either.

Harper's breathing reverberated inside her head, her beating heart a hammer and anvil, so she held the air in for a few moments to listen.

Nothing. No scuffle or shout. No harsh rebuke from the priests or cries from Emi. Where had they gone?

On legs that felt as solid as flan, Harper crept down the wide hallway, the soft soles of her shoes virtually silent on the tiled floor. Rooms were dark and many were locked up tight. No help at all. A hospital was supposed to be filled with healing vibes, a soothing environment despite the clinical décor and smell.

But the absolute lack of color and sound was spine-chilling. Shadows claimed more territory than the feeble streams of light revealed, and all Harper wanted was to find the girl and get out of this ominous building.

When she passed the area where the men had accosted Emi, she looked around and tried to figure out which way they might have gone. A whirring noise cut through the air suddenly, making her jump and bite back a yelp of fright. What was that?

She whirled to face behind her where the metallic hum was originating. Then she noticed the small light moving near the ceiling. An elevator! And someone was riding down.

Throwing herself against the nearest door, Harper twisted the knob savagely but had no luck. She sprinted down the corridor until she passed an open door. The entryway was completely open and had a wider door frame than the other rooms.

She hurried inside and realized why. This room was designed for emergency medical treatment, and any caregivers would need to be able to flow in and out unobstructed. Unfortunately, the area was organized and clean, with no real hiding place, so she kneeled behind what looked like a crash cart and prayed whoever got off the elevator didn't come her way.

She heard the universal *ding!* that announced the elevator's arrival and listened for voices or footsteps to follow. She heard none.

The doors closed again with a soft sigh but Harper stayed where she was, focusing on the hallway and trying to pick up on the slightest movement. Her knees were beginning to ache, and she knew she'd have to stand soon.

Besides, she was doing no good by hiding here. Her first objective now was to find anything she might use to defend herself. She hated feeling this vulnerable.

Rising and blowing out a breath of relief, she took slow steps to the door and peered out. She saw no one in either direction, so she whirled back to study the room.

The glass-faced cabinets were locked, but the drawers weren't. At first she found nothing but gloves and tubes for collecting blood samples. No syringes or even scissors.

She opened a drawer that seemed to hold nothing but castaway pieces. Among the collage of leftover materials, she spotted a plastic bag with blue inside and recognized it immediately. The pack was sealed for sterility, and the blue material inside was wrapped around some sort of kit.

Ripping the plastic and unfolding the material, she found a plastic bottle with a lid, a couple of packets of cleansing swabs, a few other items she couldn't name, and *a-ha!* a scalpel.

Then her stomach churned at the thought of how she could use it. *Never mind that. Just find Emi.*

Emboldened by the sharp, silver tool in her hand, she made a quick survey of the ground floor, only to confirm that she was alone. Before she could second guess herself, she ran up the stairs, avoiding the noisy elevator that would signal her arrival, and performed a search of the second floor.

When again she found nothing, she did the same on the third floor with identical results. No one else was in the building with her, which meant the priests and Emi had gone elsewhere.

Damn! There's no way I can search this whole village, and with only a scalpel for defense. Thinking the words made Harper realize just how out of hand the situation had become, and she didn't want to fall back into old patterns. Foolish, reckless patterns.

Stopping in her tracks, she pulled out her phone and dialed Reid, sending up a quick prayer that he was available. He answered on the second ring, and Harper's body seemed to flood with icy water when the terror she'd been denying rushed forth.

Hearing Reid's deep, warm voice had broken the dam. "Reid, I don't know what to do." She sounded unnerved but couldn't help it. "The village is cleared out, but I saw Emi. The temple priests were chasing her. They took her away, but she didn't go willingly."

She heard him telling her to calm down and to tell him where she was and what was happening, but all she could do was drag in a painful breath laced with fear. "I was right the whole time." Her voice broke on a sob. "Now they have her, and no one is here to help but me. They have that girl, Reid."

The shadows around her multiplied as night rolled into the valley, and with it, a gathering storm. Harper gripped the phone in one hand and the scalpel in the other. "Reid, I think they're going to kill her."

26

Reid shoved his phone in his back pocket and turned to face Nishimura as the man walked out of his kitchen. He'd stopped by the condo to have dinner and conversation with his friend, but now the agenda for the evening had changed.

"I have a problem," Reid said, waving aside the offered beer. "Harper just called me. She said the girl we told you about just got taken away by some temple priests."

He tilted his head forward and met Nishimura's eyes. "The last time we were here, you told us there was nothing to worry about if we stayed away." He could feel his own pulse throbbing in his neck. His vessels running rampant with fear. "I'm afraid Harper isn't going to do that. She'll try to help this girl if she can."

"No. No." Nishimura set the bottles on a nearby table, paying no notice when one bobbled and almost spilled. "Call her back now. Tell her to go to her home and stay there, Reid." The man licked his lips. "She must not interfere. The laws of the village religion answer to no one."

Reid was already concerned, but his friend's shaking hands chilled him to the core. "What are you not telling me?"

With a disheartened sigh, Nishimura took off his glasses and stared hard at Reid. "I left the village by choice, leaving only an elderly aunt behind. My parents had died and I had no siblings. No reason to stay there."

The Japanese man swallowed hard enough to make the action visible. Then he lowered his voice. "I broke the faith and told *Shinto* secrets. I didn't think anyone would ever know, but somehow they found out. Their reach is long."

He rammed his glasses back onto his face. "That picture you showed me of the man ripped in two. That punishment is not done to the one who speaks." He shook his head with misery etched on his features. "But to a family member."

Reid's head swam when he understood the man's meaning. "Are you saying they did that to your aunt? To punish you for speaking about the *Shinto*?"

"Yes! I will always bear that guilt, and I swore never to go back. Never to speak of it again." He stepped close to Reid and gripped his arm. "Now I must! Your friend will be in grave danger if she tries to stop what is meant to be. They will not tolerate intrusion."

"My God." Reid ran a hand through his hair, and his shoulders clenched. The village was two hours away. He might not make it back in time.

"If the girl bears the mark, the one your Harper showed me, then there is nothing to be done. Fate has been decided."

"What?" Reid gave Nishimura a shocked look. "You said you didn't recognize the symbol."

The man shook his head again. "I am sorry. The warnings of my childhood still echo through my nightmares. I did not want to cause you or your friend harm. Like I did my aunt."

Nishimura stepped away and looked out the expansive window in his living room. To the bright city lights that couldn't prevent shadows of his past from reaping vengeance.

He turned his head, giving Reid his profile. "That *kanji* symbol is the most revered of the *Shinto* church. The one commandment that must always be obeyed."

He turned back to Reid, his normally happy face burdened with dread. "That symbol is reserved for a very special occasion.

The most sacred of rituals."

Reid stiffened as he waited for his friend to explain.

"That sign," Nishimura said, "is the mark of the penance stone."

悔
恨

Harper didn't know what to do or where to go. She hadn't found any sign of Emi, and the darkened streets were difficult to search.

So many of the homes were empty and offered no radiant light to guide her steps. Even the sky was cloaked, the whirling storm swallowing any moonbeams before they could fall on the village.

Never had she seen a place so dark and deserted. And the sweeping wind carried no sound.

Staying close to the buildings she passed, she made her way to the older side of town. She had to check the temple but would take every precaution. When lightning cracked across the sky and thunder resounded soon after, she found a reason to be grateful for the violent weather.

If she couldn't hear the movement of others, they couldn't hear her, either.

This is insanity. She'd chanted this inside her head once every few minutes and knew her plan was foolhardy, but a young girl's life was at stake. An innocent who'd tried time and again to make Harper see the truth.

Now she had no choice but to help Emi, if only she could figure out where to look for her.

Guilt could be a powerful thing, even if undeserved. She'd blamed herself for not sensing her sister would need her. For not going to the library and walking Haley home.

Twins were supposed to share a special intuition. So why

hadn't Harper known sooner that Haley was afraid? That she was alone in the dark.

"I would have run screaming through the night, Haley. I would have come if I'd known." She rarely spoke aloud to the memory of her sister. To her spirit. But the emotions charging through her now were reminiscent of another time and another missed opportunity.

Harper wiped a hand across her cheek, unaware she'd been crying. Then another drop hit her chin. Not tears, but rain.

As the shower gingerly pelted the arched bridge where she crouched, Harper decided to make her move. She ran, stopping only when she'd been enveloped by darkness. The towering homes cast black shadows on the already dim streets, so she made her way to the temple easily.

No movement on the outside, she noted, watching from a hidden corner. Covert actions were becoming her norm, and she was surprised to find her hands steady. Her mind clear.

The temple rose toward the wicked sky, its upper tiers visible only when lightning struck. No lights burned inside that she could detect, so gathering her fortitude, Harper raced to the massive doors and pushed.

If anyone waited on the other side, she would be found out. It was a risk she had to take.

Cracking the door open and peeking into the temple's main worship area, she saw only candles set on the table up front. Flames flickered on wicks all around the dais as well as the mountain sculpture. She slipped inside and listened intently.

Then she pushed herself on, tossing aside any small amount of good sense. Turning a deaf ear to the voice of reason that told her not to go upstairs, she took the steps two at a time. When she reached the top, she found herself staring down a hall that turned sharply to the left.

The corridor followed the shape of the square building with closed doors on one side and windows with wood blinds on the other. Reaching for the large brass loop of the first door, she tried pushing and pulling, but it didn't budge.

She pressed her ear to the ancient wood and held her breath. No noise. No movement. With renewed purpose, she hurried along the hall, checking each door. The results were the same every time, and she didn't know whether to be relieved or frustrated.

She was terrified of meeting up with those fierce priests but had accepted reality. When she found Emi, she would have to face the men who shadowed and watched her every move.

At the end of the hall, Harper found more stairs and followed them up to an identical setup, just in reverse. Intermittent doors led to the interior of the tower, but now they were on her right. She performed the same careful inspection again for the third and fourth floors.

Once she'd finished, she felt confident the temple was void of all life and definitely any evil *Shinto* ceremonies. She would certainly have heard those damn bells.

She should have been reassured, but instead, the pressure ratcheted up. She was running out of time. As far as she knew, she was already out of time. Emi could be lying dead somewhere, her body not to be discovered until the light of day. If ever.

Harper raced down the stairs, making quick work of the back and forth route. If she ran into anyone, she would be trapped. The stairwells led either up or down with no detour.

When she entered the worship hall, she couldn't stop herself from sprinting straight through to the doors. With every minute she'd spent inside the temple, her anxiety had increased. The high ceilings and empty spaces did little to quell her sudden claustrophobia, and the pelting rain was a welcome sensation.

She took greedy gulps of the fresh air but didn't pause long enough to catch her breath. She still had a search to perform, and with the village empty, most buildings would be locked against her.

She had to think rationally. Where would they have taken Emi? If the priests were going to hold a ceremony or ritual, they would do so in a sacred location.

A memory flashed in her mind then, and she remembered one place she'd never been. Because it was forbidden to outsiders.

Fatigue was beginning to take its toll on her body, but Harper pumped her legs and ignored the cramp of muscles. Once she got to her bike, she could regain her strength. She would ride through the countryside, then forge her way up the mountain.

The more she thought about it, the more convinced she became. She needed to find Emi in a hurry.

And now she knew where to go.

悔
恨

Harper stopped and leaned against a tree trunk to rest, wiping the wetness from her eyes and face again. The rain had lessened, but the wind and thunder seemed to be making up for the loss. Above her, the forest thrashed and swayed as gales rushed through, tossing the trees about.

When she'd reached her house, she'd thought of calling Reid again, but knew he'd only demand to know where she was and what she was doing. He'd tell her to stay at the house until he got there. To wait for him.

And while Harper would like nothing better than to have Reid at her side, she couldn't wait for him. Too much time had already passed.

She checked the clock on her phone and noted she'd called him only forty-five minutes ago. Even if he'd left Oda City that very minute, he'd still have over an hour left to drive.

Emi couldn't wait that long, so neither could Harper.

Pushing herself up from where she leaned against the rough bark, Harper started up the trail again. Soon she came to the fork in the path where Emi had fled the day she'd run from Harper. The same place the priest had caught her and had beaten her with the leather strap.

The priest had been adamant that Harper not go any farther up those stone steps. The fact that she and other Chuujitsu visitors were prohibited from seeing what waited at the top of the hill only made her that much more determined to go there.

Judging by the position of the slope, the steps would lead her to the southeast side of the mountain. She should have a view of whatever lay beyond the valley and possibly the road Reid would return by.

If she found Emi and no threat seemed imminent, she might have time to call him and give him her location. She patted the phone in her pocket, now protected by the rain jacket she'd dashed inside the house to grab.

She needed the phone to stay dry and functional, or her grand plan to hide in the woods would be useless. She'd have no way of contacting Reid, and she wouldn't be able to return home. Not if she succeeded in stealing Emi away from the priests.

The steps were slick from the rain, and moss squished beneath her feet in some places. From her position at the bottom of the steps, she couldn't see any lights.

As she climbed to the top, she glanced to the surrounding forest. The creeping ferns and thick underbrush seemed sinister, as if hiding an evil that only came out at night.

Focusing on her ascension, Harper kept an eye on the top of the staircase. Anyone looking down would see her, and now she cursed herself for not thinking better of the parka. Sure the material protected her and the phone, but it was also a bright saffron-yellow.

Regardless, she might as well stay dry until she found out

what was up there. When she had a mere ten steps to go, adrenaline kicked in and started the now-familiar rush of panic. She still couldn't hear or see anything, but fear was playing tricks on her once-rational mind.

Were they up there waiting for her? Had they seen her moving along the trails at a distance?

Now she was near the last few steps, and a roof came into view. No vicious priests pounced on her. No one cried out an alarm. The *tap-tap-tap* of light rain repeated its rhythm between the howls of wind and rumbles of thunder.

The building in front of her seemed peaceful, and Harper was beginning to wonder if the men had whisked Emi out of the village entirely. Beneath a streak of lightning, she caught a glimpse of the building. The structure was made of wood and had tile or stone shingles, but that was all she could tell from where she was.

She was looking at the back side of the building and was momentarily confused by the strange positioning. Then she remembered something she'd read about shrines only facing east or south. The practice had something to do with *Feng Shui* and the attraction of bad luck.

She sloshed her way across the sodden ground and around to the front. Here was the proof that she'd discovered a shrine. What looked like small, wooden houses sat out front with rows of candles inside, and a large golden pot.

The wide, shallow receptacle was molded into a lion's face, and while she couldn't recall a name or its use, she was sure she'd seen pictures of similar pots outside of other shrines.

Standing here now, she felt an eerie vibe that permeated her body. If this was indeed a shrine, it had to be the one dedicated to the local *Shinto*. To the *kami* revered by the village. The angry mountain.

And Harper was suddenly more afraid than she'd been all night. What if she was too late? What would she find inside?

Emi's body, sacrificed on a stone slab or strung up like some sick form of ornamentation? Would Harper finally know the true meaning of the penance stone?

She stepped over an ornate offering box at the top of the steps and put both hands on the double doors. These didn't push inward like the heavy ones at the temple. Instead, they were made like *shoji* screens and slid easily to each side.

For a moment, her vision went black as her body fought the possible horrors that might be waiting inside. Then the center of the room cleared and panic ebbed. She could see the entire room now and almost collapsed from yet another letdown.

She was relieved to find the shrine empty, but with each crescendo of expectation, her body and mind took a beating. She closed the doors behind her and went to sit in one of the pews. The décor here was simple and clean, not like the opulence of the temple.

She sat on the plain wooden bench and searched for any other options. Where else could they possibly be? She'd scoured the entire town except for actually entering the locked homes and businesses. That was far beyond her capabilities, and more to the point, the idea was ludicrous.

So where was Emi?

Minutes passed, and she selfishly admitted she was grateful for the reprieve. Her body was exhausted, muscles aching from exertion. Her skin was cold and drenched from the rain.

She looked again at the phone. Still an hour before Reid could get here.

She'd left him worried about her and what she might do. Now, as she glanced at the phone, a message told her she'd missed a call. From Reid. The phone was silenced, so she hadn't heard it ring. She might as well call him back and put his mind at ease.

She'd come to a dead end and had no choice but to go home and wait for him.

Her finger was hovering over the call button when she heard a sound. Deep and repetitive, the same level of vibration over and over. She ran to a window to get a better view of whatever was making the noise.

The shutters were closed, but she was able to pry one of the slats open. Just enough to see outside.

She hadn't come around the shrine on this side, or she might have seen the trail that veered back into the forest and along the edge of the mountain. She considered exploring the path, but only briefly, because the humming was coming closer, and soon she could make out its human quality.

Voices were chanting, much like the priests had that night in the woods when she and Reid had watched the ceremony. The ritual they'd believed was the final act.

Now Harper knew they'd been wrong. Oh, had they been wrong.

A procession made its way up the stone steps she'd just climbed, several priests carrying lanterns that dangled from chains. She knew they were priests by the tattoos on their chests and backs. The circles of ink were fully visible, because tonight they were without their usual brown robes.

They were bare from the waist up, dressed only in wide-legged pants of black silk. Their torsos gleamed as if their skin had been oiled, but their appearance wasn't what made Harper shrink inside.

A familiar figure was in the middle of the group, her black hair loose and raining down the back of her crimson robes. The girl marched as if being led to the gallows, or possibly an even worse fate.

As the procession followed the mysterious path into the trees, Harper knew she'd be taking the very same walk. She would call Reid on the way, because she had to get outside to follow the priests and their prisoner. She couldn't risk losing them. Not now.

Not when she'd finally found Emi.

27

Keeping the glowing lanterns in her sights was easy, since the flames stood out in the nighttime forest. Finding the path in the dark was another matter, especially since she had to keep lifting her eyes to track the parade of priests.

Harper stumbled over a protruding root and had to clamp her lips tight to muffle the grunt that expelled. She wasn't sure how this confrontation would turn out, but grappling with multiple men in the dark with only a scalpel for defense just didn't seem like the wisest course of action.

She wanted to stop and call Reid, to give him her location, but every time she paused long enough, the flames got lost in the dense tree leaves. As if on cue, the glowing orange spots blinked out again, one by one.

Startled into action, Harper rushed forward on the trail until she saw why the lanterns had disappeared. Up ahead the trees were gone, and myriad stone stairways had been set into the mountainside. They didn't go straight up but along the edge, back and forth in a gradual ascent, like switchbacks on steep mountain roads.

Torches placed sporadically along the way illuminated the treacherous climb, and stone markers lined the cement pathway to guard against falling off the side.

There was no way she could lose her quarry now. When the priests and Emi reached the top, she'd make a run up behind them.

She took out her phone to call Reid. He should be back in the village in another half hour or so, and she was more than ready to have some help. She didn't want to put him in danger, and the thought of his being hurt sickened her.

But she couldn't leave a disabled child to be slaughtered by maniacal temple servants. Despite Emi's teenage years, her mind was that of a child. Simple and sweet. Guileless.

And defenseless.

Harper almost cried out when the words flashed across her screen. [[No service]]

"Damn it!" She pushed it back in the pocket of her jeans and got ready to move. The priests were almost at the top, and Harper had no idea what was inside the mountain.

She couldn't lose them again.

The yellow of her rain jacket was just too visible, so she tore it off and gave thanks that she'd worn moderately dark clothing that day. She might not be seen if she hurried and kept to the inside of the stairway, closest to the mountain. Tall grass grew on the land between sections of stone, so that would provide her additional cover.

Trying not to make too much noise, she hurried along the cement walk, then took the first set of stairs. Soon they jutted to her left and went straight up the face of the incline before taking her back in the direction she'd started. Only now she was above the original trail.

Back and forth she climbed until her thighs burned, and her breaths came fast, hard and abrasive to her lungs. More torches were above her now, and she could see an entrance.

What had once been used for mining operations was now decorated in worship of *gekido-yama*. The angry mountain.

A black hole led inside, and she could see tall poles embellished with gold and scarlet ribbons. The long streams snapped furiously in the wind, while torches flickered and danced with every gust.

At least the rain had slacked off some. And she had her scalpel. What more could she ask for?

Reid. I need Reid. She didn't delude herself into thinking she wasn't scared. She was. Terrified. But she couldn't stop thinking about the red book and the symbol on Emi's hip. That *kanji* sign was important, and while she didn't know exactly what was planned, she was certain it would involve Emi's death, unless she did something to stop it.

Reaching the top, Harper staggered to the side of the entrance, again having to catch her breath. She was gasping and couldn't go inside until she quieted. Peering inside, she saw only darkness and wished desperately for a flashlight.

When she was ready to go in, she took out her phone again and hit the screen. She'd have to settle for LED illumination. Then she crept forward, mindful of the uneven floor.

Yes, this was definitely a mine and the supporting beams were verification. She could see where tracks had once run through the tunnel, but the rails had since been removed. She followed the main corridor, checking as she went to make sure she didn't pass any offshoots.

If the inner layout turned out to be a maze, she was going to be in trouble.

Finally, she rounded a bend in the passageway and saw the faintest glow. *The lanterns!* She'd gained ground on the priests, and now they seemed to have stopped moving.

Edging as close as she dared, Harper put her phone away to conceal the light and watched. She listened.

The group was in the middle of a cavernous room, and from what she could tell, other tunnels branched out from this central location. The priests had hung their lanterns from a metal structure in the center of the room. Almost like a gazebo, the circular design surrounded an area of smooth stone flooring, also perfectly round.

Harper felt as if a shot of epinephrine hit her heart and made it close in on itself. An oval table sat in the very center of the floor, eerily lighted by the flickering lanterns that encircled it. Harper couldn't tell what it was made of, but she was betting on granite. On stone.

The priests were surrounding Emi now, moving closer as if to make sure she had no way out. One of the men spoke harshly to her and grabbed her arm. The girl cried out and shook her head.

Harper gripped her scalpel. She was fully aware that this was a lost battle, but she was ready to rush in just the same. She would strike, and cut, and slice if she had to. They were not hurting that innocent girl.

Another man came up behind Emi, taking her shoulders in his hands. Then the others moved in, each taking hold of her body to lift her off her feet. They were putting her on the table. This was it!

Harper's brain fired red hot, making it easier not to think. Just to act.

When Emi cried out in one long moan, Harper revealed herself and took three strides forward. "Stop!" she yelled, hoping she sounded more authoritative than she felt. She flashed the sharp metal in her hand to show she was serious.

The priests all froze mid-action, and amazingly, they each stared at her and let Emi go. They eased away from the oval table and dropped their hands. Harper was shocked by their acquiescence but pushed ahead, ready to take full advantage.

"Emi," she called as the girl looked over at her. Harper waved her free hand. "Come here." She waved again and tried to smile, but the attempt felt more like a strained grimace.

She was still shaking where she stood, knowing the men might rush her at any moment.

Emi slowly sat up and smiled at Harper. She swung her legs off the side, allowing the rich, silky material of her red robe to sway for a moment before she jumped down.

With her eyes still locked on her rescuer, the girl walked easily through the throng of priests. And not one of them touched her.

When Emi was about ten feet away, she stopped and folded her hands together across her abdomen. "Oh, Harper. Harper. I knew you would come. I knew that you would save me." She tilted her head. "I could tell right away that you were the one."

Harper started to speak, but the air in her throat seemed to turn solid. She was stunned. "Emi, you…"

"Can speak?" the girl finished. "Yes. Most proficiently, too." Her smile changed, the curve becoming sharp and sinister. She came forward in incremental steps. "Despite the fear you nurture, inside you there is a great spirit. A fighter. And that only adds to your value."

"My value?" The earth seemed to shake beneath Harper's feet. What was this? She'd come to help the girl, but didn't recognize this person standing in front of her. She wasn't meek or mute. And definitely not helpless. In fact, Emi was the one in control.

Harper thrust the scalpel forward. "Don't come any closer. What the hell is going on?"

Emi inched toward Harper despite the threat, her dark eyes sparkling as she whispered. "You are so clever. So smart. You figured most of it out but were always missing that one critical piece."

"What piece?" Harper knew she should run, but her legs were paralyzed. Her mind was shutting down and taking her body along with it. "What do you want? If you're part of this, then go. Die. Or do whatever you were going to on that table. I have nothing to do with this."

Now anguish cracked her voice. "I was trying to *help* you. Why did you come to me in the first place if you weren't in danger?"

"Oh, but I was," Emi said. "Without you, I would have died tonight. Now that's not necessary." She lifted a hand and gave one short jerk. The priests marched forward. At Emi's command.

Why were the men suddenly following her lead? Was Emi's family that powerful, or was she just the only one able to speak English?

Maybe Emi was using Harper as some sort of leverage.

The girl moved even closer as the men circled around Harper, too quickly for her to get away. Emi closed in as Harper trembled.

She was so afraid. So confused. With eyes on the duplicitous teenager, Harper didn't see the man leap forward until it was too late. He wrenched her wrist until the scalpel clanked to the floor.

Another man rushed in to help hold her still, but all she could do was stare at the girl who'd played her for a fool. The supposed innocent who'd strung her along the whole time. Guided every action. And led her straight to hell.

"Why?" Harper whispered. She didn't recognize the tense, horrified voice as her own.

"Because, Harper." Emi walked over and leaned in. She spoke in a low, raspy voice. "You are special, too."

悔
恨

Reid's car skidded to a halt on the gravel, sliding in right behind Saya's. He'd called her as soon as he'd left Nishimura's, hoping she might get back to the village in time to talk Harper into waiting for Reid before doing anything.

The wall's iron gate swung wildly in the wind, evidence the storm had yet to blow itself out. He was halfway across the garden when Saya burst out the front door. "She's not here! I looked everywhere, and she's not answering her phone."

"I know," Reid said, his voice raised over the howling gusts. Everything was wrong. How had this happened? Why hadn't he taken the threat more seriously? Harper had seen it from the very first, but he'd dismissed her worry as vivid imagination or the fear she clung to so tightly.

Now regret smothered him. He remembered Harper telling him how she wished to turn back time and save her sister. He understood that desire. He would give anything to go back to the morning he'd left for Oda City. He would have insisted she go with him.

"Where do we look? Should we split up?" Saya's distraught voice broke into his self-recriminations.

"No. We stay together." He used his arm to gesture toward the house. "We should go in and get flashlights." He looked down at Saya's feet, glad to see she'd worn sensible clothing and shoes.

"Do you really think they'll hurt Harper?" she asked as Reid rummaged in the closet. "Maybe she won't be able to find them or stop them. Then they'll leave her alone."

A serpentine ripple of dread rolled down Reid's back. "I don't think so." He looked into Saya's deep brown eyes. "Nishimura told me everything."

When he brushed past her, Saya grabbed his arm. "What are you talking about? What more is there?"

"Those marks inside Harper's house were meant for her. If the priests catch her…" he couldn't say the words out loud. He didn't want to give them any power. "We have to save her," he told Saya before turning to head for the door. "And I think I know where she went."

悔
恨

Harper's skin felt bruised and chafed. The priests had shown no concern for her comfort when they'd held her down and stripped off her clothes. The fear of rape had passed quickly when, just as roughly, they'd dressed her in a silky, crimson robe.

Just like the one Emi wore.

Her struggles had gained her nothing. There were simply too many of the priests, and they were stronger than their modest, monk-like attire would have suggested. They wore only black pants, revealing thickly muscled torsos.

And Harper could only fight for so long. She was worn out, beaten and defeated in every way possible. With her hands and feet secured, she could only lie on the oval table as several priests rang bells around her. Up and down her body they moved, cleansing her.

For whatever sacrificial ceremony was to come.

Emi circled around and around, like a tiger eyeing its next meal. When rage resurfaced in Harper's gut, she narrowed her eyes at the girl. "You can at least tell me what you meant. How could I possibly be special? I'm not part of your religion."

Emi made a *tsk-tsk* sound, then gazed up into the soaring cavern. "Very well. Every three years, the village of Chuujitsu must pay the highest price for its continued prosperity. We give the *gekido-yama* the most sacred of sacrifices."

She stopped circling and smiled at Harper. "Blood. Human blood. But not just anyone's will do."

She held up a finger like a teacher making an important point. "The elders from long ago decreed the most valuable offerings. Those who would be considered special. First, and easiest to find, is the pregnant female."

"Ugh." Harper was disgusted. "That's barbaric." She couldn't imagine the horror of losing not only your own life, but that of your unborn child. "For a mountain?" she spit out. "A fucking pile of *dirt*?"

The slap was quick and unexpected. Emi curled the fingers of the striking hand into a fist as she glared at Harper. "Watch your mouth. We don't have to make this easy."

Harper bit her lip. This was easy? She didn't know what came next or how painful it would be, but two of the priests had left the cavern, and apparently, the ritual wouldn't continue until their return.

She shivered. What would they bring back with them?

"The second sacred sacrifice is a person like myself," Emi said, pacing around the floor again. Fire from the hanging lanterns reflected orange on her black hair. How had Harper not seen this girl's evil?

"I was born at a very specific time, when the full moon is darkened by the earth's shadow," she said spreading her hands with dramatic flourish. "A child born under a lunar eclipse is marked immediately." Emi's face darkened as one hand went reflexively to her hip. "I cannot be offered until after my seventeenth birthday has passed, but I am still worth more than the pregnant female."

Now she stopped and pointed at Harper. "But *you* are the real prize." Her mouth turned up at the corners. Cruelly, fiendishly. "The surviving twin. My culture reveres twins, and bringing the two souls back together for the mountain is the greatest atonement."

Nausea struck Harper, and she started struggling again. "You bitch!" After flailing uselessly and wearing herself out, she collapsed against the stone table and fought against tears. She wouldn't give Emi the satisfaction.

But the thought of Haley's death brought a new level of pain. Her sister's murder would now be the cause of her own. An insidious fall of dominoes.

Harper screamed to release some of the anger.

"Now, don't get so worked up." Emi laughed lightly, her relief at being passed over for this year's sacrifice making her almost giddy. "Your death will serve many people."

She stopped and came to Harper's side. She patted her restrained arm. "You will be a worthy sacrifice. Remembered always. In fact, I will light a candle for you in the temple." She kissed Harper's cheek. "In gratitude."

Harper seethed but was powerless to do anything. How could this girl know anything about her? Especially personal details of her life. She'd only come to this village because...

She froze when she thought of Ms. Hayashi, the leasing agent who'd specifically picked Chuujitsu for her residence. The woman must have learned the details of Harper's life. Her past.

Then she'd delivered a surviving twin straight into the heart of this madness.

How far past the village limits did this religion reach? Did they have people everywhere in Japan?

As she mused over the implications, the two priests returned to the cavern. They were carrying a large tub of some kind, filled with a white substance. They set the container next to the table, and one man lifted the contents from inside.

When Harper saw what he held, when he grabbed one of her ankles, she renewed her fight to get away. "No. No! What are you doing?"

Paying no mind to her screams or the jerk of her hands, the priests each helped hold her down so the man near her feet could perform his task. The white material in the tub was some kind of wrapping, and now that it was on her skin, Harper could feel its cool moisture.

"What is this?" She looked to Emi, and despite her burning hatred for the girl, she begged, "Please."

Heaving a sigh, Emi explained, "The bindings contain a plaster mix, a very special blend with unique properties."

The man was now winding the long, cold strip around Harper's calves, while two others kept her legs pressed together. The man cinched the material with a hard tug. Tighter. Tighter. The material squeezed her skin.

"I don't understand," Harper said, too terrified to be embarrassed by the catch in her voice.

"You will," Emi said before turning to the men and speaking to them in Japanese. She walked away as Harper cried for help.

Soon the bindings were over her thighs. She tried to roll her hips to slow the man down, but the others held her firmly in place.

When he wrapped her stomach, then her ribs, Harper could no longer fully expand her lungs. She started to panic. Her heart raced, and her breaths were too shallow. The heightened anxiety only made things worse.

The huge, dark room grew blacker in front of her eyes. Pressure closed in on every side just as darkness did her vision. Darker, darker.

Then she fell into a void.

悔
恨

The next time Harper opened her eyes, she jerked and tried to move her arms. The priests were no longer holding her down, but the man with the bindings was standing nearby.

That's when she realized she was in a different place. The room was smaller, like an alcove. The ceiling of earth was mere feet above her now.

I must have passed out. "Where am I?" she said on a whimper.

Then Emi was there. "I'm glad you're awake. You need to hear the rest. You see," she smiled, this time with a touch of sadness, "I had to make you fear for me, so you would try to save me. So you would follow me when I let myself be seen. When I called out."

"The clinic," Harper said. "And every other time. It was all a premeditated plan." Her head was fuzzy. Nothing made any sense.

"We couldn't simply take you," Emi said. "The surviving twin is the most special, but also the hardest to claim."

She paused, then confided to Harper, "All of the meetings, the drama, it was my idea. I promised the temple I could deliver you in exchange for myself, but there was one caveat."

Harper only looked at the girl and waited.

"You had to come into the mountain of your own free will." Emi smiled. "I was quite worried near the end, but you found me, Harper. You saved me."

"Now." She clapped her hands and spoke to the lone priest. He approached and began wrapping Harper's neck, the only part of her body that was still uncovered. Other than her head.

"No, wait. I'll suffocate." Harper channeled her energy to her legs, but her body was numb, and the wrappings were getting stiffer.

"Don't even try," Emi said. "This method has been perfected over many centuries. The plaster will dry, but as your body decomposes and leaks, the wrapping will soak that up as well and harden even more. Your form will lie here for the rest of days. An effigy of the life that was given up to the mountain."

"Before I go, I'll give you a gift. The answer you've been searching for." Emi stood back as the priest bound Harper's jaw. "That symbol on my hip and in your home. That *kanji* signifies the offerings we make."

Now another priest came forward to help clamp Harper's mouth closed as the other man wrapped. She groaned against the material as they roughly swathed her head, leaving only her nostrils uncovered. Why would they do that? Didn't they want her to die?

She blinked rapidly when they bound her eyes, but soon the plaster forced them closed. Scratchy fluid leaked into her eyes and burned.

Helpless and terrified, Harper whined, because there was nothing else she could do. Yes, they wanted her to die. Just not quickly.

Emi's voice was beside her head again. "You, Harper Gray, will last here forever, paying reparations for the sins of my ancestors. Over time, you will become one with the bindings. Hard. Everlasting."

The girl drew an expectant breath, then whispered, "*You* are the penance stone."

Futility overwhelmed Harper. Emi and the others had moved away, and she didn't think anything could be worse than the loss of voices. Even the terrible sound of her murderers was more comforting than being here alone.

The silence was sharp as broken glass. It invaded her soul.

Then she heard something else and knew she'd been wrong. There was something worse.

The scratches and clunks she heard now were easily recognizable. Stone against stone. The scrape of spreading mortar. That's why they'd brought her to the smaller room. The alcove had been carved from the mountain itself.

And now they were walling her inside. Making her one with *gekido-yama*.

Her nose flared as she fought for air, and a part of her welcomed the unconsciousness that was pressing down on her again. But the absolute darkness allowed her mind to turn elsewhere. Away from her impending death.

Her thoughts turned to Reid.

Just when she'd found him, she would lose him.

Inside her plaster coffin Harper shivered. The cold was taking over, stealing her last bit of heat. *Reid. I'm sorry I didn't listen to you. Please forgive me.*

The noise being made by the remaining priests was coming from somewhere above her now. They must be closer to the top. Closer to sealing her off from the world completely.

They would leave her isolated in a way she'd never dreamed off. Never wanted.

Where even Reid couldn't find her.

When the last stone was put in place and no more scrapes filled the small enclosure, Harper pictured Reid's warm smile and his amazing green eyes. He was the last thing she thought of.

Then, destroyed by agony, she sensed the darkness coming for her and had no strength left to fight.

Beneath the tightly-wrapped material, she screamed.

28

"Get down," Reid said, grabbing Saya's shoulder to push her behind a thick shrub. They'd been making their way toward the stone steps in the mountain forest when he saw lights bobbing somewhere above.

"Someone's up there, but they aren't as close as I thought." He glanced at her, wide-eyed and crouched by a tree. "Sorry. You okay?"

"Yeah. Now that I know you weren't a priest jumping from the bushes to chop my head off." She smiled, but Reid could see the strain on her face, and the fear she was trying to conceal. He had to give Harper credit. When she'd finally decided to pick a friend, she'd done well in choosing Saya. The Japanese woman was as fierce as she was loyal.

"They're coming this way, though," she added, standing with him to take a look. "We should take cover."

He saw reason in her suggestion but couldn't move his legs. He suddenly felt as if his insides had been sucked out. "If they're coming back, they must be finished. What if Harper is…"

"She's not," Saya said with more force than necessary. "We'll find her, Reid. If there wasn't a chance to save her, then Nishimura would never have sent you here."

Reid prayed she was right. He couldn't lose Harper. He clenched his fists, the skin stretching tight over his knuckles. He had to get to her in time. *He had to.*

Life wasn't fair, he knew, but Harper had already suffered so much. He didn't want to imagine what she was going through right now. Somewhere on this dark, cursed mountain.

He and Saya eased back into the woods and waited for the lights to descend. A troop of priests passed by, and the sheer size of their force made Reid killing mad. Harper would never stand a chance against so many.

He didn't even know he was moving forward until Saya wrapped her arms around his waist and put all of her weight into holding him back. "No," she whispered harshly. "You won't do her any good that way. I need you, Reid. Harper needs you."

Her plaintive tone got through. He nodded to her that he was all right. Back in control.

But the anguish rolled out of him as he watched their retreating backs. "I'll kill them if they hurt her. I'll fucking kill them."

The rational scientist in Reid was replaced by the enraged male protecting his woman. Primal. Possessive. Dangerous. And as soon as the last priest vanished down the trail, he bolted from their hiding place to race up the stairs.

He heard Saya keeping pace. Once they reached the top, he edged closer to the building they found there. "This must be the shrine Nishimura mentioned, and the temple priests just came down from here."

He walked around the side of the shrine, but as he drew near the front steps, he slowed. Then he stopped. "Saya." All the dread and trepidation for what they might find inside was in that one word.

"I'll go," she said, coming to stand in front of him. Her eyes were liquid brown pools. "Let me look first."

"No." Reid shook off the tremors that had temporarily stopped his heart. "We'll both look."

With no more words, they each took one side of the doors and slid them apart. He exhaled so hard a banner hanging near the door fluttered. Harper wasn't there. "Thank god."

"Nishimura knew they would take her up here to the shrine," Reid said. "But regular villagers aren't allowed to know more than that. Only temple servants." He made sure they hadn't missed anything inside before following Saya back out.

"Over here," she called, her voice low so it wouldn't carry, but urgent. "There's a trail that leads to the old mine shafts." She kneeled and shone her flashlight on the ground. "The soil is torn up. A lot of people tramped through here. And recently."

"Let's go," he said. "She has to be this way."

They made quick work of the path in the woods and kept running once they made it to the steps. Both were spurred on by a sense of emergency, and neither voiced the fear they likely shared. The mines went all through the mountain interior.

If Harper was alive, they still might never find her.

Reid had to stop when he reached the final level of steps. He was dragging in breaths, and so was Saya. When she caught up to him, they walked the rest of the way up.

Two torches on poles flanked the entryway and ribbons fluttered in the wind. The celebratory adornments pissed Reid off all over again. He ripped down the ribbons and kicked one of the torches. "They won't have her," he said. "No matter what, I'm taking her out of here."

A male voice called out from deep within the tunnel. Too late, Reid realized his outburst had alerted men inside. Some of the priests must have stayed. "Get behind me, Saya," he growled, picking up the torch pole he'd just broken and smashing the lantern end against the stone wall.

He held the splintered end at the ready, and for Reid, killing mad wasn't just an expression anymore.

"Forget that," Saya huffed. She lifted her hands and fell into a fighting stance that was far too natural to be new to her.

Only two men were striding down the tunnel, and they weren't at all prepared for the attack that met them at the exit.

Reid used his wooden rod to bash one of the men on the side of the head. The priest staggered. So Reid hit him again.

The other priest had taken up a position similar to Saya's, and the two of them sparred, each striking and blocking in turn. In a sudden move, the priest swept one leg and took Saya's out from under her.

He didn't have a chance to regain his footing before Reid jumped him and rained his fury down on the man's head. After three solid hits, the priest fell to the ground with his friend.

"Thanks," she said. "Guess I'm out of practice."

"You were great," he said. "I can't wait to tell Harper." The small surge of humor and warmth dissipated as they looked down the long stretch of shadowed tunnel. Again they set off at a jog and quickly came to a large room with multiple shafts.

"Oh, no. *Oh, no.*" Saya was getting frantic.

Reid ran ahead to check out the strange setup in the center of the room, searching for any clue to what had gone on inside the angry mountain. Then he spotted wet stains on the perimeter of the circular stone floor. The moist trail led away from the table. "This way," he called out, already tracking the disturbance in the soil.

As he entered one of the other tunnels, he pulled out his flashlight again. Torches and lanterns lit most of the stairs and inside the cavern, but the smaller passages needed more light.

Saya caught up again and shone hers as well. "What is that stuff?"

"I don't know, but it's fresh. And more importantly, it isn't blood." The trail of milky stains stopped at a wall, and Reid stood staring for several seconds. "The tracks end here. They just disappear as if—" Comprehension rocked him to his core.

"As if they went inside the wall." Saya slapped a hand to the stones. "They're wet. This masonry is new."

"Harper!" Reid shouted, slamming his palms on the wall. He didn't care who heard him. An army of priests couldn't stop him now.

He dropped his makeshift weapon to pound on the stones, but then picked it back up to chisel at the wall. "The grout is fresh. We can get this down."

Saya searched madly for a tool of her own, then raced back to the construction in the main cavern. She came straight back with two metal hooks. "Here. This is better. They were holding lanterns."

The hard metal slid through the mortar as if it were nothing more than dry sand. Reid paid no heed to the scrapes and gouges he made to his knuckles. The need to see if Harper was alive pounded through his arteries.

At last a stone slid backward, and he rammed it the rest of the way through, trying to see inside. "It's too dark. Saya, the light." She handed him the flashlight, and he thrust the front end through the hole. The beam danced haphazardly before he realized what he was looking at. "Is that…"

Instead of facing the horror that lay inside the room, Reid forced every bit of his rage into the rocks next to the hole. He pushed and pulled in a frenzy of motion until they loosened and gave way. Stones from above tumbled down when the ones beneath dislodged, but he didn't flinch from the onslaught.

Saya was helping pull out stones as well, widening the hole into the open space behind. When she paused to shine her light inside, her other hand flew to her mouth. "My, God. Reid!"

He was already shoving himself through the narrow opening they'd created. He couldn't see her face, and her body seemed smaller somehow, but Reid knew the mummified form on the stone slab was Harper.

"She's not moving," he said, going to her side and running his hands up and down the outside of the wrappings.

Saya went to Harper's feet while Reid used his fingers on the tight bindings. "I can't get a grip on anything."

"Do you have keys?"

"Yes!" He pulled his keychain from the pocket of his jeans and willed his hands not to shake.

"Use your keys to work on her face. She needs air," Saya instructed. She started ripping with her own keys near the ankles and began peeling it back. "It's starting to dry and harden. What is this stuff?"

Reid was working desperately to cut the strips on Harper's head without scratching her skin, but making sure she could breathe was all that really mattered. When he finally cut through a segment, he peeled the material and stretched the hole he'd made to reveal her face.

She was so pale. So still.

"Harper," he said shaking her. She didn't respond, and he couldn't tell if she was breathing or not. Her neck was still covered, so he couldn't check for a pulse. With a sound of frustration, he put his head to her chest, then fell silent to listen.

Nothing. He couldn't hear anything through the bindings. "Please, Harper." Now he tore at the bindings to get them off of her head. Her neck. How long had she been like this? Was it too late? "Please, baby. Come on."

He stopped occasionally to pat her cheeks, to shake her shoulders. "Saya, help me up here. I have to get her out to see if she's breathing."

Saya moved to the other side of Harper's shoulders and started pulling. When they'd made enough progress, her smaller fingers were able to slip inside. "Wait," she told Reid. "Stop moving."

She held still for a few seconds, then gave him a smile that was elated yet still concerned. "She has a pulse, but it's slow. Her skin is freezing."

Suddenly, Harper gasped a deep, guttural breath and jerked her head to one side. She opened her eyes and looked up to the craggy ceiling, as if she didn't really see it, or Reid and Saya hovering over her with anxious expressions.

Gulping in several quick breaths, Harper finally had enough air to cry out, "Haley!"

Then she broke into sobs.

29

"What's happening?" Harper asked as she picked up on familiar voices. Her eyes were clouded over and felt dry and scratchy.

"You're okay now," a male voice said. Hands held her face on both sides, then released her again. Her skin was tingling, pinching, and she could feel a tugging sensation on her shoulders, her arms.

"Where did she go?" she said in a slurred voice. "Where's Haley? I saw her."

The movement around her slowed for a moment, then resumed. "Harper, wake up. We have to get you out of here." A woman's voice, but not Haley's. Lifting her hands to her crusty eyes, Harper wiped to clear a strange residue from the corners.

"Try to sit up," the man said, and like a bell of clarity ringing deep inside, she recognized the voice.

"Reid?" she asked, a quiver in her voice.

"I'm here, baby. You're safe." He hugged her tightly, and this time, she clasped onto him as well.

"Thank you. Thank you." Harper was talking to him as much as the heavens above. "I saw my sister, Reid." The tears threatened again. "I guess I was unconscious. I don't know. But it doesn't matter, I know she was there."

Harper knew she was emotional and babbling, but the climb back to lucidity was fraught with joy and loss in equal proportion. She started remembering where she was, Emi, the priests—and she was so happy to be alive. Free from that awful, choking plaster.

But at the same time, the divine sense of warmth and affection she'd felt was receding. She'd touched something on the other side, when she'd been lost in the darkness. She'd *felt* someone. "I think she came for me," she whispered. "My sister."

Now Reid pulled her to a sitting position and took her face in his hands again. He looked into her eyes. "She was there for you." He kissed her chalky forehead. "She didn't want you to be alone."

"I know." Harper sniffed and met his green eyes with a new and powerful certainty. "But I wasn't supposed to go with her. Not yet."

"No," he echoed. "Not yet."

"Reid," Harper said, "I want to be here. With you. I want to live. No, more than that. I want to have a life. No more hiding." She pressed her lips to his, hard, with all the fervent passion running through her. "I love you so much, and I should have told you. I never should have held back."

The sobs were building in her chest again. "I don't want to be alone anymore."

"You never will be," he said. "And I should have told you, too. So here it is, in this little hole in the wall. Literally." He smiled. "I love you, Harper Lee Gray, and I'm going to hold you to what you just said."

"Good." She looked at Saya who'd given them as much privacy as she could, but was doing double-duty by looking out the hole in the wall, keeping watch in case any fanatics returned.

"Saya," she said, smiling at her friend when she faced her. "Thank you."

"You'd do the same for me." She held out her hands to help Harper stand. "We need to go. Do you think you can walk?"

Harper gave a dry laugh. "I can walk to Tokyo if it means getting the hell out of this village."

With his serious face back in place, Reid said, "We just have to make it back to Harper's place where the cars are parked."

He went to the stone wall and squeezed one leg through first, then his upper body. Harper was unsteady but grew more confident with each step. Every muscle fiber burned as life rushed back to help her move.

Reid held her hand as she climbed out, while Saya supported her from behind. "I'm just glad they dressed me in this robe before wrapping me up," Harper said, shocked at her own attempt at humor. Shouldn't she be devastated? A blubbering mess?

Saya smacked her on the butt as she made the final push through the wall. "Well, since I'm back here, I'm *really* glad you've got clothes on."

The laugh rolled out of Harper, and there was her answer. No, she wasn't going to fall apart. She wasn't going to starve herself, and she wasn't going to hide. Those days were over.

Reid and Saya had saved her life in more ways than one. And while their friendship and love had brought her back from the brink, the brief communion with her lost sister had been the final approval she'd needed to truly move on.

Some might say she'd dreamed or hallucinated, but Harper didn't care. She'd recognized the familiar connection, the special bond shared only with her twin, and that's what she'd sensed in the deep recesses of near-death. Pure and unwavering love.

And a sisterly shove back toward the light when Reid had called her name. *Thanks, Haley.* Harper stood and took Reid's hand. *I love you, too.*

Reid held a broken rod in his other hand, and as nimbly and quietly as possible, the three of them made their way back through the main cavern. Harper shivered when she passed the table but kept going. She refused to look back.

They stepped over the two priests lying in the shaft near the exit. One of them moaned as he started to stir. "We have to hurry," Saya said. "Unless you want to give him another knock on the head."

"Let's just keep moving." Harper needed to get as far away from this mountain as she possibly could. She didn't want to waste a single second, and despite what the men had done to her, she just couldn't stomach any more violence. "Please." She pulled on Reid, and he came without argument.

The storm was back in full fury. Tempestuous clouds shot lightning toward the earth, and rain continued to pound. Harper actually enjoyed the cleansing streams. She smoothed her hands over her eyes and face as the showers turn her robe from dusty white to dark red.

Neither wet steps nor rolling thunder slowed her as she raced with Reid and Saya, down the steps and through the woods. When they passed the shrine, Harper took the lead and gazed down the single line of stone steps. The stairs would lead them to the forest trails, then back to her house. "I don't see anyone."

With no other encouragement needed, Reid and Saya joined her to hasten down the final section of the forbidden ground. Harper had finally seen beyond the mysterious staircase, and she never wanted to go back.

They were almost at the bottom, almost to the trail, when a man's voice echoed down the mountainside. He was raising the alarm and telling the others that their sacrifice had escaped. Harper looked at Reid. "Guess I should have let you hit him."

The three of them ran the rest of the way, darting to the right with Reid taking point. He knew this section of forest paths better than any of them, and soon they saw the roof of her house jutting through the tree line.

Reid came to an abrupt stop, throwing up his arm to block the women. "They're already waiting for us," he said. "Damn.

We needed the cars." Taking a moment to consider their options, he stared quietly into the woods.

Eventually he sighed and looked to Harper. "We can go the long way, around the back side of your house. We can pick up the trail that leads down toward the river, but it will be a long walk." His eyes were worried. "Can you make it?"

"Absolutely. Anything to steer clear of them." Harper didn't need to clarify. Though most *Shinto* practices were peaceful and loving, she would never look at robed priests the same way again.

Moving backwards down the path they'd just traveled, they picked up a separate route that carried them deeper into the woods, up the mountain, and toward the west. After an hour of walking, they emerged and found themselves in the old cemetery.

"I know where we are now," Harper mused. "These trails are like a spider web, all interconnected at some point."

"Not far and we'll be able to see if they're also waiting at my house," Reid said as they crossed the darkened graveyard. "If the way is clear, I'll sneak in and get you some clothes."

"No," Harper said, grabbing his elbow. "You called Nishimura. He'll meet us where you told him to. I'm not that cold, and we just have to cross the river."

During their hike, Reid had gotten a hold of his friend and asked him to come pick them up. They'd agreed on a secret place near Reid's house. Nishimura had already been en route, worried about Reid and Harper and willing to risk his own safety to see to theirs.

On the other side of the cemetery, the path descended until they came upon the old steps that led to the abandoned *Shinto* gate and worship area. "Here is where the river was once revered," Harper said. "I think I would have liked that *kami* better."

The lack of moonlight made for a dark trip through the

forest, and as they rounded the bend, they realized another problem. Their adversaries had done away with their telltale lanterns, so Harper and the others hadn't seen them.

Until they were practically face to face.

"Go!" Reid said urgently, pushing Harper down the incline. They hadn't made it to the trail yet, but the slope was gentle enough to run down. Tall grasses brushed their legs as they ran, and the two flashlights were practically worthless at the speed they were moving.

Harper could hear the priests gaining ground, so she pulled on another reserve of energy and dashed forward, trying to put some distance between her and the bloodthirsty zealots in pursuit.

"There! To the bridge!" Reid was right behind her and Saya to her left when Harper understood what bridge he meant. But the swinging ropes and planks were nothing compared to the hell she'd endured this night.

Her feet hit the wooden slats at full speed, but the instability of the structure wobbled and threw her off rhythm. The undulations made Harper lose her balance, and she stumbled and fell to her knees.

Saya was there instantly, trying to get her back up, but she was adjusting to the strange sensation of weightlessness as well. When they both stood and grasped the rope railing, Harper saw Reid standing with his legs apart, wielding the pole he still held like a bat.

Several priests had followed them onto the bridge and were closing in on them. Then Harper caught a flash of red as the moon broke free of the clouds. Emi was there as well, and in an imperious voice, she spoke to the priests. They stilled.

"I knew you'd come here when you couldn't go home," she snarled to Harper. "In fact, I know you much better than you ever thought to know me." Emi directed her next words to Saya in Japanese, and Harper could only imagine what the girl was saying. What she was promising or threatening.

When Saya laughed, the sound made Harper smile. "Forget it. I don't want anything else you and your village have to offer."

"Very well," Emi said before huffing through her nose. "Then we'll simply take her." She looked at Reid. "You can't beat us all."

Reid was rigid, his wide shoulders braced for attack. "But I can slow you down, and that will be enough."

The reality of what was about to happen sunk in and instantly infuriated Harper. She wouldn't leave Reid here to be beaten by the priests while she made her getaway. She wouldn't run and leave him to suffer in exchange for her freedom. Her need for self-protection had cost her too much already.

She wasn't going to risk the man she loved.

"There won't be any fighting," Harper called out, matching Emi's arrogant tone with one of her own. "Saya," Harper said sharply, "Translate, and tell the priests exactly what I'm saying."

As the water gurgled far below, Harper embraced her newfound strength. She would stand with Reid and Saya. She would not abandon them, because they hadn't abandoned her.

They'd gone into the depths of the *gekido-yama* to save her. Now it was her turn.

"I am a surviving twin," she said, then nodded at Saya to let her know she wanted the single declaration translated. Saya spoke loudly to the priests in Japanese.

"We already know that," Emi said, taking a step forward.

"I must go into the mountain willingly for the sacrifice to be worthy." As Saya spoke again in Japanese, Harper moved up to stand with Reid. She put her hand gently on his arm until he lowered the staff.

With her eyes locked on Emi's as the young girl seethed, Harper spoke clearly and firmly. "I will not go willingly into the mountain." The force of her words carried up into the air and to the mountain itself. Beneath her, the rushing river lent its power, its approval. "I will not be your sacrifice."

Emi started prattling in Japanese again, speaking to the priests in their native language. But the men ignored the girl. They were listening to Saya instead.

Reid spoke suddenly beside her. "It's almost midnight. You must make reparations before the dawn of the first growing day." He spoke English for Harper and let Saya deliver his message to the priests.

Harper assumed this new information had come from Mr. Nishimura. She didn't know the full story, but she could see the priests were deeply disturbed by Reid's announcement.

"You're running out of time," Reid said. "You must still offer a penance stone."

"Shut up!" Emi screamed. "You don't belong here. You know nothing of our religion!"

"We know enough," Harper said.

Two of the priests were arguing now, and Emi turned back to them, still angry and authoritative as she spoke. One of the two men who'd been disagreeing spoke loudly to the other priests. Harper thought it might be the same man who'd once hit Emi with the leather strap.

After the man gave his directives, a line of priests encircled Emi and took her by the arms.

"No! No!" She yelled something more in her language, but soon the fury in her commands turned to fear and pleading. One of the men stepped forward to bind her wrists before they began to drag her away. She continued to fight, but was soon overpowered and lifted off her feet.

Harper, Reid, and Saya all stood silently and watched. Even after the mob disappeared into the woods, the young girl's screams carried back to them.

Reid moved to Harper and spoke quietly. "Are you going to be okay with this?" He winced when Emi shrieked again. "She probably won't survive the night."

Harper lifted one brow as she turned her head to watch the river flow away from the village. As she watched the waves escape. "I won't feel guilty, if that's what you mean."

He nodded, eyes shining in the dark.

"I'll be fine," she said before stepping away. She put her arm through his for support as they made their way across the bridge. "In fact, I may just light a candle for her." She sniffed. "In gratitude."

The remainder of their journey was peaceful, and with the threat of capture gone for good, Harper relaxed enough to feel how sore her body was.

When they reached the edge of the forest near Reid's house, he said, "We don't have to hide anymore, but I still want to take a look around first."

He walked through the trees and entered the cabin. After a few minutes, he reappeared on the porch and waved for the two women to join him. He had a cell phone to his ear.

When Harper neared him and he disconnected the call, she asked, "Nishimura?" pointing to the phone.

Reid nodded. "He's on his way back now and will take us to get the other cars. He wants to leave right away."

Reid touched Harper's dirty cheek. "I'll explain all of it to you later, but Nishimura is in danger here. He's broken the *Shinto* law again and is still considered one of the villagers. They can't catch him with us."

Harper nodded. "Of course. But I want to ride with you." She wrapped her arms around him. "I might be a little needy for a day or two. Hope you don't mind."

The smile he gave her heated her more than any hot shower ever could. But... she still wanted that shower.

She lifted her mouth as he bent to brush his silken lips over hers.

"I don't mind at all," he said against her lips. "In fact, I don't plan on letting you out of my sight anytime soon." He let his forehead rest against hers. "You're safe," he whispered, as if he needed to remind himself as much as Harper.

"When we get to my house, I just want to grab my laptop," Harper said. "As far as I'm concerned, we can send someone else back to pack up my things."

"And mine," Saya seconded. "I'll miss my students, but I won't be able to help them by staying here. Not anymore." Her brown eyes were troubled. "But I can't stand the thought of leaving them here. In this hateful place."

"We'll do something," Harper said. "Once we're gone. I don't know what, but between the three of us, we'll come up with something. Speaking of which..." She glanced between the two of them. "Where are we going?"

Saya lifted her hands and grinned. "There's plenty of room at my parent's place in the city. But I'll warn you, Harper—my extended family comes around pretty often. There will be a lot of people and very little privacy."

With Reid's arms around her and Saya's indomitable grin shining, Harper drew the first full breath she'd taken in years. She laid her head on Reid's shoulder and said, "Sounds perfect."

Epilogue

Harper hung up the phone and turned as Reid walked into the bedroom. Behind him, the steel-blue waters of Boston Harbor were framed by the open door leading out to the balcony. When he lifted a questioning brow, she nodded in grim acknowledgement. "That was Saya calling from Tokyo. The Office of the Prime Minister is about to hold a press conference."

Reid took two steps toward her. "Have they gone in?"

"Yes." Harper knew what he was asking. "The teams have completed a search of Chuujitsu." She put a fist to her stomach as it tilted. "And the mountain."

Her face warmed as relief rolled through her, along with the burgeoning hope that the horrors of the village were over. At last, the Japanese government was taking the allegations against the *Shinto* temple seriously.

Reid turned the television on, already set to a national news channel. The banner across the bottom of the screen identified the press conference, and they both listened quietly as the man's announcement was translated for English viewers.

Finally, Reid spoke aside to Harper. "Japanese authorities know we were telling the truth. They've seen for themselves just how many secrets the temple and its mountain have been hiding."

Secrets, she thought, putting a finger to her lips. A nice euphemism for corpses.

Noticing her continued silence, Reid moved into her line of sight and locked gazes with her. "The sacrifices have stopped. No more stones will be offered up to the mountain." He grasped her gently by the shoulders. "You did it, Harper."

She took a deep breath then exhaled shakily. The smile that

bloomed on her face was triumphant. "No. *We* did it. Together." Nagging anxiety had been her constant companion for months, but the weight in her stomach dissolved as the television continued to tell of bodies discovered and an investigation that might last for weeks.

But Harper wouldn't need to worry anymore. Her part in the tale was over.

She glanced out the balcony doors, and as the sunset gilded the ocean horizon, all she could think about were the lives that would be spared.

Four months after that fateful night in the village, their efforts had finally paid off. Harper, Reid, and Saya had driven out of Chuujitsu and had launched an immediate campaign to expose the *Shinto* temple, their barbaric laws, and their practice of human sacrifice.

Saya had notified the police in Oda City as soon as they and Nishimura had returned. Despite their insistence that a girl was in need of rescue, the officers only made it as far as the village before temple priests intercepted them. And convinced them that everything was fine. That the allegations were false.

Who would doubt a priest? So the secrecy had continued.

Harper had tried to save Emi in the end, even after everything the girl had done, but time had simply run out.

No one had believed the three American tourists, so they'd decided to take their crusade to a larger audience.

On the heels of her latest release, Harper had revealed the sordid story, piggybacking on the publicity her new book had brought in. She gave interviews and stirred international interest. She'd been in the spotlight for weeks, a testament to how far she'd truly come since her solitary days of hiding behind locked doors.

The finishing touch, though, was Reid's dissertation. His inclusion of Chuujitsu and their ancient laws had garnered academic acclaim. His colleagues stood with him, launching their own version of investigation.

Once his paper was accepted and published, the full weight of the anthropological community was behind them. Not to mention several women's and children's advocacy groups.

So now, weeks later, the world's critical eye was turning away from Harper. And was taking a closer look at Chuujitsu.

The reporters assembled at the press conference were clamoring, calling out questions and fighting to be heard. Harper picked up the remote and clicked off the TV.

Today was not a day for wallowing in bad memories, but a time for new beginnings and celebration. For looking forward. Instead of focusing on shadows, she drew in the fresh, salty air and reveled in the joy of being alive.

No more being haunted by the past.

"You don't want to watch?" Reid asked.

"No. I think it's time we moved on." She went to him and let him envelop her, his strong arms providing everything she'd ever need.

"Besides, I'd rather talk about the future." She lifted her eyes to his with a curious smile. "Have you made a decision?"

Reid had received offers from several prestigious universities. He'd more than made a name for himself and could accept the faculty position of his choice.

"I have," he said, angling his head and curving his mouth slyly. "I was thinking about D.C."

Harper's chest buzzed with gratitude, her heart melting a little bit more for the amazing man she'd found. Or rather, who'd found her.

"George Washington University? That will be close to my parents in North Carolina." She beamed but then stilled, her attention focused solely on him. "Are you sure you don't want to stay in Boston? Teach at your alma mater?" She bit her lip and added, "I know you're not close with them, but this is where your family lives."

Reid's green eyes seared her with affection as he reached out to cup her cheek. "Harper." He kissed her softly. "*You* are my family."

He found her lips again, and this time the kiss was filled with warmth and promise. As his mouth moved against hers, the last knot of tension released in Harper's stomach. She eased her head back with a sigh. "We can let go of the village now. We can move on."

Reid slipped his hands around her waist, caressing her back and creating swirls of heat and longing. "Yes." He nipped her upper lip. "And I'd like to start moving on right away, if it's all the same to you."

Joy and desire merged into one as she quirked her mouth and studied his handsome face. "Only if you tell me you love me first."

"That's an easy price to pay." He laid his forehead on hers and whispered, "I love you, Harper Gray." Then he touched her cheek. "The bravest woman I've ever known."

Moved beyond words, Harper gripped him tightly, breathing him in as her heart ran warm, as if filled with liquid gold. "I love you," she said, shivering.

Reid tangled his hands in her hair, and his lips met hers again in a heated promise of forever. With mouths melded, they moved together toward the bed. In love. Full of hope. And ready to see what life had in store for them.

Seagulls called and dipped through the air, their cries carrying in on the breeze. And while Harper and Reid made love, their bodies were bathed by the light of the setting sun.

Wind and warm sunbeams entered the room freely, thanks to her new outlook on life. With the love and support of a good man, she did feel brave. She felt safe.

And more often than not, these days...

She left the doors wide open.

If you enjoyed this book, we would love to read your review on your favorite retail or review site.

Thank you!

Suza Kates writes both paranormal romance and suspense. She lives in Savannah, Georgia with her family and three ridiculously spoiled cats.

For more on Suza and her books visit

www.suzakates.com